Taylor Bu...
stamped a...   ...ght.

He wasn't a m... ...and maybe a
kiss with and then walked away from unscathed.
So why in blazes hadn't she just said no?

She shut the door behind him and leaned against
it as her basic honesty made her admit that she
wanted this one evening—wanted to test that
shiver of attraction she felt toward him, and
see if it was reciprocated. She wasn't some
impressionable young thing. No cowboy was
going to put any dents in *her* carefully guarded
heart.

When Ashley was done with the silent pep talk,
she realized she had to be dressed, made up and
combed out in a little over twenty-five minutes.
And ready to resist the most intriguing man she
had met in years.

Lordy, but she was looking forward to tonight!

Dear Reader,

Welcome to Silhouette **Special Edition**…welcome to romance. This month we have six wonderful books to celebrate Valentine's Day just right!

Premiering this month is our newest promotion. THAT'S MY BABY! will alternate with THAT SPECIAL WOMAN! and will feature stories from some of your favorite authors. Marking this very special debut is *The Cowboy and His Baby* by Sherryl Woods. It's the third book of her heartwarming series AND BABY MAKES THREE.

Reader favorite Christine Rimmer returns to North Magdalene for another tale of THE JONES GANG in her book, *The Man, The Moon and The Marriage Vow*. The wonderful Joan Elliott Pickart continues her newest series, THE BABY BET, in Special Edition this month. *Friends, Lovers…and Babies!* is book two of the MacAllister family series. Also in February, Pamela Toth introduces the Buchanan Brothers in *Buchanan's Bride*— it's the first book in her series, BUCKLES & BRONCOS. Sharon De Vita's *Child of Midnight* is her first for Special Edition, a passionate story about a runaway boy, a caring woman and the renegade cop who loves them both. And finally, Kelly Jamison's *The Wedding Contract* is a marriage-of-convenience story not to be missed!

So join us for an unforgettable February! I hope you enjoy all these stories!

Sincerely,

Tara Gavin
Senior Editor

Please address questions and book requests to:
Silhouette Reader Service
U.S.: 3010 Walden Ave., P.O. Box 1325, Buffalo, NY 14269
Canadian: P.O. Box 609, Fort Erie, Ont. L2A 5X3

PAMELA TOTH
BUCHANAN'S BRIDE

SPECIAL EDITION®

Published by Silhouette Books
America's Publisher of Contemporary Romance

To Marcia Book Adirim, editor and friend, with many
thanks for your encouragement and support.

 SILHOUETTE BOOKS

ISBN 0-373-24012-0

BUCHANAN'S BRIDE

Copyright © 1996 by Pamela Toth

This edition published by arrangement with Harlequin Books S.A.

® and TM are trademarks of Harlequin Books S.A., used under
license. Trademarks indicated with ® are registered in the United States
Patent and Trademark Office, the Canadian Trade Marks Office and in
other countries.

Printed in U.S.A.

PAMELA TOTH

was born in Wisconsin, but grew up in Seattle, where she attended the University of Washington and majored in art. She still lives in Western Washington, and she enjoys reading, traveling and quilting when she isn't spending time with her two daughters and her Siamese cats. Three of her books, *Two Sets of Footprints*, *Walk Away, Joe* and *The Wedding Knot,* have won the *Romantic Times* WISH Award and she has been nominated for two *Romantic Times* Reviewer's Choice awards.

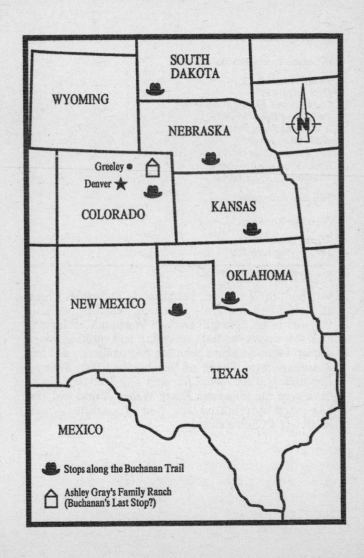

WYOMING

SOUTH
DAKOTA

NEBRASKA

N

Greeley •
Denver ★

COLORADO

KANSAS

NEW MEXICO

OKLAHOMA

TEXAS

MEXICO

Stops along the Buchanan Trail

Ashley Gray's Family Ranch
(Buchanan's Last Stop?)

Chapter One

"Hellfire and damnation!"

Glaring at the pancake-flat tire on her pickup, Ashley Gray wasn't sure if she wanted to laugh or cry. What she felt like doing was kicking the tire as hard as she could, but the way her luck had been running, she'd sure as shootin' break a toe.

She was hungry and road weary. She had finished out of the money at the rodeo in Nebraska and she was traveling alone, since her friend Heather had gotten herself engaged to a bullfighter. Now Ashley was looking at a delay she couldn't afford on her way to Wichita.

What next, she wondered as she glanced down the ribbon of dark road. It glistened with rain from an unexpected shower before disappearing into the night. The only pair of headlights in sight were her own. Her cotton shirt was getting soaked, and water had begun to drip off the brim of her Stetson.

From the horse trailer behind the pickup, Ashley's pinto gelding added a trumpeting complaint at the delay. No doubt he wanted his dinner.

"Easy, Spinner," she called, reaching into the cab of her truck to flip on her flashers and grab an old denim jacket. As she shrugged into it, a car went by without slowing and sent up a spray of dirty water that dampened the leg of her jeans.

"Thanks for stopping," Ashley muttered. At least she knew how to change a tire; her brother had made sure of that before she'd hit the road over a decade before.

By the time she had dug her flashlight from under the seat and dragged out the jack and the spare, the end of her strawberry blond braid was soggy, too. As the hiss of tires braking on wet pavement snapped her head around, the braid slapped wetly against her cheek.

Shielding her eyes with her hand, she blinked into the beam of light from a truck that had pulled onto the shoulder behind her trailer. The passenger door opened. In the glow of the cab, she got a glimpse of two men. One was bareheaded and the other wore a dark Stetson.

Great. All Ashley needed to complete her day was a couple of drugstore cowboys looking for fun. She'd been taking care of herself for years, since before she had started competing professionally, and she wasn't about to let some two-bit tenderfoot slow her down now.

"Howdy. Need some help?" called the man who'd been riding shotgun. The driver killed the high beams and turned on the four-way flashers before he got out and slammed his door.

Ashley raised her flashlight, and the tension in her shoulders eased up when she recognized the passenger as a roughstock rider from the pro circuit. He was tall and blond, with a mustache and a friendly grin.

She lowered her light as he came closer. "Thanks for stopping," she said. "I've got a flat, but I can handle it. If you're in a hurry, I don't want to hold you up." The rain, at least, had slowed to a light drizzle. The night was quiet and dark around them. Anyone with sense had gone to bed hours ago.

"I'm Donovan Buchanan," the man said as he stopped a few feet away. He was wearing faded jeans with tears in the knees and a Western shirt. "This is my brother, Taylor." With a jerk of his thumb, he gestured to the even bigger cowboy standing behind him.

She already knew both their names. Briefly, she glanced at the other man. Standing in the shadows, he touched a hand to the brim of his black hat. He had the height and heavy shoulders of a steer wrestler, as she knew him to be.

"My name's Ashley Gray. I've been on the road for hours and I'd hoped to be closer to Wichita by now."

"We've been to a wedding," Donovan replied. "We're going to Wichita, too."

Ashley didn't like the idea of being alone on the dark road, but she knew how tight the schedule between rodeos could be. No doubt the two men had been driving for hours. "I can manage, if you need to get going." She glanced at Taylor standing silently behind his brother. His jaw was shadowed by a day's growth of whiskers, but she couldn't make out his expression.

"I've seen you around," Donovan said. "You're a barrel racer."

"That's right, I am." Ashley smiled, even though her mind was on the tire, the long drive ahead and her empty stomach. The rain had finally stopped, but she was still damp and tired to the bone.

Taylor moved around her and picked up the lug wrench she'd left on the ground. In the glow from her flashlight, she could see that his unsmiling face had been chiseled with broader strokes than his brother's and his sideburns were darker.

"If you'd aim that this way, I'll take care of the tire," he told her. He had a strong nose, straight, dark brows and his voice was deeper than Donovan's.

"Sure thing." Relieved, she stood over him, eager to get done so they could all be on their way, as he squatted down by the wheel. She was eyeing the width of his shoulders beneath his lightweight jacket when Donovan spoke up again.

"Need some help there, bro?"

Taylor grunted something Ashley assumed was a negative reply.

"I can hold the light if you want to hop in our truck," Donovan suggested to her. "It's warm if you're wet from the rain and there's coffee in the thermos."

Ashley tore her gaze away from Taylor's broad back. Next to him, Donovan's more conventional handsomeness paled. She didn't feel right leaving the two men to do everything, and she'd already had enough caffeine. "Thanks, but I'm fine. I'd just as soon stay here." Another car went by, swerving so it didn't splash Taylor, who was positioning the jack.

"You been to Wichita before?" Donovan asked.

"Oh, sure," Ashley replied. "I've been just about everywhere."

"I know the feeling," Donovan replied. "At least Wichita's got pretty decent purses and a friendly crowd."

She knew that both men were tops in their chosen events, usually making the finals in Las Vegas every year. You couldn't stay on the road for long without seeing the same faces over and over. In the beam from her light, she watched Taylor nimbly loosen the last of the lug nuts and set it in the overturned hubcap.

"Need some help with the wheel?" Donovan asked him.

"Nope."

Donovan grinned at Ashley and asked how she had been doing.

"I finished out of the money this last time," she admitted, noticing the shiny horse trailer behind their big cab-over-style camper. The equipment all matched and was probably a lot newer than her own pickup and two-horse trailer. A silent testament to their success.

She preferred to sock her money away in the bank—what was left after expenses and entry fees.

"You'll do better in Kansas," Donovan said confidently. He was tall for a bullrider, but leaner than Taylor.

She hoped he was right. Her funds were running lower than she liked. It had only been bad luck that the barrel her horse had barely nudged tipped over and cost her a ten-second penalty, but those things happened.

"I've seen you ride that pinto," Taylor said as he worked. "You're good."

The unexpected compliment startled her. "Thanks," she replied. She had seen him, too. The way he took down a steer was a perfect blend of strength and grace, but she couldn't very well say that.

"You hauling two horses?" she asked instead.

Taylor kept working without looking up.

"Yeah, his Appaloosa and the mount I use for hazing," Donovan replied.

She wondered if they had a ranch somewhere, as did so many of the big-name competitors. As she wanted someday, too. A place to go when she wasn't on the road. Somewhere to retire, although she couldn't picture that day ever coming. She loved the life too much to think about quitting.

Taylor freed the damaged tire and ran his hand over the tread.

"What do you think caused the flat?" she asked.

"Feels like you picked up a nail. Shouldn't be a problem to have fixed."

"That would be a relief," she murmured. While she could afford a replacement, she'd rather not part with the money just now.

Apparently, Taylor heard her. He glanced up, and his expression held a gleam of understanding.

"Sure I can't help with that?" she felt compelled to ask.

"No, thanks. I'm almost finished."

Donovan distracted her with a question about her horse. He turned toward her trailer and then he clutched at his side with a groan.

"Damn," he grumbled. "I keep forgetting."

"Did you have a wreck?" Ashley asked.

"Just a small one," he replied with a rueful grin. "You could say that a rank little bull named Baby Dynamite and I parted company on a sour note."

Ashley shuddered. A derisive snort made both of them glance back at Taylor. The spare and the hubcap were in place. He had straightened to his full height and was brushing the dirt off his hands, but he didn't look their way.

"You're lucky that bull didn't step on your head," he muttered.

"Can't get any sympathy from someone who only does those sissy timed events," Donovan drawled. "No offense to you, darlin'."

His words sidetracked her. Normally, she would have objected to his familiarity, but Donovan's expression was so openly flirtatious that she found herself returning his smile instead. Barrel racing, her specialty, was a timed event, too.

"Dropping onto a seven-hundred-pound steer from a speeding horse isn't exactly what I'd call sissy stuff," she felt compelled to point out.

If Taylor appreciated her defense, he gave no sign of it. Donovan, though, stroked his chin thoughtfully. "Looks like you got a fan here, bro."

Ashley's face grew warm, but Taylor ignored his comment as he stowed her tools and the flat.

"It's not safe for you to travel alone like this," he told Ashley in a tone that made her hackles stand on end. "Donnie will ride with you and I'll follow you in my truck."

"I've got one bossy big brother and I don't need two more," she shot back. "Nor do I want a bodyguard." She flashed a glance at Donovan. He winked, grinning, and her hand itched to smack him. "I'm a big girl and I can take care of myself."

"Obviously," Taylor drawled with a telling glance at the tire he'd just changed. "Then we'll just follow you till we get somewhere you can have that fixed."

Before she could sputter an objection, he had circled the front of his truck. "You don't want to be driving without a spare, especially not at night." He climbed behind the wheel and pulled the door shut. As the pickup's engine roared to life, she glanced at Donovan.

"Might as well do what my brother says," he told her with a shrug. "It saves time in the end."

Frustrated, Ashley switched off her flashlight. She was about to go around to Taylor's window when Donovan opened the door of her truck expectantly. She hesitated, then changed direction when he held out his hand to assist her.

She glanced back at the other rig, but the headlights came on and she couldn't see if Taylor was looking her way.

"Thank you for stopping," she told Donovan as she climbed into the cab. No point in getting angry; they had stopped to help her.

"Sure thing."

"Thank your brother for me, too, would you?"

"No problem." The glow from the dome light made his blond hair shine. "See you down the road." Carefully, Donovan pushed her door shut. "Good luck in Wichita," he added through her open window before he turned away.

Ashley started the engine, flipped on her lights and checked her side mirror before easing back onto the road. Taylor pulled out behind her. She kept glancing in her side mirror, conscious of his following her, and she couldn't help wondering if Donovan had remembered to pass on her thanks.

When she finally slowed and pulled in at the first gas station that was still open, she asked the teenage attendant about getting the flat fixed. Then she waved dismissively at Donovan, who had rolled down his window.

"I'm all set," she called.

"You want us to wait?" he asked.

Still smarting from Taylor's implication that she couldn't manage on her own, she shook her head. "No, that's okay. You go on ahead."

Before she could thank them again, he turned and said something to Taylor. Then they shifted and pulled away as Donovan shouted a last goodbye, no doubt eager to get on down the road. Suddenly feeling absurdly alone, Ashley turned on her heel and followed the young attendant as the sound of the other truck faded to a growl in the distance.

"Pretty girl," Donovan mused aloud as he and Taylor headed down the dark road.

Taylor didn't bother to respond. His brother never missed an opportunity to meet an attractive woman. Not that Taylor would have left her stranded at the side of the road without stopping to help, even if Donovan hadn't spotted her stalled truck first. Even if their headlights hadn't picked up the sight of her rounded backside as she bent over the front wheel.

For all Taylor cared, she could have been wearing that newfangled thong underwear and it wouldn't have made any difference. Women were a peck of trouble, and he'd already had enough of that to last a lifetime.

"Did you notice those big brown eyes of hers?" Donovan went on as if the two of them were having an actual conversation. He was used to Taylor's silences. "And I think I saw some itty-bitty freckles, like little specks of cinnamon sprinkled across her face." He glanced at Taylor, who put on his turn signal and changed lanes to let a small car pass them.

Oh, he had noticed her eyes, all right—dark and melting, like expensive chocolate, surrounded by a thick sweep of lashes. And the stubborn chin she'd thrust out when he told her she shouldn't be driving alone. As if she really didn't appreciate their help. No doubt she had been relieved as hell to see them. Why didn't women just say what they really wanted, instead of always playing games, daring a man to search beyond the obvious and guess at their true feelings?

Taylor's fingers tightened on the steering wheel. Damned if he could figure them out.

"Nice body, too," Donovan continued as Taylor tuned in a new radio station without taking his eyes off the road ahead. "Legs that went on for miles." He sighed loudly and smoothed down his mustache with one finger.

Did he think Taylor was blind? He had noticed her before, astride her black-and-white pinto, her red-gold braids flying from underneath her cowboy hat while she circled those barrels as tight as bark on a tree. She was a knockout, all right. Despite those long legs his brother had mentioned, she didn't clear Taylor's shoulder. She'd had to tilt her head back to look into his face, and still she'd managed to stare down her haughty little nose at him.

The image made him grin before he realized what he was doing. He gave Donovan an exasperated glance. "Do you want to stop for some coffee now or wait until we get there?" Taylor asked.

His brother's drawl was unrepentant, his green eyes snapping with humor as he shifted one booted foot. "Why? The idea of some little cinnamon pastry whet your appetite, big bro?"

Ashley crouched low over the saddle as Spinner exploded into the arena and headed for the first barrel of the cloverleaf pattern. Dirt flying, they circled it cleanly as she clung to her horse. All she could hear was his thundering hoofbeats and her own urgent cries as they headed for the second barrel. Spinner slammed on the brakes, muscles bunching, and they went into another tight turn. Shouting encouragement, Ashley urged him on to the last big drum. As soon as they'd rounded it, too, they flew back down the arena with a final burst of speed.

Her heart was still racing when their time was announced and she realized they had won the go-round. Acknowledging the applause from the crowd with a wide grin and a wave of her hat, she patted the pinto's neck as they trotted to the gate. "Good boy. Great job."

Spinner blew loudly, bobbing his head and jangling his bridle. When Ashley dismounted, her knees were shaky from the adrenaline rush. The time, well under sixteen seconds, was one of her personal best. She was giving her horse a hug when another barrel racer stopped beside her.

"Nice job." The other woman's comment sounded sincere, even though Ashley's time had bumped her out of third place and a share of the purse.

"Thanks, Gwen." Ashley didn't stop to talk. Her first responsibility was to take care of her horse. He needed to be cooled down and fed before she ate the salad she'd left in the tiny fridge in her camper.

She planned on watching the steer wrestling later. Not for any special reason, she told herself, just for something to do.

Spinner snorted and she glanced over her shoulder to make sure he was okay. When she did, she recognized Taylor Buchanan bearing down on her. He was wearing his black Stetson, a red plaid shirt and dark jeans with an ornate silver buckle. Startled, Ashley hesitated as Spinner stopped beside her and pawed the ground impatiently. For once, she ignored her horse.

Taylor saw her and touched the brim of his hat with his free hand as he started to walk past her. His sideburns were medium brown, she noticed, as were his straight brows. She wondered what he looked like without his hat.

"Excuse me," she said. It was the first opportunity she'd had to thank him directly for changing her tire. She ignored the impulse to point out that she had managed to arrive safely.

He stopped, towering over her own five-and-a-half-foot height, and scowled down at her. The polite little speech she'd prepared melted away like ice under a hot Texas sun. Usually she could talk to anyone.

"Congratulations," he said in his deep, quiet voice. "That was quite a run you just made."

"You were watching?" The idea flustered her even more.

A light that could have been humor glinted in his eyes. They were a bright, shocking blue. "Yes, ma'am."

Her mind went blank. "I owe it all to my horse," she blurted, and then almost groaned at her own idiocy.

To her surprise, Taylor seemed to take her remark seriously as he gave Spinner a thorough perusal and a pat on the neck. "He's beautifully marked. Did you train him yourself?"

She nodded, cheeks hot. "My brother breeds horses in Colorado and he specializes in pintos. He gave Spinner to me."

"You've done a good job with him."

"Thanks." Tentatively, she smiled.

Taylor's eyes narrowed fractionally. "Well, I'll see you later," he said.

Ashley realized he was about to walk away and she still hadn't thanked him.

"Wait!" she exclaimed.

His dark brows rose and she couldn't help noticing how attractive he was, with his strong jaw and weathered face. Here was a man who didn't spend all his time in covered arenas. Tiny lines fanned out from his eyes, and deeper grooves ran from his slightly crooked nose to the corners of his unsmiling mouth.

"Yes?" he prompted.

She realized she was staring and her gaze careened away. "Where's your brother?" she asked, completely rattled as she made a show of glancing up and down the wide aisle. "I haven't seen him around."

When she looked back up at Taylor, his expression had inexplicably hardened. "Donnie will be along any minute, if you want to wait. He had to replace the cinch on his saddle."

Before Ashley could spit out the thanks that she'd meant to tell Taylor in the first place, he touched his hat brim politely and walked quickly away. This time, she didn't even try to stop him.

As Taylor headed toward the barn, he fought down his annoyance. How could he begrudge Donovan his easy popularity with women? His younger brother went out of his way to be friendly, he was never at a loss for words and he was as handsome as sin. Taylor, as Donovan was fond of pointing out, was usually frowning and silent. And he was so big he made women nervous.

Apparently Ashley Gray was one of those who preferred good looks and charm to glowering intimidation. And who could blame her? The two times they had run into each other, Taylor had been as stiff and silent as a stone statue. One glance into her warm brown eyes and his mind had stuttered to a stop. He had quizzed her about her horse, when all she wanted was directions to his golden-boy brother.

Try as Taylor did to banish her sassy image from his consciousness, she refused to go. Only later, when he had backed his horse into the corner of the box at one end of the arena and focused every bit of concentration on the steer he was about to pursue did she finally fade.

"Hey, darlin', why so glum?"

Ashley was still thinking about Taylor when she looked up to see his fair-haired brother coming toward her. He was leading his horse, a showy palomino, by the reins. No doubt Donovan was riding as hazer for Taylor in the steer wrestling to come.

She returned his smile readily, wishing Taylor were half as approachable. Donovan's easygoing manner was a direct contrast to his tongue-tying movie-star looks.

"I wanted to thank Taylor for changing my tire," she said as Donovan pulled up beside her. "But I didn't get a chance."

He glanced around at the stream of contestants and spectators. "I just passed him. He's gone to get his horse."

Ashley bit her lip. "Oh, I saw him a few minutes ago. It's just that when I tried to talk to him, I..." How could she explain without making a fool of herself? She made a futile gesture with her hand.

Donovan tipped back his hat, his green eyes crinkling as his smile widened. "Let me guess. My big brother treated you to one of his fiercest frowns and you forgot what you were going to say."

Ashley's mouth dropped open. "That's it exactly!" she exclaimed as color stained her cheeks. "Is he always so..." Again, words failed her. The man was Donovan's brother, after all.

"So intimidating? Abrasive? Downright unfriendly?" Donovan finished for her.

"Well, yes," she admitted, relieved that he understood. "I ended up asking for you, instead."

"Well, sweetheart, I'm flattered," Donovan drawled as his mischievous gaze danced over her.

"Oh, no, I didn't really mean it," she blurted without thinking.

Instantly, his grin disappeared. He placed his free hand over his heart and dipped his head. "Now I *am* disappointed."

For a second, she was afraid she'd hurt his feelings, until he looked up and winked. Before she could say anything more, they both heard a voice announcing that the steer wrestling was starting in a half hour.

"I'd better let you go. Besides, I need to take care of my horse," she said.

For a moment, Donovan looked as if he meant to say more. Then he tugged at the brim of his hat and clucked to his own mount. "See you later, darlin'," he said over his shoulder.

"Good luck," Ashley remembered to call after him as she watched him go. A couple of pretty young girls in Western dress turned to watch him, too. When he bowed and tipped his hat, they dissolved into giggles.

Ashley knew he had a reputation as a flirt. Taylor, on the other hand, appeared to be more of a loner, except for his brother's companionship. Ashley vaguely remembered hearing something about him and a woman, but she couldn't think what. Maybe one of her friends would remember. Of course, she would have to be careful how she worded her question, or the others would tease her unmercifully.

Gossip about the men and women who rodeoed—who was dating whom, who had broken up and who was available—was second only to speculation about which barrel racer was expected to win which event, who had a new horse and who was going to be at the next show down the road. The last thing Ashley wanted was for her mild interest in Taylor's background to be blown out of proportion.

No, she reconsidered as she left the building with her horse. The very last thing would be for Taylor to find out she was asking about him. Something warned her that he wouldn't welcome her curiosity, no matter how mild.

With a groan, she realized that she would have to hurry if she meant to take care of Spinner and get back in time to watch his event.

Taylor glanced over at Donovan and then directed his entire concentration to the frightened Mexican steer that was about to break the barrier in front of them. The timer wouldn't drop his flag to stop the clock until Taylor had succeeded in wrestling the steer to the ground.

Without taking his gaze off the animal in the chute alongside him, he tightened his hand on the reins and sucked in a breath. The steer broke from the chute and Taylor urged his horse after it.

From her seat in the stands, Ashley leaned forward and watched the rider in the black Stetson as his horse raced alongside the running steer. She was vaguely aware of Donovan's palomino on the steer's right, forcing it to "lane"—to run in a straight line.

She held her breath as Taylor leaned down from his speeding horse and gripped the wicked-looking horns. As soon as his right foot cleared the stirrup, his mount veered away. Legs stuck out in front of him, Taylor dug his heels into the dirt to slow the steer, swung it expertly around and grabbed its nose, twisting its neck and throwing it to the ground.

A loud cheer went up from the crowd as the timer dropped his flag. Taylor got to his feet and slapped his hat against his leg as the steer shook himself and bolted for the exit.

From her seat in the stands, Ashley could see that his hair was medium brown and slightly wavy. He waved to the crowd as his time was announced, his horse trotting behind him. Ashley watched him walk back to the gate until her friend Evie poked her.

"Don't start drooling over that bulldogger. He's a loner." Evie was another barrel racer. She and Ashley were serious competitors in the arena and close friends the rest of the time.

"What do you mean?" Ashley asked as he disappeared and the gate closed behind him. "Do you know him?" Normally, she paid little attention to gossip, but she was curious about him and Evie seemed to know about everyone.

"I've met him. I heard that ever since his divorce his heart's been wrapped in barbed wire. He dumped his wife because he was jealous of her singing career," Evie confided. "Hasn't gotten serious about anyone since. He sees a gal a couple of times and then drops her."

Briefly, Ashley told her about his stopping to help her, omitting his arrogant comment about her traveling alone. "Maybe he's still looking for the right woman," she suggested lightly.

Evie shrugged. "You remember my friend Jill from Montana?"

Ashley nodded. She remembered that Jill wasn't happy unless she had a man in tow.

"She was really hung up on Buchanan, but he broke off for no reason at all."

Ashley sat back in her seat and chewed on her lip thoughtfully. Jill was hardly a test case. But why were Taylor and his brother so different from each other? Was he as self-contained as he appeared, or was there more to him than met the eye? She was definitely curious, but look where curiosity had gotten that poor cat. Best she kept hers to herself. Or, better yet, forgot about it altogether.

"Whatever happened to Jill?" she asked.

"Got married, I think," Evie replied after she had blown a bubble with her gum. "I could sure go for that other Buchanan brother. The blonde. Now there's what I call a hunk. Yummy mustache, great buns and he's a bullrider, too." Bullriding was the most dangerous of all the rodeo events, and fatalities weren't that uncommon. The men who rode bulls were looked on either as dashing heroes or total lunatics, but they had an undeniable appeal.

Ashley realized she was glad Taylor didn't ride bulls. Dropping from a running horse onto a frightened longhorned steer was dangerous enough. At least barrel racing was pretty tame in comparison, although there were occasional wrecks when a horse slipped and fell trying to take a turn too tightly, or a rider lost her seat.

Ashley opened her mouth to say something else about Taylor and then realized that if Evie even suspected her grudging interest in him, there would be no peace. Prudently, Ashley remained silent.

"You going to the dance tomorrow night?" Evie asked her. There was always a Saturday-night dance at the rodeo. It gave everyone a chance to socialize and blow off steam between competing and the dash down the road to the next event, where they would do it all over again.

Ashley loved everything about the pro rodeo circuit, including the endless travel, the people and, most of all, the competition itself.

"Sure, I'm going to the dance," she said. "Penny and I will stop by your camper and pick you up on the way, if you want."

Evie agreed to the plan and then left to find a couple of the other barrel racers, while Ashley stretched her legs out in front of her and watched the rest of the steer wrestling. When no one beat Taylor's time, she found herself almost as pleased as she'd been when she won earlier.

Without stopping to analyze her feelings, she left the grandstand and ran into some friends she hadn't seen in a while. Later, she made her way through the crowd to the campground behind the rodeo arena. The evening was mild. As usual, the area was clogged with pickup trucks, campers and horse trailers. Dogs barked and children shouted as they played. The smells of livestock and cooking food hung in the still air. As Ashley walked back to her own rig, she exchanged greetings with several cowboys she knew.

"Good run today!" a calf roper shouted.

She signaled her thanks with a smile and a wave.

"Hey, Ashley, you goin' to be here for the dance tomorrow night?" hollered a bareback rider she doubted was old enough to shave.

"Sure am," she called back.

"Save me a slow one, will ya?"

As she promised she would, she spotted a dusty black rig parked on her right. Donovan was sitting beside it in a lawn chair, polishing a pair of ornately tooled boots.

When he looked up and saw Ashley, he got to his feet and greeted her.

"Taylor made a good run earlier," she said, glancing around but seeing no sign of him.

"Sure did." As usual, Donovan was smiling.

Ashley realized she'd missed his event while she was talking to her friends. "How did you do?" she asked.

He shook his head. "I got the only bull in Kansas who wouldn't buck. Came in fourth."

"I'm sorry." She knew the rider scored half the points and the bull or bronc the other half. If the animal refused to cooperate, there wasn't much a cowboy could do to improve his score.

"Hey, darlin', want to go to the dance with me tomorrow night and cheer me up?" Donovan asked as he stood holding one shiny boot. A Stetson the color of vanilla ice cream was pushed back on his blond head.

She liked Donovan, but to her he paled next to his brother, and she didn't want to give him the wrong idea. "I'm sorry, but I'm going with a couple of friends," she replied. "I could save you a dance, though."

His smile widened, etching deep creases into his tanned cheeks and making him even more attractive. "I'll look forward to it," he said.

As soon as Taylor knew that Ashley had left, he pushed open the camper door and stepped down to where Donovan was standing, wearing a silly grin.

"What was that all about?" Taylor asked, even though he had heard the exchange through the camper's open window. "I would have thought she'd jump at your invitation."

Donovan gave him an appraising glance before he sat back down and began buffing his boot. "What gave you that idea?"

"She was looking for you earlier." Taylor remembered his disappointment that she had only spoken to him because of Donovan. Taylor couldn't blame his brother for finding her attractive. He did, too. Her brown eyes seemed to look right into him. Hell, maybe she looked at everyone that way, for all he knew. No reason to start acting like a fool.

Donovan held up the boot he was polishing and examined it carefully. "You probably heard what happened," he said. "I made my move and she shot me down." He uttered a sound of disbelief. "What woman says no to a man she's interested in just so she can go to a dance with her girlfriends?"

Taylor couldn't fault his logic. "Maybe she's just playing hard to get," he suggested. Some women liked to string a man along, hiding their real feelings until he was as trussed up in confusion as a hog-tied calf.

Donovan dipped the rag into the polish and rubbed at a spot on the toe of his boot. "I know the difference between a come-on and a thanks anyway," he replied. "Much as I hate to admit it, Ashley didn't even bother to look sorry." His expression revealed his disappointment. "Maybe she likes the strong, silent type."

Suddenly, Taylor found his mood lifting. Without analyzing his feelings, he drawled, "Maybe you're just losing your touch, Donnie boy."

Donovan's eyes narrowed. "Oh, yeah? And maybe the lady's just not interested in cowboys."

It was Taylor's turn to make a rude sound of disbelief. "Yeah, sure."

Donovan sat back in the lawn chair and looked up at last. "Then you go ask her."

The brothers had been daring each other since they were boys. Donovan knew Taylor couldn't let such a direct challenge go unanswered.

"That's not fair," he argued instead. "She's already said no to you. She may turn me down on principle."

Donovan thought for a moment. "Then ask her out tonight."

Silently, Taylor mulled over the idea. It wasn't as if he didn't find her appealing, because he did. It had been a while since he had sought out feminine companionship, and he'd had a lot of practice keeping his feelings under control. As attractive as Ashley was, he wasn't really worried about losing his head. That was a lesson he had learned the hard way. On the other hand, perhaps it would be simpler to let Donovan's challenge go unanswered, for once. What was a little teasing compared with the idea, remote as it might be, of starting something he didn't have any intention of seeing through?

"She's probably got plans for tonight," he told Donovan, rolling down the sleeves of his dressy Western shirt and snapping the cuffs.

Donovan was bent over his other boot, his hat brim hiding his face, but Taylor heard him make a noise. He was clucking. Like a chicken.

Telling himself he was too old for such childish taunts, Taylor forced out a dry chuckle as he turned on one heel and walked away. Surely there was someone else he could find to talk to who wasn't always trying to run his life.

Chapter Two

Ashley peered into the narrow mirror mounted over the sink in her tiny camper. She had just finished washing up and was wrapped in an old towel, about to brush out her hair and put on fresh makeup, when she heard a knock on the door. Probably one of the other women, looking for someone to grab a bite with or needing to borrow some hair spray, a pair of earrings or even a clean shirt. Sharing and helping each other out was an integral part of life on the road and one of the reasons Ashley loved it so much.

Without stopping to put on her robe or think about her tangled hair, she pulled open the door.

Taylor Buchanan was standing on the ground outside, head tipped back so he could look into her face. While Ashley tried to hide her surprise, his startled gaze slid down to the top of her towel.

"I guess I caught you at a bad time."

Ashley's face went hot and she ducked behind the door of the camper. "What can I do for you?" she stammered.

For a moment, he remained silent. Then his lips twitched. "Damned if I can remember," he drawled. "Maybe I'd better come back some other time." He took a step backward, looking like a man about to flee.

"No, that's okay." Afraid he might not come back at all, Ashley was torn between curiosity and regret at the way she was dressed. Or undressed. And wishing that her wrap was at least luxurious velour or fluffy Egyptian cotton instead of the ratty, faded towel that was about one washing away from the rag bag. She felt a little silly cowering behind the door, but she didn't want him to go and she couldn't very well invite him in. "What did you want?"

If her question provoked any inappropriate responses, Taylor wisely didn't let on. He was freshly shaven, she noticed, and he had on a clean shirt and jeans. This time his ornate belt buckle was gold. She recognized it from the Pendleton Roundup out in Oregon.

He studied her with a brooding expression, as if he was turning something over in his mind. His face was impossible to read. "I wondered if you'd already eaten or if you'd like to go somewhere for a late dinner?" he asked abruptly.

A dinner invitation from him was the last thing she expected to hear. If he wanted to shock her into dropping her towel, he had darned near succeeded.

She meant to say no. There was something about Taylor Buchanan that put her survival instinct on full alert—and she always listened to her instincts. This time, though, the message got scrambled somewhere between her brain and her mouth.

"Sure," she said, surprising herself. "I haven't had anything since breakfast but a salad. Just give me a few minutes to dress, okay?"

If he was pleased that she'd accepted his invitation, he gave no sign. Instead, his gaze strayed back to the towel. "I like what you're wearing now." The glint was back in his eyes. "That shade of blue looks good with your hair."

Her hair! She'd raked it loose of its habitual braid with her fingers, but she hadn't even put a brush to it. No doubt it was hanging around her face like frayed rope. She inched the door closed.

"I'd rather change into something else," she told him. "This gets drafty. How long do I have to get ready?"

He glanced at his watch. "A half hour? Is that enough time? I need to go by the barn first, anyway."

She didn't know if she should be insulted or amused by his generous offer. Just how much repair work did he envision her making? "I'll do my best," she said dryly.

His eyes narrowed as if he was trying to decide how to interpret her tone. "Wear something casual and we'll try that steak place down the road a ways. Unless you'd rather go somewhere different?"

"Steak's fine."

"I'll be back in thirty minutes." Still looking slightly wary, he touched the brim of his hat and left.

For a moment as she stared at his broad back, panic filled her. Taylor wasn't a man you shared dinner and maybe a kiss with and then walked away unscathed. He had *dangerous* stamped all over him. Why in blazes hadn't she just said no?

He had already disappeared around the corner of her camper, so she couldn't very well chase after him with her towel flapping. And tell him what? That she had come to her senses? Remembered a previous engagement? Gotten cold feet?

Well, that last one might be true if she stood here any longer. She shut the door and leaned against it as her basic sense of honesty made her admit, if only to herself, that she wanted this one evening—wanted to test that shiver of attraction she felt toward him and see if it was reciprocated. She wasn't an impressionable buckle bunny, new to the circuit. No rodeo bum, not even a successful one like Taylor, was going to put any dents in her carefully guarded heart.

When Ashley was done with the silent pep talk, she realized she was still wearing only a towel. Even her eyelashes were naked. She had to be dressed, made up and combed out in a little over twenty-five minutes. And ready to resist the most intriguing man she had met in years. Just the kind of man, she suspected, that her brother had in mind when he'd warned her about cowboys in general and rodeo bums in particular.

Lordy, but she was looking forward to tonight!

"So, can I get you anything else?" the waiter, who looked barely old enough to be out of high school, asked Ashley as he set down her plate. She eyed it with dismay while he served Taylor's T-bone. After confiding that this was his first day on the job, the poor boy had already given Taylor the wrong dressing on his salad and brought them both beer after she had asked for wine. He looked so nervous that she felt sorry for him, and she made a point of giving him an encouraging smile every time he looked her way.

"She ordered prime rib," Taylor said bluntly. He had set his hat on an empty chair and finger-combed his wavy brown hair.

Ashley winced as the waiter's smile faded. "Actually, this looks pretty good," she began as she studied the barbecued chicken he'd set before her. "Maybe..."

"Oh, no. I'm sorry." He whipped the offending plate back before she could protest. "I'll bring you the prime rib right away."

"Thank you." She caught his eye and gave him another encouraging smile, aware that Taylor watched them with a brooding expression as he took a long swallow of beer. Couldn't he see that the boy was practically shaking in his boots? "Don't worry," she added. "You'll get the hang of it."

"If I don't get the hang of it pretty soon, the boss is going to fire me," he said in a low voice as he hung his head. "I've already made too many mistakes tonight."

Ashley grabbed the plate back out of his hands. "I've changed my mind," she told him, ignoring Taylor's snort of displeasure. "I'm really in the mood for chicken, after all."

The waiter beamed, his cheeks turning bright red. "You don't have to do this."

Ashley reached up to pat his arm. "We'll put in a good word for you before we leave."

"I can't thank you enough." The waiter included Taylor in his grateful glance. "Uh, well, I'll let you eat in peace."

"Thanks, we appreciate that," Taylor drawled as he cut into his steak.

Ashley glared, but he ignored her. "Think you can manage to bring me another beer?" he asked instead.

"Right away," the waiter stammered. He glanced back at Ashley, who gave him a broad wink.

After he had left, she stared across the table at Taylor. He returned her gaze, jaw flexing as he chewed his steak.

"Well," she said brightly, cutting into her chicken. "How's your dinner?"

"Meat's tough."

"That's not Larry's fault," she huffed.

"Larry?"

"Our waiter. Didn't you notice his name tag?"

Taylor had to admit that he hadn't. He had been too busy looking at her, tempting as a hand-dipped chocolate in a black T-shirt with Cheyenne Frontier Days across the front in gold script and snug black jeans. She had left her hair loose and it tumbled past her shoulders in a lick of pure fire. Tiny gold stars danced at her earlobes, drawing his attention with her every movement.

Lowering his gaze, he cut off another bite of steak with careful precision. When he looked up again, he noticed her smiling at some point past his shoulder. He turned and wasn't surprised to see Larry grinning like a fool, his thin cheeks flushed. The cozy exchange reminded Taylor of all the times he'd caught Lorrie Ann flirting practically under his nose. How stupid did women think he was, anyway?

He toyed with the idea of tearing the waiter limb from limb, then dissected more of his steak instead. "Want me to get you his phone number?" he asked Ashley dryly. He was angry at himself for letting her behavior provoke him. He thought he'd put aside possessive feelings like jealousy. You had to care to be jealous, and he'd learned the hard way that caring could bring on more pain than he wanted to feel ever again.

Ashley looked astonished at his question. "He's probably young enough to be my, well, my younger brother, anyway," she protested, obviously unsure whether Taylor had been kidding. "I feel sorry for him, that's all. He's having such a tough time."

Taylor didn't bother to answer. This evening had been a mistake, that was for sure. When was he going to learn? Lorrie Ann always had an excuse, too, and it always sounded plausible. He wasn't long on trust these days. She'd finally wised him up when he caught her breaking in a saddle-bronc rider.

Taylor took a deep, steadying breath. Ashley was right; the waiter was young and obviously nervous. Perhaps she was only trying to be nice. Not all women were like Lorrie Ann—they couldn't be. He knew that deep down.

"How'd you get into rodeo?" he asked Ashley.

Her grateful smile almost dispelled his annoyance. "I grew up on a ranch in Colorado," she said. "I started racing barrels as soon as I could stay in the saddle. Being a part of rodeo is all I ever wanted to do. How about you?"

"The same," he said, realizing that if he asked her questions, she had a perfect right to ask them back. Talking about himself made him uncomfortable. There was so much in his past that he just wanted to forget. "Donnie and I pretty much grew up on a ranch. Rodeo was our dream." He didn't add that it had been one way to escape a life he hated.

"Was the ranch anywhere around here?" she asked as she forked up some rice.

"No. Idaho."

"I hear there's some real pretty country up there. Someday I'd like to check it out for myself." He didn't respond, so she rushed on. "Do you have other brothers or sisters besides Donovan?"

The last thing Taylor wanted to discuss—or even to think about—was his family. "I have a sister, but she's a lot younger." He returned his attention to his plate, hoping to discourage further conversation. He should have known better.

"Does she still live in Idaho?"

Taylor saw the waiter coming back with his beer. He paused until the boy had set it down and departed before he answered. "I have no idea where she is," he admitted. She had been so young the last time he'd seen her that she probably didn't even remember she had brothers. That was what hurt the most. That and not knowing if he would ever see her again.

Ashley's friendly expression faded. "I'm sorry," she murmured, obviously unsure where to take the conversation next. "I have a half brother. He's older than I am, but we're pretty close. I can only imagine how you must feel."

Gruffly, Taylor brushed aside her sympathetic comment. She hadn't a clue how he felt, and he wasn't about to enlighten her. It was less painful to keep some things buried than to drag them out and examine them like faded snapshots.

"He still has the ranch in Colorado," she added between bites.

Relieved, Taylor realized she was talking about her half brother. "He's the one who raises horses?"

"Yes, and cattle as well. Our mom still lives there, too."

"Someone else owns the place in Idaho now." Taylor could have bitten his tongue for volunteering the information without thinking. Ducking his head, he stabbed a bite of potato.

While he waited, braced for more uncomfortable questions, Ashley told him about the Blue Moon Ranch and her family. She had no way of knowing the envy that clawed at his insides at the cheerful picture she painted.

The childhood he had shared with his brother had been a hell of a lot different from the idyllic one she described.

Gradually, his tension faded. "Sounds like a nice way to grow up."

"Daddy used to call me his little cowpoke," she added with a rueful smile. "I followed him and Joe around like a puppy."

Taylor wondered about the edge her voice had taken on, but didn't ask. She was pretty and she stirred his blood. That didn't mean he was ready to trade secrets. Usually he was careful only to get mixed up with women who knew the score and wanted only what he did—a good time before they both moved on. Women, he suspected, who were as different from the one seated across from him as a half-wild range cow was from a bottle-fed calf.

Ashley had been nibbling on her lower lip, studying him assessingly. Now she set down her fork. "You haven't mentioned your parents. Are they still alive?"

Taylor shrugged, holding the hurtful memories at bay. He looked around for the waiter. Where was the boy when he was really needed, anyway? "How about some dessert?" Taylor asked.

"No, thanks. No dessert, just coffee." If she was bothered by his rudeness in ignoring her question, she didn't let it show.

When the waiter came to the table to see if they needed anything else, Ashley gave him a smile that made Taylor's breath catch.

"Coffee," he growled. "Think you can manage that okay?"

As soon as he had spat out the words, he regretted them. It wasn't the waiter's fault that Ashley was one of those women who were naturally flirtatious. He could hardly ignore her.

"Yes, sir," he stammered as he scrambled away.

For a moment, Taylor wondered if Ashley was going to ask again about his family. Instead, she studied him thoughtfully until he was tempted to fidget in his chair.

"I'm sorry if I made you uncomfortable," she said, surprising him. He hadn't realized he was that easy to read. "I might get carried away sometimes, but I didn't mean to pry."

Her unexpected apology made him feel like a prize jackass. Her questions hadn't been out of line.

He was tempted to tell her that, but it would involve more explanations, ones he wasn't willing to give. "Don't worry about it," he mumbled instead, ducking his head like a schoolboy.

Despite his attraction to her, the date was turning into a disaster. He wished that, for once, he had ignored his brother's dare. When he looked up, her eyes were dark with sympathy. She reached out to pat the hand he rested on the table. Her touch was warm; it threatened the icy wall around his heart.

Taylor's response was instinctive. He yanked his hand away and got to his feet, terrified that the wall he'd built so painstakingly would crack and his feelings, dammed up for so long, would finally come cascading out like a flash flood—humiliating him and shocking her.

Ashley's lower lip trembled as she stared up at him. He knew he was overreacting, but he could no more stop himself than he could stop the chilly panic sliding through him.

Deliberately, he wiped all emotion from his voice. "If you can tear yourself away from Larry, I think it's time we left."

* * *

He had been horrible to her, she didn't understand him at all and she was well rid of him, she told herself on the short ride back to the campground in the car Taylor had borrowed. Neither of them had spoken a word since his last outrageous crack about the waiter. As Taylor drove slowly down the row to her camper, Ashley refused to break the awkward silence.

People were still sitting around in lawn chairs in the glow from the outside lights, talking quietly and drinking beer, but a lot of the campsites were deserted. Or empty. Those who hadn't done well were already on their way to some other rodeo hundreds of miles away in their quest for the prize money that was the only measure of their standings for the season.

When Taylor stopped the car and went around to open her door, Ashley didn't meet his eyes. "Thank you for dinner," she murmured in a parody of politeness as he followed her to the back of her camper.

"Yeah, sure." In the glow from a nearby lantern, his expression was harsh and unrelenting. Only his eyes were shadowed by the brim of his Stetson.

She wished she could read his meaning, wished she could tell if there was some complex emotion behind that wall of ice as she suspected—even wanted to believe—or just more ice.

It made her sad that she would probably never know. At the bottom of the steps to the door of her camper, she turned. His head dipped and the beams from a slowly passing car illuminated his eyes for an instant. Long enough for her to see the flare of desire. Despite her confusion, an answering spark burst to life within her.

Dismayed by her weakness, she scrambled up the steps.

"Good night," she said over her shoulder as she yanked open her door. A man like Taylor should come with a warning label. She was a fool to be intrigued, pathetic to still be attracted.

She didn't expect a reply, and he didn't give her one. When she turned to shut her door, he was halfway to the car. There was nothing left for her to do but to slip quietly inside and do her best to put the evening behind her.

As he drove back down the rutted road to return the car he had borrowed from one of the roughstock riders, Taylor silently lambasted his poor judgment in asking her out in the first place. He would have been far better off focusing his attention on the action in the arena and forgetting about things that would only torment him with reminders of what his barren life was missing.

The warmth he saw in Ashley could overheat in a flash, scorching all it touched and leaving nothing behind except ashes and painful scars. It was safer to stay cold. Numb and alone. He had learned that lesson the hard way, and it was one he'd best never forget.

The next day, Ashley had another good run at the barrels, finishing second in her go-round. That evening she intended celebrating her success. Even the sight of Taylor's black truck still parked in its usual spot wasn't enough to spoil her mood as she hurried back to her camper to change for the dance.

"Wow, look at you!" Evie exclaimed when Ashley stopped by to pick her up.

Ashley twirled around in a circle to show off the denim skirt she wore with cowboy boots and a shirt that dripped fringe. The skirt and boots had been Christmas presents from her sister-in-law, but this was the first time she'd worn them.

"Do you like?" she asked Evie self-consciously, tugging on the hem of her short skirt.

"More important, will the guys like?" Evie said with a laugh. "Those boots better not pinch your toes, honey. I have a feeling your feet won't get much rest at the dance tonight."

An hour later, Evie passed by her on the crowded dance floor as the band played a lively number with more enthusiasm than skill.

"Told you so," Evie mouthed over her partner's shoulder.

Ashley was dancing with Donovan for the second time. He had come over to claim her as soon as she walked in, then returned several songs later to ask her again. Both times he flirted so outrageously that he made her laugh. She hadn't seen his brother, but between line dancing and partnering other cowboys out celebrating a win or forgetting a defeat, she hadn't left the floor.

"Heard you had dinner with my bro last night," Donovan said as he raised their joined hands and she ducked beneath his arm.

"That's right, I did." She wondered how much Taylor had told him about the evening, and whether he was coming to the dance. Not for anything would she admit her interest to Donovan.

"Don't think he said anything, because he didn't," he continued, dispelling her concern. "I just know how contrary he can be if he sets his mind to it."

"Why would he bother to ask me out and then be contrary?" Ashley demanded the next time the dance steps brought them together.

Donovan shrugged. "I never said he always showed good sense. He's my brother, though, so I have to stick up for him."

Donovan's expression showed that he was kidding, as he so often did. Ashley wished she could ask him about the family Taylor seemed so reluctant to discuss, but this was neither the time nor the place. Especially if Donovan had the same apparent aversion to family that Taylor did.

Instead she admitted, "We didn't exactly hit it off. It was no one's fault, but it didn't work out."

As Donovan again raised his arm so she could twirl beneath it, she thought he looked disappointed. In other circumstances, she might have been offended that a man as handsome as her current partner seemed to be matchmaking for someone else.

After he finished spinning her around, the number came to an end. Ashley scanned the crowd and her gaze collided with a piercing blue one. Taylor was standing by the door wearing his habitual black hat and a matching shirt with a jagged red and white stripe across the chest. When she spotted him, his jaw bunched and he looked away.

He danced the next number with the rodeo secretary, who had gray hair and a photograph of her grandchildren on her desk in the trailer where she collected entry fees and paid out prize money. Ashley's partner was an old family friend who often worked as a pickup man. When the music stopped and he returned her to the sidelines, she saw Taylor working his way in her direction as a skinny bronc rider pulled her into a lively two-step. By the time he spun her back around, Taylor had disappeared.

She didn't see him again until she danced with Donovan for the third time. Taylor had his arms around a pretty girl she'd never seen before. Telling herself it wasn't jealousy she felt burning inside her like acid, she turned her back on him abruptly.

For a moment, she had forgotten all about Donovan, who dropped his arms in confusion.

"That must be a step I haven't learned yet," he said gallantly as she stumbled against him.

Embarrassed, Ashley apologized.

"No need," he replied with a grin. He glanced in Taylor's direction and then raised a brow at Ashley. "You okay?"

"I'd like to sit down," she replied. "These boots aren't broken in yet, and my feet are starting to hurt." If Pinocchio had been more than just a fairy tale, her nose would have poked out Donovan's eye.

"Sure thing." He slid his arm around her shoulders and walked her from the crowded floor.

"Would you like something to drink?" he asked as the number ended and the band announced they were taking a break.

"No, thanks. I'm fine." She wondered if Taylor had noticed her new skirt.

"I'll find us a place to sit, then." He began looking around for empty chairs.

Ashley realized the energy that had propelled her since her earlier ride had finally drained away, leaving her feeling as flat as stale beer. The big room she had thought so filled with laughter and fun earlier now seemed only hot and noisy.

"Actually, I think I'll go back to camp and turn in," she replied. When he offered to escort her, she saw Evie stick up her arm and point to her watch. Making her excuses, Ashley thanked Donovan and left him to enjoy the rest of the evening. Before she turned away, another woman came up and claimed him.

As Ashley made her way to the door, exchanging greetings and turning down pleas to stay awhile longer, she was careful not to look around. Taylor could dance with two women at once if he chose to; it had nothing to do with her.

The next afternoon as she pulled out of the campgrounds behind the huge covered arena, she realized that her path probably wouldn't cross Taylor's for weeks— given the number of rodeos there were to choose from all across the country. By the time she stopped for coffee and a sandwich a couple of hours later, she almost had herself convinced it didn't matter.

She hated traveling alone. Over the years, she had almost always had someone, usually another woman, riding with her. It helped with expenses and made the driving easier. There had been a couple of opportunities back in Wichita to pick up a rider or two, but she hadn't acted on them. Even now, she wasn't sure why. Maybe she was just getting antisocial, she thought as she pulled out of the truck stop, one of many such places she would pass on the long drive to the next rodeo. For once her usual anticipation was flagging.

Maybe she needed the time alone.

When Taylor and Donovan got to the rodeo grounds in Colorado Springs a couple of weeks later, the first thing they did was to park the truck and troop into the office to pay their entry fees and check the schedule. Then they got their horses settled in their allocated stalls and drove out to the informal campground behind the arena.

Taylor noticed an old green pickup parked there, but it was towing a small camp trailer and there was a little boy playing out front. The rig probably belonged to a roughstock rider, since he wouldn't have to bring his own horse on the road. The stock contractor furnished the broncs and bulls, and often provided the portable fencing used for the chutes, as well. All a rider needed was his gear and his guts.

"This okay with you?" Donovan asked, slowing the truck by an empty spot. "It's not too far from the barn."

"Sure thing." As soon as he'd braked, Taylor was out of the cab. He watched closely while Donovan backed up the empty horse trailer.

Was Ashley here? He hadn't seen her since the dance back in Kansas, but that didn't mean he'd forgotten one thing about her. Like the skirt she'd worn. It hadn't begun to cover those long, wraparound legs. Just thinking about them made his mouth go dry. Or the way her dark eyes had softened with concern at dinner while he dodged her questions.

Somehow, she had slipped through a crack in his armor. He needed to see her again, if for no other reason than to prove to himself that she was just a flesh-and-blood woman and not a fiery-haired tease—flitting in and out of his dreams like an R-rated Tinkerbell.

Donovan poked his head out the truck window, distracting him. "How'm I doing?" he asked.

Taylor glanced around and made a chopping motion with his hand. "Close enough." As the brake lights flashed on, his mind switched gratefully to the first year they'd been on the circuit.

They'd gone to rodeos in towns so small they weren't on any map, ridden in open arenas that were little more than corrals surrounded by wooden benches. There were no barns or showers. They'd slept in the pickup bed or shared a cheap motel room with as many as four other cowboys.

When they did win, the purses often barely covered expenses. Sometimes they chose between meals and entry fees, but they had hung in until they both began winning steadily enough to buy a battered camper and to eat on a fairly regular basis. Neither one of them had ever mentioned quitting. The past few years had brought them both a measure of success they'd only dreamed of when they'd lived on old John Tulley's ranch. This life with its dizzying success and crushing failures, elation, anguish and injuries was all Taylor had ever wanted.

Now Donnie cut the engine and climbed down from the cab, stretching the kinks from his back and shoulders. Did he ever think about what it was like growing up? Taylor wouldn't blame him if he didn't. For the most part, it was too painful to remember.

"It's gotta be a woman," Donovan remarked, effectively derailing the train of Taylor's thoughts. "Who is it—that tall brunette I saw you with at the last dance or the little redhead we met in Tulsa?" While Taylor gave him a disgusted look, he snapped his fingers. "I know, it's Ashley, isn't it? You never did say anything about how your date with her went, but you didn't go near her at the dance the next night."

Taylor managed a crooked smile. What would Donnie say if he admitted what he had been thinking about? "Actually, it was all three women," he drawled instead. "I've been trying to make up my mind."

Donovan came over and slapped him on the back. "Sure, bro. Let me know what you decide. Now let's go have a beer and see who's showed up here so far."

His suggestion suited Taylor just fine. It sure beat thinking about either Ashley or the distant past. Together the brothers ambled toward the beer garden in the big arena. As they walked by the green pickup he had spotted earlier, he saw that it wasn't even a Jimmy like Ashley's, it was a Ford.

"Good luck later," Ashley called to one of the other contestants. As she turned to hurry down the tunnel out of the arena, she slammed into what felt more like a brick wall than a human one. Big hands whipped out to steady her as she grabbed for her hat, which had fallen down over her face when she reared back her head.

"Why don't you—" she started to say as she lifted up her Stetson.

"Maybe you'd better slow down and watch—" A familiar deep voice stopped abruptly as her startled gaze collided with Taylor Buchanan's chilly blue one. For a moment, his fingers tightened on her upper arms as if he was about to shove her away.

"Are you okay?" he asked instead.

Suddenly aware that her hand was still pressed against his wide chest, she snatched it back. "Yes, I'm fine." For a moment she thought he was going to add something more, but then his mouth flattened into a grim line. "Excuse me." He stepped carefully around her and hurried away.

Cheeks flaming, Ashley began to move in the opposite direction. She dragged in an unsteady breath. Obviously, their unexpected run-in hadn't fazed him at all, while her arms still tingled from the imprint of his hands. She was bound to see him now and then—if she had any sense at all, she wouldn't let him disconcert her like this.

When she caught up with two of her friends who were going to watch the bareback bronc riding, she was still annoyed at her own vulnerability.

"Was that Taylor Buchanan I saw you with?" Stacy asked as they found seats in the grandstand.

Evie's eyes widened with curiosity. Ashley had confided that their date hadn't gone well.

"I wasn't actually with him," she said shortly. "He almost mowed me down. You'd think someone that big would watch where he was going." She felt vaguely guilty for stretching the truth, but the collision had been partly his fault.

"I wouldn't mind running into him," Stacy purred. She had long black hair and a curvy figure. Evie had once referred to Stacy as a carnivore who ate rodeo cowboys for breakfast. "Maybe he'd take me to the finals in Las Vegas with him. He's way up in the standings."

"Trust me, you wouldn't last that long," Evie told her.

"Better qualify on your own," Ashley teased, ignoring her own sudden irritation at Stacy's comment. Who was Ashley to care whether the other woman set her sights on Taylor Buchanan or any other cowboy?

Before Stacy could reply to either of them, the announcer introduced the first contestant, a man Ashley knew only slightly but Evie had once dated, and the three women turned their attention to the other end of the arena.

Later that night as Ashley was walking back to her camper after checking on Spinner, she heard a burst of derisive masculine laughter coming from the shadows behind the big barn. Probably a couple of cowboys sharing a bottle, she thought as she kept walking.

From that same direction came a faint bark and then a sharp yelp of pain. She glanced back over her shoulder, but she couldn't see anything clearly beyond the pool of light. When she hesitated, wondering what she should do, she heard another yelp that turned into a heartrending whine.

Ashley looked around for help but there was no one else in sight. She was about to hurry on to the campground in search of aid when another burst of jeering laughter made her decide to investigate the noise instead. Stomach knotted, she stepped out of the light.

As she cautiously inched closer, a movement in the deep shadows by the back fence caught her eye. It was still too far away to see what was going on. Hesitating, she looked toward the campground again, but it appeared deserted.

Quietly, Ashley sneaked up behind a Dumpster. Peering around it, she could make out four figures in the gloom. They looked like teenage boys. She heard another whine and saw a dog huddled against the fence. He looked hurt. While she tried to decide what to do, one of the boys took a long drink from a bottle and then threw it at the poor animal. The bottle missed its target and Ashley hoped the dog would run, but it was either too scared or too weak.

Sickened, she was about to step out from behind the Dumpster and demand that they stop when she noticed another man hurry toward them.

"What the hell are you kids doing out here?" he yelled as she crept closer.

At the sound of his voice, Ashley's heart lurched into her throat. Good Lord, the man confronting the boys was Taylor and he was hopelessly outnumbered.

Chapter Three

As Ashley peered into the gloom, she saw the four boys whirl and fan out slowly, surrounding Taylor. Suddenly, the teenagers looked a lot more menacing.

"Why don't you mind your own business, cow-poke?" sneered the tallest of the group.

"Let the dog go," Taylor replied. His voice was as calm as if he were ordering a pizza.

Ashley inched along the side of the Dumpster, fear rising in her throat. Despite Taylor's size and strength, there were four of them and only one of him.

"Who's gonna make us?" challenged the same boy who had just spoken. He appeared to be the leader.

They could have knives, she realized. Or worse, a gun. If she went for help, Taylor might be hurt before she got back.

"Just leave the dog alone," he urged. "I don't want any trouble."

"Then you should have minded your own damn business, tough guy."

Ashley had hoped they would leave. Instead, they began to circle around Taylor, who remained silent. If only a half dozen more steer wrestlers would suddenly appear.

"You gonna take us on to save this poor doggy?" taunted the boy who was doing all the talking.

"If I have to."

Ashley knew she had to do something, and quickly. Taking a deep breath, she stepped away from the Dumpster and walked through the darkness toward the little group.

"The others are coming," she said in a clear voice. "And the police have been called."

Taylor spun around at the sound of her voice. "Ashley! What the hell are you doing here?" It was clear he was less than thrilled to see her.

She forced a smile to her trembling lips. The boys were watching her and one made a low comment she didn't hear. They all snickered.

"We've been looking for you," she told Taylor firmly as she went to his side, hoping he wouldn't say the wrong thing. "Your brother and two of his friends were right behind me." As a bluff it was mighty weak, but it was the best she could come up with on such short notice.

One of the boys uttered a crude curse and glanced warily around. "Let's get out of here." He lowered his fists. "That mutt ain't worth the trouble."

The leader squinted into the shadows. After a moment that seemed like half a lifetime, he gave an indifferent shrug. "Yeah, I hear ya." He took a threatening step toward Ashley.

Taylor shifted in front of her protectively, the muscles in his shoulders and arms bunching. She was grateful, but they were still outnumbered. If the boys didn't leave soon, they'd realize she was bluffing.

"We got better things to do," drawled the leader. "Let's book."

Relief nearly buckled Ashley's knees. As she watched, afraid to breathe, he turned and trotted off into the darkness with the other three close behind him. Now that the danger was past, she started to shake all over. Tears rolled down her cheeks.

"What the hell do you think you were doing?" Taylor demanded, grabbing her shoulders.

"What were *you* doing?" she echoed, wrenching loose. "There were four of them and they looked so mean. What were you thinking of, confronting them all by yourself?"

He shrugged. "I heard the dog whining. They were only boys."

"Boys kill people," she cried, fighting hysterical laughter. "I was just trying to help."

To her surprise, he yanked her roughly into his arms. She felt him press his face against her hair. For a moment, his solid warmth enveloped her, making her feel safe once again, and then he let her go.

"Thanks," he said quietly. "I appreciate it."

Before Ashley could respond, the dog whimpered softly. In all the excitement, she'd almost forgotten about the poor creature.

"We've got to get him out of here, in case they come back." Slowly, Taylor crouched down and began moving closer.

"Be careful," Ashley whispered. "If he's scared, he could bite you."

Stretching out his hand, Taylor began talking in low, soothing tones. Hesitantly, the dog stretched out his head and sniffed his fingers. Then the animal whimpered softly, a plea for help.

"He's been badly frightened," Taylor muttered, "but I can't see where he's hurt. It's too dark here."

Ashley stayed perfectly still, watching the two of them. Taylor was so patient, so caring. This was a new side to him that she was seeing, a side she had hoped was there, beneath the ice.

"Good boy," he crooned. "It's okay, we won't hurt you." The dog let Taylor pat his head as his tail thumped weakly against the ground. Taylor skimmed his hands over the animal's trembling body. "The boys were throwing rocks and bottles," he told Ashley. "I think he's bleeding."

"I heard him cry out," she said. "I was trying to see what was going on when you rode in on your white horse."

Taylor glanced at her over his shoulder. "It would have been really stupid for you to come back here alone. Those boys were trouble."

She hadn't thought of the possible danger until she had seen Taylor confront them. "It didn't stop you," she replied as he straightened and peeled off his jacket.

From what Ashley could tell, the dog looked like a terrier mix. He was medium sized, his short hair matted and dirty, and he had pointed ears and dark eyes.

"I hate to move him without knowing where he's hurt, but we need to get him to a vet," Taylor told her.

"Is he wearing a tag or a collar?" Ashley asked.

"No. He's probably a stray." Taylor checked the luminous dial of his watch. "Damn, I'll have to put him in my camper for now," he said as he glanced up. In the dimness, she could see that his face was set in harsh lines. "My event's about to start. He'll probably be okay until I'm done and then I'll look for an all-night clinic."

"I can take him to the vet," Ashley said. The poor thing could have been hurt worse than they thought.

Taylor wrapped the dog in his jacket and lifted him carefully. Then he headed toward the light of the campground with Ashley hurrying to keep up.

"We don't know anything about him," Taylor said as they walked. "He could get frightened and turn on you. Maybe I can find someone else to take him."

When they got to where Ashley's truck was parked, she put a detaining hand on Taylor's arm. "We're wasting time," she told him, scratching the dog's chin. Immediately, he licked her fingers. His eyes were as round and dark as buttons.

She stroked his head. "Look. He's really very sweet. We'll be fine." She opened the passenger door and waited. In the light, they could see that the dog had a swollen place on his head and several cuts. Taylor set him down on the seat and pulled a bandanna from his pocket. He tied it around a deep gash on the foreleg that was still oozing blood.

"I'll stop by the office on my way out and ask if anyone knows about an emergency clinic that might be open," Ashley added impatiently.

"I could skip my event and go with you," Taylor replied. "It's not that big a deal."

"Don't be ridiculous." His offer warmed her, but she knew how far he'd come to compete, and how crucial one win could be in the standings at the end of the season. Luckily, her event had been first tonight. "We'll be fine."

"Okay. Take this." He handed her two folded bills.

She hadn't thought about how she was going to pay the vet. Her own funds were still low. "Thanks." She tucked the money into her shirt pocket. "I'll let you know what happens." Circling the truck, she hopped behind the wheel. Taylor shut the passenger door. She glanced at the dog, whose head was down, and started the engine.

"Be careful," Taylor admonished, stepping away from the truck.

"I will." Slowly, she accelerated. The dog didn't move, and she hoped she could get help in time to save him. Damn those boys, anyway.

With directions to the closest after-hours pet clinic, she drove into town. The vet was still there and she examined the stray right away.

"His cuts and bruises look pretty superficial, but that gash on his leg needs stitches," she told Ashley after she had inspected him carefully. "He's malnourished and he has no tag or identifying tattoo. I'd say he's been on his own for a good while now. When I've got him patched up, I'll call animal control to fetch him."

"I'd like to wait and make sure he's really okay," Ashley said, relieved that his injuries weren't more serious. He seemed like such a sweet little thing as he watched her with apparent trust.

"I'll be keeping him here for the rest of the night. If you want, you can come back in the morning, though, before he's picked up."

Ashley agreed and pulled the money Taylor had given her out of her pocket. She was shocked to see that the two bills folded together were both hundreds. Giving one to the vet as a deposit, she extracted a promise that animal control wouldn't take him away until she came back the next day. Before she left, she patted the dog gently on the head. He really was kind of cute. Or he would be when he was cleaned up. In the light from the clinic, his fur looked gray under all the dirt.

"I'll be back," she told him as she scratched under his chin. "You take it easy." Giving the vet an embarrassed glance, she asked, "Are you sure he'll be all right?"

"If you hadn't brought him in, he might have bled to death. Those cuts would have certainly gotten infected. He's in no danger now, though, and he should be feeling a lot better by morning."

A little while later, Ashley was just pulling up back at the arena when Taylor hurried over to her truck. "How's the dog?" he asked.

His obvious concern warmed her. Alone, she probably wouldn't have been able to save him and might very well have gotten hurt trying. Taylor's willingness to go out of his way for a helpless animal made her see him in a whole new light.

"He's going to be fine," she replied. "The vet wants to keep him overnight, so I'm going back in the morning to check on him."

"I'll go with you." Taylor's tone left no room for arguing, but she didn't mind. On the contrary, she was pleased he took such an interest in the dog she was already thinking about keeping.

"He reminded me of a little mutt we had where I grew up," Taylor found himself telling Ashley the next morning while they were driving to the vet's office. Funny, he hadn't thought about Scruffy in years. She used to follow him and Donovan down to the bus stop when the weather was halfway decent, and she'd often be waiting there for them again in the afternoon.

"Did your dog look like Tramp?" Ashley asked. She was wearing faded jeans and a flowered shirt. Her glorious hair was twisted into pigtails that reminded him of braided copper and tied with ribbons that matched the blue in her shirt. On her, the hairstyle looked anything but childish.

Ignoring the insistent pull of attraction, Taylor raised his eyebrows. "Tramp?" he echoed.

She glanced down at her hands, and he saw that her cheeks had gone pink beneath its smattering of freckles. "He reminds me of the dog in that Disney movie *Lady and the Tramp*," she confessed. "Kind of gray and with the same square muzzle and pointy ears. Oh, take a left at the next corner."

"All that gray may just be dirt," he replied as he slowed and put on his turn signal. Although he hoped the dog would recover, the main reason Taylor was going to the vet's this morning was because of Ashley. He knew he should stay away from her; they got on like cowboys and bucking bulls, but he hadn't been able to resist the chance to spend time with her.

"I'm sure the local animal shelter can find a good home for the pup," he said as they drove slowly down a side street. "Somewhere that has a fenced yard and kids he can play with. He seems friendly enough."

"The vet's office is in that brick building on the right," Ashley said, pointing. "If Tramp is ready to be released, I'm taking him with me. I've decided to adopt him."

Surprised, Taylor glanced at her profile as she stared straight ahead through the windshield. Her chin was thrust out, as if she expected an argument. The way Taylor saw it, Tramp would be a link between the two of them, a reason to seek her out without anyone getting the wrong idea.

"That's a great idea," he told her, his mood lightening. "He'll be company for you on the road, and he might even prove to be a decent bodyguard."

"I don't need a bodyguard," she said quickly as he pulled into a parking place and killed the engine. "I can take care of myself."

Prudently, Taylor swallowed his grin. Her prickly attitude reminded him of a little barn cat, all big eyes and bravado, spitting at anyone who tried to pet it. Before he could come up with a suitable response, she was out of the truck.

"Come on. I want to see how he's doing."

Still amused, Taylor followed her into the small veterinary clinic. It smelled like antiseptic and sounded like a zoo. As Ashley stated their business to a middle-aged receptionist in a white uniform, he heard high-pitched barking and the persistent yowl of an angry Siamese cat from the back of the building. Obviously, Tramp wasn't their only patient.

"Excuse me."

He glanced up to see that Ashley had turned away from the counter and was looking at him. "Here's your change," she said. "I'll write you a check for the vet bill as soon as we get back to the arena, okay?"

Automatically, he took the money she thrust at him. "I don't want you to pay me back," he said as the receptionist disappeared through a swinging door. "I'm just glad he's okay."

Ashley nibbled on her lower lip. "But I'm adopting him," she said. "And I don't expect you to pay his vet bill."

Taylor studied her face, wondering what it was about her particularly that he found so compelling. Taken individually, her features were pretty enough, but not unique. Big brown eyes, a straight little nose with a touch of arrogance. Full lips stained a shade of pink that made his mouth water above a chin that demanded independence. Hair like a river of fire. Put them together, though, and they made him wish for things he'd sworn off long ago.

She frowned and he realized he'd been staring. "No, I don't want your money," he said firmly. "I meant to pay the bill. I'm doing it for Tramp, not for you," he added with a burst of inspiration.

Her protest died on her tongue. "Thanks," she said with a smile that damn near made him drool.

He was about to say something stupid when the receptionist returned, leading a newly transformed Tramp on a leash. Ashley's attention shifted from man to dog with unflattering speed.

"Tramp!" she exclaimed, squatting and holding out her arms. Tramp glanced up at Taylor, stub of a tail wagging slowly, and then he, too, ignored his would-be savior and went straight to Ashley.

At least the dog has an eye for beauty, Taylor thought wryly.

The vet, wearing a white smock and a gold name tag, came out next.

"I want to take him with me," Ashley told her.

The other woman smiled. "He's a nice dog. When I called animal control, they didn't have any reports that answered his description. Since there's no way to know if he's had his shots, I can do them before you go, if you'd like."

"Good idea." Ashley glanced at Taylor. "I'll pay for them," she said firmly.

He shrugged. "Suit yourself." At least she wouldn't be traveling entirely alone anymore.

After the vet had finished with Tramp, she brought him back out and handed Ashley a tube of cream. "Put this on the cuts every day until they're gone and watch for signs of infection. Snip the stitches on his leg after five days and be sure you get them all out."

When Ashley had put the tube in her pocket, Taylor scooped up the dog. When his tongue snaked out to lick Taylor's cheek, both women chuckled.

"The only other things he needs are good quality food and fresh water," the vet continued. "And lots of love."

"I think he'll get that," Taylor drawled when he saw Ashley's adoring expression. It stunned him to realize he was jealous of a damn dog.

Ashley left that afternoon with Tramp sitting beside her in the truck as if he had been born to it. He and Spinner had made friends before she loaded her pinto in the trailer, and she wondered if he had been around horses before, too, or was just naturally friendly.

Too bad he couldn't talk. He might have some interesting stories.

When she drove out of the campground towing her horse trailer, she was disappointed to see that Taylor's truck was already gone. She hadn't asked where he was headed next, and he hadn't mentioned it. Donovan would have told her, but she hadn't run into him before she left.

When Taylor had dropped her and Tramp off at her camp spot, she'd thanked him again for rescuing the dog and taking her to the vet's to pick him up. Taylor had spent a couple of minutes patting Tramp and talking to him in a low voice that sent shivers down her spine, then gave her only a brief goodbye before he walked away. It was easy to see that whatever interest prompted him to ask her out had been thoroughly exorcised.

"Need a break?" she asked Tramp a couple of hours later. "There's a rest stop right ahead."

He'd been asleep on the seat, but he raised his head at the sound of his name. Talk about smart; he was a quick study. She repeated her question. This time, he sat up and gave a huge yawn. Then he yipped politely.

"Okay." She was enjoying their one-sided conversation. "We'll pull over and I'll walk you on your new leash." On the way out of town, she had stopped to buy a bag of dog food and a few other necessities. Tramp had sniffed everything thoroughly before she put it all in the back of the pickup except for the red leather collar, which he wore proudly, the matching leash and his water dish.

When Ashley signaled and turned off at the rest stop, the first thing she saw parked alongside the rest rooms was a shiny black pickup towing a matching horse trailer. Donovan was standing next to the driver's door waving at two young women driving away in a red convertible. When Ashley pulled in next to him, he grinned and moseyed over.

"Is this the mutt I keep hearing about?" he asked as she snapped on Tramp's leash, stuffed a small plastic bag into her back pocket and let him out of her truck.

"This is the one," she replied. "Tramp, this is Taylor's brother."

Donovan squatted and held out his hand. To Ashley's surprise, Tramp thrust his paw into it and wagged his tail. With a chuckle, Donovan gave the paw a shake and then scratched behind Tramp's ears.

"He seems like a good dog," Donovan told her as he straightened. "Now I won't worry so much about you being on the road alone. I'm not sure he could change a tire, though."

"That's what big strong cowboys like you are for," she teased back, wondering where Taylor was. She tried to put the burly steer wrestler out of her mind, but so far it just wasn't working.

"Yes, ma'am," Donovan murmured, bending closer. "If you need me, just whistle."

"I can't imagine what she'd need you for, bro," drawled a familiar voice. "She's already got a pet."

Taylor touched the brim of his hat and greeted Ashley, then bent to pet Tramp's head.

"Uh, would it be okay if I gave him something?" Taylor asked, his voice uncharacteristically hesitant. "I picked up a little present I thought he might like."

His sheepish expression raised Ashley's curiosity. "Sure," she said.

Taylor reached into his shirt pocket and pulled out a shiny bone.

"It's nylon," he explained as he held it out to Tramp, who sniffed it eagerly. "It's supposed to be ham flavored and it'll keep his teeth clean."

Delicately, Tramp eased it out of Taylor's hand. Holding the bone in his teeth, he glanced around as if making up his mind.

"Thank you," Ashley said, touched by Taylor's thoughtfulness. "It will give him something to do while we're on the road."

"That's what I figured."

When Tramp began to fuss again, she remembered his promised potty stop. Gently, she took the chew toy from his mouth and tossed it onto the seat in her pickup.

"You can have it when we leave." To her surprise, Taylor went with her when she crossed the narrow road to a small field and let Tramp explore. All around them were weeds and wildflowers. The sun warmed her bare head. When the season started back in February, they played mostly in covered arenas. When the weather grew milder, more rodeos were held outside. Ashley preferred competing in the open air; it seemed more authentic than the huge modern arenas.

"Has he given you any problems?" Taylor asked as the dog sniffed a clump of tall grass with interest.

She shook her head. "He's good company." Slanting a glance up at him, she added, "Better than some people I know. He pays attention to what I say and he doesn't interrupt."

Taylor chuckled. "Sounds good. Where are you headed next?"

"Amarillo. What about you?"

"Us too." He looked to see if Tramp was done with his business. "I guess we'd better hit the road."

Ashley didn't comment on the coincidence, but when she crossed back to where the trucks were parked and Taylor mentioned it to Donovan, he was quick to invite her to stop for supper with them on the way. Ignoring the flash of annoyance in Taylor's eyes, she accepted.

Only when she was back on the road did she allow herself to wonder if his reaction had been because his brother had thought to ask her or because she had accepted.

She shook her head while Tramp watched curiously from where he lay holding his new toy with his forepaws. "I wish I could tell what he's thinking," she muttered.

He cocked his head, listening, and then went back to gnawing on the bone. By the time Ashley saw the sign for the truck stop where they had agreed to meet, Tramp was asleep again and she was more than ready for a meal.

* * *

She watched Donovan stay on a huge bull long enough to finish in the money, but she missed Taylor's ride because she was with the farrier when he replaced one of Spinner's shoes. Her gelding had thrown it during her barrel run. Consequently, she was out of the money again. Neither of the Buchanans were around when she pulled out later that same night, headed for another rodeo and another chance at the prize money that would keep her on the road.

While she sped south to a smaller show in Lubbock, she wondered when she'd see the brothers again. They hit the major shows, where the competition was better and so were the purses. Ashley divided her time between those rodeos and the ones where she had a good chance of earning enough to at least pay for gas and food.

Some of the biggest stars chartered planes or hired drivers to get them from one place to another. Even less successful competitors sometimes pooled their money in order to get to the events with the most promise any way they could. No matter what level they were on, they were all scrambling to win the money that determined their standings at the end of the year. The top fifteen in each event went to the finals in Las Vegas for ten days in December. It was what they all aimed for, the culmination of why they all did what they did.

Ashley had made the finals the past two years, missing by a handful of dollars the year before that. Last year she had finished third, and all she could wonder at the time was how her father would have felt had he lived to see her. Would it have finally been enough to earn a few treasured words of praise from him or would he have said, "Third's great, honey. Maybe next year you'll get second or even first." Then he would go on to tell whoever else was listening how well his stepson, Joe, had done in college rodeo, while Ashley wore a smile that stung like a new brand and blinked away the tears she'd promised herself she would never shed again.

Since her father had died before she ever made the finals, she would never know what he might have said. But after years of listening to him sing Joe's praises, she had a pretty good idea.

"She won in Lubbock last week," Donovan said as he and Taylor geared up for their go-round in the steer wrestling. He figured if Taylor was too proud to ask around about her, he'd spare his big brother the trouble. "Nancy Evans from Billings ran against her. Said she and her horse both looked great."

Taylor didn't say a word, but Donovan noticed he didn't ask who Donovan was talking about, either.

"Keep your horse tight on the steer," he said instead, as he rolled down the cuffs of his shirt and snapped them. "You let the steer swing wide last time and I almost ended up eating dirt."

Donovan stepped into his chaps and pulled them up. They were black, trimmed with silver conchae, and they matched the saddle he used when he was hazing. He didn't bother to reply to Taylor's complaint. Donovan's palomino had never let a steer swing wide in his life. Donovan knew what was bothering his brother, but now sure as heck wasn't the time to bring it up, not when Taylor was about to face a long-horned steer whose only thought was to outrun him.

"Come on," Donovan said after he'd fastened Taylor's number to the back of his shirt. "Let's get the horses. We're up pretty quick."

Taylor gave him a long look but didn't say anything. He knew what Donnie was up to, asking everyone who came through if they'd seen Ashley. He should be irritated, but he knew his brother was trying, in his own annoying way, to help. What Donnie couldn't know was that there wasn't enough help on the circuit to fill up the emptiness inside Taylor. The emptiness he was terrified someone would finally notice and comment on. The emptiness that had been eating at him since he was twelve—that he still had no idea how to fill after all these years.

Pushing aside the fears that threatened to destroy his concentration and leave him open to injury or worse in the arena, Taylor slapped his brother on the back. "Come on," he said in a hearty tone, "I'll show you how it's done."

Amid the hoots and guffaws of the other cowboys in the dressing room, Donovan gave his chaps a last tug, reset his hat as he dodged a half-full spittoon and went ahead of Taylor to where their horses were waiting to be saddled up.

Chapter Four

In the next couple of weeks, Ashley hit five rodeos and finished in the money at all but one. She was on a roll. Tramp rode beside her on the bench seat of her pickup as if he had been born to the Gypsy life, making her wonder how she had ever done without him.

Taylor no longer popped into her thoughts every time she glanced at Tramp, although she still searched for his big black rig whenever she parked her camper in a makeshift rodeo campground. She refused to check his progress in the *Pro Rodeo Sports News,* but she eavesdropped unashamedly whenever she heard his name mentioned. It didn't count as interest if she wasn't actually asking about him, did it?

A medium-sized rodeo in a small town in South Dakota whose population quadrupled during this one weekend a year was the last place she expected to run into the brothers Buchanan. When she walked into a tavern to meet some friends and spotted Donovan's familiar cream-colored Stetson in the knot of cowboys at the bar, she figured his more taciturn brother probably wasn't far away.

"Hey, pretty lady!" Donovan exclaimed as he got to his feet and bent to give her a smacking kiss on her cheek. His mustache tickled, stirring no more than mild pleasure. The man was drop-dead gorgeous—perhaps she needed a hormone supplement.

"Buy you a beer?" he asked over the sounds of music and conversation that filled the room. The air smelled like smoke, fried onions and trail dust.

She returned his friendly hug. "Thanks, but I'm meeting someone. Have you been staying out of trouble?"

"When it's the only option." His green eyes gleamed with amusement. "I've been following your progress. Told you things would turn around for you, didn't I?"

"That's right, you did." She was flattered that he had bothered to check on her, but that didn't keep her from sneaking a look around the room. A black hat caught her eye, but the shape was wrong. Evie waved from a big table in the corner. Ashley waved back.

"I've got to go," she told Donovan. "My friends are already here. Want to join us?" Wouldn't Evie choke on her bolero tie—she thought Donovan Buchanan was the cutest thing since red silk panties.

"We're leaving to play pool as soon as Taylor shows up." Donovan introduced her to the two men with him.

"You'd have more fun with us," said one, a successful young bullrider wearing a buckle as big as a dinner plate and a wedding ring. "We might even let you win."

She was tempted to tell him she could beat him at pool without his help, then decided it wasn't worth the bother.

"Yeah, we're fun guys," agreed the man next to him. He was pleasantly homely, with a gap in his tobacco-stained teeth and a high, shiny forehead. "Even if Cochran can't find his pool stick with both hands."

Cochran, the one with the ring, aimed a mock punch at his shoulder. "Least I've got a pool stick to grab," he drawled.

"Yeah, come on with us," Donovan said. "You can be my partner and we'll beat the boots off these yahoos." When she hesitated, he added, "Taylor should be along any minute, if you'd like to say hi." Donovan's expression remained openly friendly, but his gaze had sharpened imperceptibly.

"I'd better take a rain check," Ashley replied with reluctance. "My friends are waiting."

"How long are you sticking around?" Donovan asked.

"I'm leaving right after my ride. I need to be in Colorado by tomorrow." Her family had promised to meet her at the rodeo grounds on Saturday, and she was looking forward to seeing them. She hadn't been home for a couple of months now.

"Greeley?" he persisted.

"That's right." She glanced around again, wondering if Taylor had given her a thought during the past weeks.

"Why don't you wait until we're done tonight and we can caravan," Donovan suggested. "I don't like thinking about you on the road alone."

"I'm not alone," she replied. "I've got Tramp with me."

Donovan's smile widened. "I forgot about him. How's the mutt doing?"

"That's what I was going to ask," remarked a voice that sent shivers down Ashley's spine.

Refusing to show her pleasure in seeing him, she turned to greet the man she'd been subconsciously looking for everywhere she'd gone.

"Hi," she managed in a casual tone. "Tramp's doing fine. His cuts are healing and you'd think he'd been a Gypsy in a former life. He seems to like traveling." While she spoke, her gaze roamed Taylor's face. If anything, she had forgotten just how attractive he was. Below the brim of his cowboy hat, his eyes glittered as he returned her searching look with a slow perusal of his own.

"I invited Ashley to join us for a beer," Donovan interjected, breaking the silence, "but she's here to meet some friends."

At his brother's words, Taylor reined in his interest. "Don't let us keep you, then."

He almost regretted his cool dismissal when her chin hiked up a notch and the warmth left her eyes.

"Good seeing you." Her glance shifted to the men with his brother. Phil and Brian were two bullriders Taylor privately thought carried most of their muscle between their ears. As they made fools of themselves trying to coax Ashley to ditch her friends and go to another bar with them instead, Taylor glanced at his brother.

Donnie was watching him with a speculative expression.

"How about it, Tay?" demanded Brian, before he could stare Donovan down. "Don't you think she should come with us?"

Ashley was already shaking her head, politely regretful, so he was saved from having to answer. Her hair had been corralled into some kind of curly ponytail, making him itch to set it free. Tiny gold guitars dangled from her earlobes.

"I really have to go," she said, tucking aside a rebellious strand of hair.

Taylor watched her hand, fascinated. It was small and slim, with long fingers and short, rounded nails. Looks were deceiving; he knew if he stroked his fingertips across her palm he'd find calluses and competence there. Thoughts of other contradictions a patient man could discover made his mouth begin to water.

Annoyed, he swallowed and hitched his gaze back to her face. She was watching him, a tiny frown puckering the smooth expanse of her forehead.

He raised his brows in a passable imitation of faint puzzlement. Dealing out her goodbyes like a hand of cards, she managed not to look at him again.

Letting her walk away wasn't easy, but the idea of spending the evening watching Donnie's buddies drool over her held even less appeal. After she'd gone to join her friends and he'd turned away to settle himself at the long, padded bar, conversation turned predictably enough to the stock each of the others had drawn for that evening.

It wasn't until after Phil and Brian left that Donovan brought up Ashley's name again.

"She's headed for Greeley, too," he said.

Taylor's interest flared like an old Zippo with the flame turned up too high. "I suppose you suggested that we follow her," he said, willing to shift the responsibility to his brother, despite his own concerns for her safety. He hated to think of her out there alone somewhere and needing help again.

"I knew you'd want me to." Donovan took a long drink of beer, as if he had no idea Taylor might be waiting to hear what she'd said. "She's planning on leaving right after her event. Maybe a word from you would persuade her to stick around."

More likely it would send her packing even faster. Still, she might be a threat to his peace of mind, tattered as it was, but she wasn't dumb. Surely she would understand the sense in waiting for them.

As it turned out, he almost missed the chance to persuade her. He was checking out the limp on a buddy's horse when she took her turn at barrel bending. By the time he realized and hotfooted it back to the campground, she was pulling out of her spot, Spinner loaded in the trailer behind her.

Ashley was surprised to see Taylor hurrying toward her, waving his hands. Her first thought was that Donnie had been hurt. Then she realized Taylor would have been at his side if that were true.

Curious, she braked the truck. "What's up?" she called through her open window. If he had come by before to check on Tramp's progress, it hadn't been while she was around. She'd thought Taylor might take an interest, since he'd been instrumental in the dog's rescue. Not that he didn't have other things to think about besides a stray dog or a woman with hair the color of faded carrots and a talent for nosy questions.

All the more reason to wonder why he was chasing her now.

Seeing Taylor, Tramp began to bark. He climbed onto her lap, tail wagging, and poked his head out the open window.

Thank God he hadn't done this in rush-hour traffic, she thought as she pushed him aside.

"Hi there, fella!" Taylor exclaimed as he stuck his hand in the window. Tramp immediately bounded back into her lap and submitted to having his ears scratched.

Watching Taylor's long fingers work their magic, Ashley was half tempted to lean forward and rub her cheek against the back of his hand. She swallowed a bubble of hysteria. Clearly, the company of horses and dogs was no longer enough for her.

"Okay, that's it," she scolded, pushing Tramp off her lap. Even after he returned to his side of the bench seat, he continued to watch Taylor intently. She might as well not even have been here, for all the notice she was getting from either of them.

"Another couple of weeks and his hair should cover that scar," Taylor said, reaching his hand in the open window to ruffle Tramp's ears. His action brought his face close to hers.

"I hate to break this up," she said briskly, "but we were heading out. See you down the road."

Taylor's gaze locked on hers, and she heard his breath catch. He was so close she could have leaned over and kissed him. "I'm glad I got to see Tramp before you two left. I've been wondering how he was doing."

Was it her imagination, or was there a message hidden in his words?

"Obviously, he missed you, too," she replied, watching Taylor's blue eyes darken. She could see the smudgy ring of violet surrounding the lighter irises, as well as each individual eyelash that fringed them.

"I'd like to spend some time getting to know the pup better." His gaze drifted to her mouth. It was her turn to struggle for breath. If he still found her attractive, what kept him from doing something about it? "We're heading for Greeley as soon as Donnie's rear end parts company with a bull named Big Ben," he continued. "Why don't you stick around and we'll follow you out?"

Ashley turned to look at Tramp, who was trembling with barely suppressed excitement. She was grimly aware that she knew just how he felt. "What do you think?" she asked as if he could understand every word. "Shall we wait for these cowboys?"

"That's a yes," Taylor drawled at Tramp's rapid-fire reply. "Why don't you park this thing and help us load up our horses? It'll save us some time."

As she complied, holding the Appy's lead rope a few moments later while the two men settled Donovan's palomino into the trailer, she couldn't help thinking what a shame it was that Tramp had to wait in her truck, since he was the one that had wanted to stay in the first place.

"After this next rodeo, I'll be going back to Mesquite with Will Parks for the Bullriders Only competition like we talked about before. You'll need to line up a hazer while I'm gone."

As the two brothers drove down the road behind Ashley's rig, Taylor mulled over Donovan's announcement. He knew his brother had been thinking about the move since the start of the season. He was too good a bullrider to pass up the huge purses being offered in the bulls-only events that were springing up all over the country. Many of the top roughstock riders managed to combine them with regular rodeo, earning a small fortune for their efforts.

"No problem," Taylor replied, keeping his eyes on the road. "I'll find someone. You're making a smart move."

Donovan expelled a long breath. "Thanks, bro. You know I hate leaving you. Sure you don't want to switch to bulls?"

Taylor chuckled. Ahead of them, Ashley's brake lights flashed on and he slowed down. "No, thanks," he drawled. "You know I'm too big to ride roughstock." He spared Donnie a glance. "Hell, you're too big, if you want the unvarnished truth." Most bronc and bullriders were smaller, wiry men. "Besides, one daredevil in the family is enough. I'll stay with steers. One of them might stick me with a horn, but at least I know he won't try to stomp me into the ground afterward, just for laughs."

Donnie's expression was resigned. He knew the dangers. Years ago they had chosen the events for which their individual skills seemed the strongest. Each respected the other's decision. Not that there wasn't a certain amount of teasing involved, though.

"The secret's in staying on the bull," Donovan said wryly. "And not falling off so you don't get stomped into the ground."

"Yeah, but you gotta bail out sooner or later," Taylor replied. "And those bulls don't care if the eight seconds are up or not. At least a good union bronc loses interest when the buzzer goes off."

"Sometimes they do," Donovan countered.

Taylor recalled that Donnie had dislocated his shoulder several years before when a feisty little mare named Sweet Georgia Brown slammed him into the fence right after the buzzer.

"No matter," Taylor said, knowing he was going to miss having his brother with him. Donnie was one of the few people he felt truly at ease with. He'd survived the same tough breaks Taylor had, and although they disagreed on the reason behind it all, Donnie knew him as no one else did.

For a fleeting moment, Taylor wished he had the words to tell his brother how much he cared. Then he pushed the impulse aside. Just because men refused to go around with their hearts on their sleeves didn't mean they couldn't have feelings. Donnie knew Taylor loved him, even if he didn't say the words.

He remembered when Ashley had unknowingly strayed into private territory and the way he had rejected her interest. He knew she'd been hurt by his rebuff, but some things a man just didn't want to drag up and hash over. Still, despite his determination to keep his distance, here they were following her taillights like a fox after chickens. Obviously, his self-control needed work. He didn't much care for being led around by the hormones.

"Ashley would make a good hazer," Donnie commented as they slowed and turned onto another road. "She's a damn good rider and she told me once that her pinto has pretty decent cow sense."

Immediately wondering when Donnie'd had the opportunity to talk to her about her horse's cow sense, Taylor rejected the suggestion. "Don't worry your pretty blond head," he said, earning himself a punch on the shoulder. "I'll get one of the other steer wrestlers to haze for me."

"I'm not *worried*," Donnie grumbled. "I just think Ashley would make a good hazer. Give you an excuse to keep the same schedule."

"I don't need an excuse," Taylor denied sharply. God, was he that transparent? He ran a hand over his face, feeling the start of bristles on his jaw. He was tired, that was all.

"Sorry," he said after a moment in which only the plaintive strains of a heartrending country ballad filled the cab of the truck. "I just think hazing's too dangerous for a woman."

"Hazing? Dangerous?" Donovan exclaimed. "Compared to sticking on a horse that's spinning around those barrels like a cork in a whirlpool, what's so risky about hazing? All she has to do is ride alongside the steer for a couple of seconds and keep it from swerving."

"I know what a hazer does." Taylor chewed the inside of his cheek, trying to come up with something to give his objection a little backbone. "I'd just feel better if I had a man riding with me," he added lamely.

Donnie hooted and slapped his knee. "What century did you just walk out of?" he asked with a grin. "Or are you worried you'll be so busy watching Ashley that you'll trip over the poor steer?"

"You're nuts." Even to Taylor's own ears, his tone lacked conviction. "I guess I can use who I want," he grumbled, knowing he was grasping at some pretty puny straws. "You'll be off doing your own thing, anyway."

Instantly, Donovan's expression sobered. "You're really okay with that, aren't you?" At least he had been distracted from the subject of Ashley Gray.

"Course I am. You just take care, or I'll beat you up myself." Clearing his throat, Taylor brought up his own tentative schedule, comparing two good-sized rodeos that would be running the same weekend and asking his brother's opinion of both.

"I'm so glad you all came." Ashley was sharing a big booth at a restaurant in Greeley with her mother, her brother, Joe, and his wife, Emma. Their son, Kenny, who was a senior in high school, was driving up with his best friend, David, and their girlfriends in time for the rodeo.

"You already said that," Joe mumbled around a bite of his hamburger. He managed a grin and his gray eyes were lit with teasing laughter. Joe was in his forties now, but the silver running through his sideburns and the creases in his cheeks only added to his rugged handsomeness.

Emma gave him a playful swat on the shoulder. "All you've talked about for two weeks was seeing Ashley again," she reminded him. Unlike her husband, she had no gray in her curly black hair, and her face bore only the faintest smile lines around her deep blue eyes.

Ashley watched the two of them exchange a glance. When Joe looked at his wife, contentment softened his habitual expression of quiet authority.

Ashley's eyes filled with moisture that she quickly blinked away. Most days rodeo filled her life, but sometimes, when she saw two people who shared what Joe and Emma so obviously did, she felt a pocket of emptiness deep inside that she suspected winning would never fill. Long ago, she had abandoned the idea of a permanent address with a picket fence and climbing roses. Once in a while, though, she still longed for a special man who would look into her heart and find her worth loving. A man like Taylor Buchanan, she realized with dawning dismay.

"How's Spinner doing?"

She realized that Joe was speaking to her. "Fine," she replied, knowing he would razz her unmercifully if he had any idea how sentimental her thoughts had become. He had more than a dozen years on her, and when she was little he had seemed more like an uncle than a brother. It wasn't his fault that she'd had to compete with him for her father's attention. Joe had been a star athlete and a good student. He'd been more of a son to her father than she could ever be. Tagging after them, she had never felt really included, not even when her dad mussed her hair and called her his little cowpoke.

It was Joe who swung her up on his wide shoulders when her legs got tired, telling her she was as pretty as any princess. He dried her tears after her father advised her to get good grades because she was too much of a tomboy to catch a man. The way Ashley saw it, she had failed him both as a son and a daughter.

"Honey, how have you been?" her mother asked now. Her hair was almost white, the delicate angles of her face beginning to soften with age. Her smile, though, was exactly as Ashley remembered. She had done her best, but a mother's love couldn't fill the hole left by a father's disapproval. "Are you eating right?" she asked. "You look thinner."

"I'm taking good care of myself." Ashley didn't remind her that she had to stay in shape to compete. She knew her mother failed to understand why she chose the road and rodeo over a home and family of her own, but her skill in the saddle gave her a solid sense of self that nothing else ever had.

When they were done eating, Joe glanced at the check and left some bills on the table. "We'd better get over to the fairgrounds," he said, pushing back his chair. "The boys will be there, and I know Kenny's looking forward to showing off his new girlfriend."

"Is she nice?" Ashley asked as she slid out of the booth.

"She's real sweet," Emma replied. "He's taking her to the prom."

It was hard for Ashley to realize her nephew would be graduating from high school in less than a month. It didn't seem so long ago that Joe had found him hiding in the barn, a scared little boy running away from people who'd taken him in for the foster-care dole.

Kenny's sudden appearance had gotten Joe and Emma
started as foster parents. They had married, adopted
Kenny and filled their big old house with a parade of
other children.

"I'm looking forward to meeting this girl," Ashley
replied. "She'd better treat him well or she'll answer to
me."

"Get in line behind me," Joe drawled.

Taylor was hanging up the pay phone he'd been using
to schedule future entries when he saw Ashley arrive at
the fairgrounds with a small group of people he didn't
recognize. While he watched, a tall man in Western dress
scooped her into his arms and swung her around. At the
sound of her laughter, a bolt of jealousy set Taylor's jaw
so hard that it damn near cracked his molars.

Before he could think twice, possessiveness he knew to
be way out of line had his feet moving in their direction.
He might not have the right to yank her out of the
stranger's arms, but he could at least find out who the
hell the other man was.

As Ashley glanced up to see him bearing down on the
group, he noticed her resemblance to the older woman
standing next to her and realized who the man had to be.
By then it was too late to retreat.

"Taylor!" Ashley exclaimed over the tall cowboy's
shoulder. "Come and meet my family."

Equal measures of relief, embarrassment and dismay
poured through him as he relaxed his knotted muscles
and advanced, red faced.

She introduced him to her mother, four teenagers
whose names were a blur and the other couple. Taylor
hadn't even noticed the pretty woman with Ashley's
brother, who extended his hand with the steadily assess-

ing gaze of a man used to screening his baby sister's boy-friends. Taylor kept his own handshake firm in Joe's iron grip and his smile polite.

"Have you and Ashley known each other long?" Joe asked.

Taylor nearly grinned when he saw her cheeks go pink. "We're just friends," he replied, knowing as he spoke that the words weren't entirely true. At least he didn't want them to be, despite his efforts to the contrary.

"Let's go in and get our seats," Ashley said, after she'd named his event and explained briefly how they had met.

"You know I don't like you traveling alone." Joe looked ready to say more on the subject. Before he could, Ashley linked arms with Taylor.

"Come with us," she invited him a little desperately.

He was about to refuse, determined to have a private talk with his hormones, when her mother spoke up.

"Yes, please do," she said. "You can explain the rules to me."

Taylor suspected she probably knew more about ro-deo than she was letting on. "I'd be happy to, ma'am," he said just the same. "I've got some time before I have to saddle up myself."

In the grandstand, he ended up sitting between Ashley and her mother, who insisted he call her Marian. Joe and his wife were in the row directly behind them, and Tay-lor would have sworn he felt Joe's breath on the back of his neck. It was easy to see that the rancher hadn't made up his mind about his baby sister's pal yet. Taylor fig-ured he must have been hell to have around when her dates came to pick her up.

Frustration had set in as deep as a spring flood by the time Taylor was ready to leave the rodeo the next day.

Every bulldogger heading on to the show in Utah was either already hazing for someone else or didn't have his own horse available. Quite often a steer wrestler or calf roper would borrow a well-trained steed and then pay mount money from his share of the purse if he won. In the long run, it was cheaper than hauling a horse from town to town. Lending out a good mount brought in a little extra income and made everyone happy.

Everyone but the bulldogger looking for a hazer to ride with him. Taylor would have asked Donnie if he could use his horse, Rio, except his brother had made arrangements to drop the palomino off at a friend's. The old bronc rider no longer competed, but he earned a good living running a rodeo school for aspiring cowboys. One of the horses he normally used in his steer-wrestling class was recovering from foot problems and he was counting on Rio for his next clinic.

When Taylor and Ashley were both getting ready to head out in their separate rigs, Donnie pulled up with his buddies in a blue sedan covered with dust. He had won the bullriding and was in a boisterous mood when he climbed out of the car and enveloped Taylor in a bear hug.

"Found a hazer yet?" Donnie asked when the back-slapping was over.

Taylor was about to admit he hadn't when he saw Ashley approaching. He knew she was spending a couple of days at her brother's ranch before she drove on to Utah.

"I'm working on it," he said instead, silently willing his brother to drop the subject.

Ashley was wearing tight jeans and a white T-shirt with Clint Black's name and image splashed across its front. She was bareheaded and her hair was pulled away from her face, the ends hanging down her back like a red-gold waterfall. Taylor had a flash of it trailing over his bare chest and ground his teeth together. What would she do if he walked up and plunged his hands into the fiery mass, just to see if it felt as burning hot as it looked?

"You should talk him into letting you be his hazer," Donnie told her, while Taylor stood by, fuming helplessly. "You could handle it."

Ashley's riding skill was the one thing in which she felt rock-solid confidence. Without thinking, she said, "Sounds like fun. It wouldn't conflict with my barrel bending, either." Steer wrestling was usually scheduled early in the program, while barrel racing came later. Bull-riding, the most popular event, was almost always the last thing on the bill.

At the sudden awkward silence, she glanced at Taylor, who was frowning. "Unless you've made other arrangements," she amended lamely.

"Nope, he hasn't," Donovan volunteered. "I'm sure he'd appreciate the help." He glanced from her to his brother. "Well, I have to go."

To her surprise, he leaned down and planted a kiss on her cheek.

"Y'all take care," he said, letting her go.

She could feel the heat flaming across her face, and she would have loved to see Taylor's reaction. Instead, she did her best to glare at Donovan, whose green eyes were twinkling with mischief.

"You be careful, too," she told him. "Good luck in Mesquite."

"Thanks, little darlin'."

She almost laughed. The man was a devil. Before she had recovered from his potent brand of charm, Donnie bade his brother a last goodbye.

"Don't forget what I said about having Ashley do your hazing," he called through the open window as they drove away.

Looking at Taylor, Ashley caught his fierce scowl, as his brother's unrepentant laughter floated to them over the sound of the departing car's engine.

"Don't you think I'm capable?" she demanded, sure she could ride as well as anyone else he might find. When he didn't immediately answer, she planted her hands on her hips and stared him down.

Taylor was the one to look away first. He rubbed one hand along his jaw and then he repositioned his Stetson on top of his wavy brown hair.

Finally, Ashley had had enough of his indecision. "Well, let me know if you need me," she told him. "I might still be interested."

"I suppose I'd better hit the road," he replied gruffly. "You take care."

Ashley wondered how he felt about Donovan going off without him. From what she'd seen, his brother was the only one Taylor was really close to.

"You too," Ashley replied. For a moment they stared at each other. She hadn't given up on the idea of hazing for him, but she had no choice but to let the subject rest for now.

He took a step toward her, looking as if he wanted to say something more. Then, leaving Ashley to wonder if she was only seeing what she wanted to, he spun on his heel and headed for his truck.

Rooted to the spot, she watched him give the trailer a final check. As he bent over the hitch, the worn denim of his jeans stretched tight over his firm rear end. Neither pocket bore the circular imprint from the flat, round

Skoal can so many cowboys carried as part of their regular gear.

As Ashley continued to stare bemusedly, he straightened and turned. The view from the front was even more enticing, the denim covering the masculine bulge of his fly bleached almost white above the long, hard muscles of his thighs. It was only when she realized that his hands were on his hips that she blinked and raised her gaze.

One of his thick, dark brows had a sardonic arch. His eyes glittered above cheeks turned a dusky red she knew wasn't from bending over the trailer.

Ashley's own face was burning with humiliation. Talk about getting caught with your tongue hanging out! She tried to think of a clever parting shot and failed. Wondered distractedly if his lips were firm and cool or soft and hot. Finally she swallowed a cry of dismay, turned away awkwardly—and fled with her pride in tatters.

"If you still want to be my hazer, you can give it a try." Taylor's voice was gruff, his attention riveted to his coffee mug.

Seated next to him at a white plastic table in front of the concession stand, Ashley was still recovering from the pleasant shock of having him seek her out. Her first impulse had been to run and hide, her second to come up with some plausible excuse for the way he had caught her gawking. Finally, since he apparently chose to ignore the incident, she heaved a silent sigh of relief and tried to do the same.

Now she was tempted to leap at his unexpected capitulation. She studied his bent head. For once it was bare, his hair furrowed as if he'd run his fingers through it repeatedly.

Distractedly, she wondered how it would feel beneath her own fingers. "Couldn't find anyone else to ride with you?" she guessed, reining in her imagination.

His mouth relaxed into a wry smile. "No one I'd trust."

She chose to take his words as a compliment. The idea that he trusted her not to run the steer in front of his horse was a small victory, but at least it was a start. Watching him over the rim of her cup as she sipped her coffee, she was tempted to string him along as partial payment for his being less than enthusiastic with his offer.

"We could make a few practice runs while the arena's open for warm-up," she suggested instead.

Taylor found the tension that had racked him since he'd caught her staring finally beginning to ease up a little. He'd hated having to approach her, hat in hand, so to speak, and ask if she'd be his hazer, after all. He had expected her to make him grovel.

"Good idea." He forced out the words, still not sure if he could keep his eyes off her in the arena long enough to grab the steer without getting trampled or digging a furrow in the dirt with his chin. Every time the image of her face, cheeks flushed, full, sensuous lips slightly parted, danced before his eyes, his body's response was both swift and painfully predictable. If only he could be certain he'd read her correctly, they'd be sharing more than coffee right now!

"I appreciate your agreeing to haze for me," he croaked.

"Now we're even."

His eyebrows shot up at her words. "Even for what?" he demanded warily. Maybe he'd relaxed his guard a little too soon. Was there some way she could tell the direction his thoughts had taken?

"You helped me by changing my tire, and now I have the chance to pay back the favor," she said innocently. "What did you think I meant?"

He flushed guiltily. "Nothing. Like you said, now we're even." Even as he said the words, he knew they weren't true. As long as he felt this pull, this raw hunger she had unwittingly stirred within him, Ashley definitely had the advantage. He didn't like it, but if she wasn't aware of her power over him, he could cope. All he had to do was keep his escalating desire firmly in check.

For a man used to rigid control of his emotions, he figured that shouldn't be too difficult.

The steer broke from the chute and Ashley started after it, intent on making sure the animal didn't swerve away from Taylor, whose horse exploded from the box on the steer's other side. Before she knew it, the whole thing was over. Taylor's time was the fastest yet.

As he walked from the arena, leading his horse, he glanced over his shoulder. "Good job," he said with a slow grin.

"You too." Pride in his performance as well as her own made her smile as she rode Spinner toward the gate. Taylor had dropped the steer in just over four seconds. As he preceded her from the arena, his wide shoulders and easy, slim-hipped stride were sexy enough to fuel any woman's cowboy fantasy.

Ashley was no exception. She dismounted behind the chutes, and the two of them watched the rest of the go-round through the fence. When Taylor's time stood, several other cowboys crowded forward to congratulate him. As soon as they were done, he turned to her with a grin.

"We did it."

Excited and relieved that she had helped him win, Ashley threw her arms around his neck. "Way to go!" she exclaimed, intending to scramble back out of his reach before he had time to react.

Before she could, his arms closed around her like barrel staves. The shock of his body flush against hers sucked the breath from her lungs and sent her heart rate into the red zone.

She hadn't allowed for his lightning-fast reflexes. She tipped back her head and glimpsed a spark of danger in his eyes, and then he lifted her feet off the ground and spun her around. Dizzily, she clung to him.

"That's my best time this season," he mouthed in her ear amid the hoots and cheers of the other cowboys. "You brought me luck, sweetheart." The endearment, combined with the press of his body against hers, was doing funny things to her equilibrium, but she refused to struggle. Not in front of the audience of fascinated cowboys.

He set her back on her feet and she thought he was going to release her. Some of her own jangled reaction must have showed on her face, because his eyes narrowed and then a smile edged his mouth. He swooped, as intent as a bird of prey, and caught her mouth with a quick, hard kiss.

The kiss scorched her to her toes. She was reaching for more when he let her go. Mortification seared her cheeks, until she noticed his expression.

He looked as if he'd been poleaxed. Slowly, his arms fell to his sides as he stared down at her.

She didn't stick around to see what he'd do next. Trembling, she pushed her way out of the raucous group of cowboys, timers, judges and flagmen and grabbed her pinto's reins. She needed some air, some quiet and some privacy—to sort out her tumbled thoughts before she faced Taylor again.

She'd only meant to tease him a little. Instead, she felt as if she'd plunged barefoot into a nest of rattlers. Whichever way she stepped, she was bound to get bitten.

Surrounded by well-wishers, Taylor watched her lead her horse down the aisle as if she couldn't escape him fast enough. Why hadn't he left well enough alone instead of using the win as an excuse to find out if she tasted as sweet as she looked? Now it was all he could do to tear his attention away from her retreating figure and try to make sense out of the conversation around him.

By the time he had made his escape and got to the barn with his own horse, Ashley was almost finished with hers. When he greeted her cautiously, she replied without looking up. No doubt his ham-handed pass had repulsed her. Stewing over an apology, he led Sergeant Pepper into the stall across from Spinner's and unsaddled him.

"Want to get something to eat when we're done here?" Taylor found himself asking.

When Ashley finally raised her head, he couldn't read her expression.

"Okay," she said quietly. "Let's just grab a burger." She named the local hangout where the rodeo people congregated.

"Fine." He thought about saying more, but she ducked to Spinner's far side and began picking out his hind foot.

Realizing that he was gaping at her when he should have been seeing to his own horse, Taylor shook his head in a feeble attempt to clear it and began the familiar ritual he performed after every competition. He was so deep in thought that he didn't realize Ashley was done until he glanced up and saw her waiting outside his stall.

It was then that he realized with a sinking feeling that all he really wanted was to kiss her again.

Chapter Five

"**W**hy didn't you stop and ask for directions?" Ashley shoved hard against Spinner's belly and tightened the cinch on her saddle while Taylor hopped from one foot to the other, pulling on his boots.

"I didn't need directions. I wasn't lost," he huffed as he straightened and fastened the cuffs on a clean shirt. PRCA regulations required that rodeo competitors wear long-sleeved shirts and Western dress in the arena.

Ashley glared at him over the top of her saddle as she jammed the tail of her own shirt into the waistband of her jeans. "Oh, sure, whatever." They'd finally pulled into the fairgrounds with only minutes to spare before the steer-wrestling event. She had run in to pay their entry fees while Taylor unloaded the horses. If they weren't ready when his turn came, he'd be disqualified.

With reluctant admiration, she paused to watch him swing into the saddle before she did the same. For a big man, he moved with a fluid grace that made her pulse skip as he urged his Appy into a few tight circles to warm the horse up.

"That shortcut Ed Brown told me about may have added two hours to the trip," he said as he rode back toward Ashley, "but I wasn't lost."

Moments later, they both dismounted. "When you've got more time, I'd love to hear your definition of lost," she replied. The announcer's voice rang out from inside the arena. "We're up next." She grabbed Spinner's reins. "Let's go."

Taylor shouted at a calf roper who was leaning against the side of a dented sedan. "Sam, would you move our trucks?"

Sam spat out a stream of chewing tobacco. "Sure thing."

Taylor tossed him both sets of keys. "Appreciate it." Leading Sergeant Pepper, he headed for the arena. "We might just make it," he told Ashley over his shoulder.

"Hey, cowboy," she called out as he was about to go through the open doorway. "Just don't take any shortcuts."

"You didn't take any shortcuts, either," he commented a little while later when the barrel racing was done, too. "You nailed that go-round down."

Her face flushed with pleasure. "I guess I did. Maybe rushing in at the last minute got our blood pumping or something." They had both won with respectable times.

For a moment, Taylor's eyes darkened as his attention strayed to her mouth. Then he shrugged. "We must be doing something right." Neither of them had mentioned the kiss after he had won before. "Or maybe we're just damn good."

"Do you miss Donovan?" she asked later as they sat outside her camper in lawn chairs with a couple of beers. After the busy evening they had just spent, it felt good to kick back and relax now.

"Yeah, I miss him." Taylor stared at the horizon, and she wondered what he was thinking.

"Have you two always traveled together since you started rodeoing?" She offered the question cautiously, knowing he disliked talking about himself. Not wanting to push him away, but curious to learn more about him.

"Not always." Taylor took a long swallow from the bottle in his hand. "A couple of times he's gone off with someone else, or I have."

Ashley suspected he was referring to other women. Jealousy flared and was quickly squashed. She had no right to feel possessive, not about his past—and certainly not his present.

"He and my ex-wife despised each other." Taylor spoke into the darkness, shocking her with the admission. She knew he'd been married and had heard the stories about his dumping his wife because he was jealous of her singing career. Ashley had dismissed the gossip because it didn't sound like anything he would do.

"How long were you married?" she asked. When he didn't answer right away, she sneaked a look in his direction. His hat was pulled low over his face. Meticulously, he was peeling the label from his beer bottle.

"Too long."

She thought he was going to leave it at that until he spoke again.

"She used to sing at the rodeo dances," he continued in a flat, quiet tone. "She had a voice to fuel a man's dreams."

Again, jealousy raised its ugly head. Ashley had never heard him talk about anything so poetically.

"Donnie tried to talk me out of marrying her. It wasn't like him to offer unwanted advice." His voice deepened. "I should have listened. When he finally told me she'd come on to him, I went nuts and decked him. We didn't speak for months."

Ashley ached for the big, proud man sprawled so uncomfortably near her. He deserved better than to have been so cruelly humiliated. "I'm sorry."

He sighed and crossed his booted feet at the ankles. "Eventually, I had to stop denying the truth." His voice iced over and she could guess what was coming next. "Lorrie Ann was like an alley cat, sleeping with anyone she thought could give her career a boost, before and after our marriage. God knows why she got hitched up with me. Maybe she thought a cowboy husband would be good publicity."

"How long ago did you split up?" Ashley asked. Did he still love her? Or had he managed to cut her from his heart without cutting away part of it, too? She didn't imagine he was a forgiving man—not when it came to that kind of betrayal. Nor did she think he would love again very readily, if at all.

Oh, Lord, had that been why he'd been glowering at that poor young waiter back at the Bum Steer? Because Ashley's friendly concern had reminded him of his ex-wife's flirting? Her stomach did a slow, sickly roll at the thought.

"Our divorce was final a year ago. I heard she married a car dealer in Dallas a few months back. Maybe he can buy her the career she wants so bad." There was an edge to Taylor's voice, faint but bitter. Bitter at being hurt, or bitter at being fooled? Ashley couldn't tell.

"I'm sorry," she repeated. "But I'm glad you and your brother are friends again."

"We've been through too much together not to be," he said cryptically. When he fell silent, she didn't ask any more questions, although she would have liked to. It was enough that he had opened up as much as he had. Perhaps he was learning to trust her a little bit more.

Or maybe he was just lonely without Donovan around to talk to.

"What about you?" Taylor demanded, breaking the silence. "Ever been married?"

"Nope." She drained the last swallow of her beer.

"Ever been close?" he persisted.

Reminiscently, she smiled in the darkness. "Once or twice."

"What stopped you?" he asked, sounding genuinely curious.

"I came to my senses," she said flippantly.

"Did you love them?"

"I was madly in love the first time," she replied. "I thought we'd be together until we were eighty, with a passel of kids and grandchildren...." She let her voice drift off.

"Why did you break up?" Taylor asked, shifting restlessly in the creaky lawn chair.

"He was showing a pig at the county fair and fell for the girl in the next stall. Her sow won best of show."

"Good Lord!" Taylor exclaimed, straightening. "How old were you?"

"Eleven, I think."

He swore softly, amusement evident in his voice. "You said once or twice," he reminded her after a moment.

She remembered Ben from college. Funny, she couldn't picture his face anymore. How could he have claimed to love her without understanding her? Their relationship had ended when she left to rodeo. He had been furious at the time.

"I haven't met anyone I'd give all this up for," she said in reply to Taylor's question. Her gesture included the jumble of campers and trailers that surrounded them in the darkness. She expected him to make a humorous comment.

"I can understand that," he said instead, his tone serious. After a few more moments seated in shared silence, he got to his feet.

"It's getting late, so I'll say good-night. Thanks for the beer."

Ashley rose, too. "Night," she echoed as he towered over her. Teasing fingers of tension danced down her spine, but he only stared into her face for a moment before turning away toward his own hulking black camper. He left her wondering what he had been hoping to find when he looked into her face, and what he might have seen there. If he thought of their kiss at all, it must not have been with the same reluctant attraction she did, or he wouldn't have left her so easily.

Each step away from her that Taylor took was pure hell, but he forced his feet to keep moving, one in front of the other. Had that been disappointment he'd glimpsed on her face?

If the raw attraction that pulled him toward her like a magnet hadn't been so damn strong, he might not have struggled against it so hard. It would have been easy to slip his arms around her and take the kiss he'd thought about for days—since the last time he had touched his mouth to hers. It would have been so sinfully easy to give in and damn the consequences.

So easy and yet so disastrously hard.

If she had been any other woman, he wouldn't be so scared to be near her, to touch her—to want her the way he did. Ashley was a complication his life didn't need. Hell, she was a threat to his very existence, pure and simple. A threat to the order he'd finally found in his life. Order within the chaos of running from town to town, saddling up, chasing steers, loading his horse and heading down the road. Too busy to think about the past or speculate about the future.

Just the way he wanted it.

He jammed his hands into his back pockets and hunched his shoulders against the force that urged him to turn around, to hurry back to where he'd left her. Instead, he headed over to his own empty camper and another sleepless night.

He didn't plan on going to the dance the next evening; he thought about visiting a honky-tonk bar and sucking up a few beers instead. Maybe shoot some pool, find a poker game or pick up a willing woman. Any of the above was bound to be easier than watching Ashley dance with an endless line of cowboys eager to put their hands on her and fantasize about her soft mouth and long legs.

Taylor peered into the tiny mirror above the camper sink and nicked his jaw with his razor. He swore at the bead of blood that appeared as a knock sounded on the door.

Without bothering to put on his shirt, he yanked it open. When he saw who was outside, whatever he'd meant to say got stuck in his throat like a wad of chew.

Ashley was standing at the base of the camper steps in a Western-style shirt and that damnable denim skirt. Her startled gaze roamed his bare chest as pink washed her cheeks and then she raised her head.

"I've got an old blue towel you can borrow," she drawled, making no attempt to hide her admiration.

It was Taylor's turn to blush. The impression that she liked what she saw kicked up an answering response somewhere south of his gut. He opened the door wider. "Did you want to come in?"

Something in his expression must have warned her that he might not let her out again. "No, that's okay. I was on my way to the dance."

"Why don't you wait a minute while I grab my shirt?"

"Double standard, Buchanan?"

"I, uh…" His voice trailed off as he struggled to keep his body's reaction to her beaming approval under manageable levels. When he saw the glint of laughter in her narrowed brown eyes, he widened his stance and braced his hands on his hips.

Her attention froze as she moistened her lower lip with the tip of her tongue.

It was all he could do not to drag her inside. "You're staring," he ground out instead.

"Sorry." Her expression was unrepentant as she tracked her gaze back up to his face. A smile hovered around her mouth.

"What did you want?" he demanded, aware that he'd lost control of the situation, unsure whether she was really attracted or secretly laughing at his expense.

"Want?" she echoed. Then she blinked, as if she was having trouble focusing.

For a moment, they stared at each other. He had actually taken a step toward her when she tossed back her hair.

"Sorry. Lost my head for a second."

She didn't sound sorry, but he could see she'd regained whatever control she might have temporarily misplaced. The laughter was back in her eyes. Maybe she'd done it deliberately, faked that unwilling interest to pay him back for catching her in her towel. Or to make up for the last time he'd caught her staring and thought she couldn't help it. He couldn't be sure. Just knew he wanted her. That it would be smart to steer clear until he had his stampeding hormones under control.

He prayed she hadn't noticed that one step he'd taken toward her.

"I wondered if you were going to the dance, too?" she asked, studying his shoulder as if it had just sprouted a tattoo there. "I thought, if you were, we might walk over together."

He took the time to let his own gaze slide down over her Western shirt. The fabric outlined the shape of her breasts like a lover's hands before disappearing into the waistband of the skirt that had already kept him awake for more than one night.

"Are you here to persuade me?" he asked with a quirk of his brow. He saw her hands clench loosely at her sides and felt bad for teasing her. Just not bad enough to stop.

Then she recovered and thrust out her chin. "Could I persuade you to do anything?"

"You can come in and try." The challenge popped out before he knew it was coming. He held the door open wider, daring her with his eyes.

His quick retort had Ashley speechless with surprise. She'd told herself that all she wanted was someone to walk into the dance with, even though she'd know almost everyone there and no one worried about coming alone.

"I'll wait out here for you," she replied, fighting the temptation to offer to help him finish dressing. Or undressing—she wasn't sure which. "But I'm only giving you five minutes."

"Ten," he countered. "I'd better down some vitamins. You're going to need a bodyguard, wearing that skirt."

Before she could think of a suitable response, he'd slammed the door. Collapsing onto a nearby picnic bench, she took a deep breath—and willed her heartbeat to slow down while she tried not to think about Taylor guarding her body.

"Ready?" he asked when he came out of the camper a few moments later.

Ashley looked him up and down and dragged in another shaky breath. He was wearing black jeans and a black leather vest over a shirt that matched the blue of his eyes and hugged his wide shoulders. His Stetson was in one hand and he'd combed back his hair. While she watched, several strands tumbled across his forehead. Her fingers itched to touch them, but he looked so wary that she fought down the urge.

"You never answered me when I asked if you were going to the dance," she said as he came down the steps.

For a moment he looked into her eyes and she wondered what he was thinking. Then he surprised her by holding out his arm. When she linked hers through it, the corners of his mouth kicked into a grin. "I guess I am now," he said softly. "I'd hate to break up a winning team."

When they walked into the dance, he dropped his arm. A bronc rider from Houston grabbed her around the waist and pointed to the crowded floor. She was about to turn him down when she saw Stacy latch on to Taylor and reach up to say something into his ear.

Swallowing the jealousy that rose up in her throat, Ashley flashed a wide smile at the bronc rider.

"What are we waiting for?" she asked.

The bronc rider's reaction time had been well honed in the arena, and she didn't have to ask twice. It was only after she had followed him onto the floor and turned to face him that she saw Stacy with someone else. Taylor was standing alone, arms folded across his broad chest. He treated Ashley to a long, blank stare and then he turned away.

She could have kicked herself for being so hasty. Guiltily, she smiled at her current partner, and waited with simmering impatience for the number to end. As soon as it did, she excused herself and headed for Taylor. He was already walking toward her, expression purposeful.

They met halfway, and no words were exchanged between them as the band slowed the music down. A man began to sing. The lights dimmed. Taylor led her to the floor and turned her into his arms. He made no pretext of holding her politely as he stared down at her. Dragging in a deep breath, he tightened his grip while she melted against him. Her hands slid up over the smooth leather of his vest to rest on his shoulders. She could feel their warm strength beneath her palms. Gently, he urged her head into the hollow beneath his chin. Their feet barely moved as she tried not to tremble each time his thighs brushed hers. All around them, the music spun a cocoon as sweet as cotton candy.

He smelled like soap and mint mouthwash. His jaw rested against her hair, making her glad she'd left her cowboy hat on her bed. She felt his breath on her cheek, his warm hands at her waist. Everything else faded. No one so much as bumped them as they drifted slowly around the floor.

Too soon the number was over and the lights came up. Ashley opened her eyes and started to back away, but then Taylor's arms tightened around her.

"Not yet," he murmured against her hair, guiding her gently toward the middle of the floor where they wouldn't be run down by the faster dancers. His voice rumbled up from his chest as the music raced and swelled around them.

Settling back against him with a contented sigh, she smoothed her hands down his upper arms, savoring their dormant strength, and then returned them to his shoulders. Closing her eyes again, she concentrated on the feel of his big body curled protectively around hers.

She thought he kissed her hair, but surely she'd been mistaken. This was all a dream, anyway. At any moment now, Tramp would wake her with a lick of his tongue and she'd realize she'd fallen asleep back in her camper and missed most of the dance.

The image of her dog snuggled next to her instead of Taylor brought a foolish grin to her lips. He must have felt the movement against his chest, because he lifted his head and looked down at her.

"What is it?" he asked.

She shook her head. Something in her face must have reassured him, because he gathered her close once again. Beneath her cheek, she felt an echo of the drumbeat from the stage. Then she realized what it was.

It was Taylor's heart, beating steadily and solidly while her own skittered along as fast as a skipped rock. Her knees shook and she curled her fingers into the soft cotton of his shirt. Immediately, his arms tightened and she sighed contentedly.

During the next slow dance, Taylor felt a hand tap his shoulder.

"Cut in?" asked a young steer wrestler he'd given a few pointers a month before.

Taylor bared his teeth in a humorless smile. "Get lost," he growled.

The youngster's grin faded and his eyes widened. "Sorry," he stammered. "No problem."

Ashley shifted in his arms. "What was that?"

"Nothing important." He realized they'd been on the floor for quite some time. "Do you want to take a break?" he asked reluctantly. "Do you want something to drink?" He hated the idea of letting her out of his arms now that he'd experienced the sweetness of holding her. Wasn't even sure that he could make himself let her go.

Her smile was bemused. Shaking her head slowly, she said, "I'm fine. Unless you want—"

"All I want is right here," he said without thinking. Hell, he'd scare her away for sure. He tensed, holding his breath, but she didn't struggle. He let out a long sigh, closing his eyes, and then he realized the music had stopped.

He swore under his breath and dropped his arms. She blinked like a baby owl just waking up and let him go. The band announced a break and she looked around. Any minute now, she'd see someone she wanted to talk to, or else another man would come up and claim her for a dance before Taylor could run him off.

He wasn't ready to let her go. His gaze swept the room and he saw the exit sign over the door.

"Want to get some air?"

Hesitating, she nibbled her lip. Her eyes had gone all dark and mysterious, screened by lashes that flickered teasingly like twin fans. Her skin glowed with healthy color above the muted hue of her Western shirt. Her lips were soft and plump, and his mouth watered for a taste.

"Okay. It is a little warm in here."

Warm, hell, he felt as if his thermostat was stuck on broil. His fingers tightened on her elbow, and he had to fight the urge to hustle her from the room. With a conscious effort, he loosened his hold.

"Sorry," he muttered into her ear as his hand slid down and captured hers. "Hope I didn't break anything."

Only my heart, she thought as she lost herself in the blue of his eyes. No doubt he was just too warm and wanted a chance to cool off. Just because he'd held her as if he enjoyed it didn't mean he wanted to lead her into the shadows and share a kiss she'd just about trade her saddle for.

"No," she mumbled. "You didn't hurt me." But he could, as easily as crushing a butterfly beneath a bull's hoof.

"Good." One corner of his mouth lifted and then he led her toward the exit. Outside, a knot of people were standing around smoking and talking. Taylor greeted a couple of men he knew, but he didn't slow down.

"Hey, Buchanan," one of the bronc-riding judges hollered, "where's the fire?"

"Back at your house when you show up drunk," another voice quipped. The remark was met with hoots of laughter.

Taylor turned to raise an inquiring brow at Ashley. "Want to take a walk down to the front gate?" he asked. "It's a pretty night."

She looked up at the scattering of stars across the black sky. The breeze was still warm, and yet shivers slid coolly along her nerve endings.

When she didn't answer right away, he slowed his steps. "Never mind," he said quickly. "It was a dumb idea." He looked away as if he were counting cars in the parking lot and tried to release her hand.

Ashley held on tight. "It isn't a dumb idea," she contradicted. A six-shooter pointed at her head couldn't have forced her to admit that her left boot was pinching her toes. Nothing was going to keep her from taking that walk with him, short of a hailstorm. Given the number of stars she had already noticed, any kind of storm was unlikely. Except for the one gathering inside her.

She tugged on his hand. "Come on. Let's go."

He released his grip long enough to take off his hat and rake a hand through his hair. Two other couples came out of the building and headed for the parking lot. One of the men could barely walk, and the woman with him was talking steadily in a low, angry voice.

"Does this mean I can't have any sugar when we get home?" the drunk asked in a loud, plaintive voice.

Ashley didn't hear the woman's reply, but she saw Taylor grin and shake his head. "This probably means you aren't gettin' any sugar until sometime after Labor Day," he muttered.

Ashley smothered a laugh. "I hope he's not driving," she said softly as the man stumbled and almost went down. She watched, relieved, as he opened the back door of a dark car and fell inside.

The sounds of other voices faded as she and Taylor strolled hand in hand along the edge of the parking lot past the huge arena. A few lights on tall poles cast a soft glow over the area. The dark car drove slowly past them, headlights illuminating Taylor's face for a moment, and then they were alone once again.

"Donnie's meeting me in Kansas next week," Taylor said as they stopped by the front gate.

Ashley knew that meant he wouldn't need her as his hazer unless his brother left again later. "You must be looking forward to seeing him."

Taylor braced one foot on the high cement base at the foot of the front gate and leaned forward to brace his crossed arms on his bent knee. He was still holding his hat in one hand, and he looked as if he could have ridden through a time portal straight out of the Old West.

"It's hard to keep in touch when we're both on the road," he said, "but I heard from Fred Robbins that Donnie did okay on the bulls."

"Do you worry about him?" Ashley asked.

He glanced at her and smiled. "All the time. He's the only family I have left."

"What about your sister?" she blurted without thinking.

A frown settled on his face and she knew the question annoyed him. "She's out there somewhere," he replied, bowing his head. "Somehow I think I'd know it if she wasn't."

She touched his shoulder. "I'm sure you're right." Would he ever open up to her? Trust her enough to share his thoughts? She had to believe he might.

He straightened and slapped his hat against his thigh. "Did you want to go back to the dance?"

His question surprised her. Had she completely ruined the tentative closeness that had sprung up between them? "I don't think so," she said. "I want to get an early start in the morning." They hadn't discussed driving together, and she didn't want to get in the habit of counting on him.

"What time's breakfast?" Taylor asked.

"Whenever the café down the road starts serving." She would have offered to cook for him, but she didn't think a few slices of stale bread, a grapefruit and the instant coffee she had back in her camper would be enough to fill his big body up. "Unless you want cold cereal," she added. "I could manage that, I think."

"I didn't mean you had to feed me," he countered. "I just figured we might go together, since we're headed in the same direction."

She shrugged, not wanting to appear too eager. "If you like."

Suddenly, he smiled. "Oh, I like, all right," he breathed, leaning closer and peering into her face.

Rattled, she looked away. Her heart lurched into her throat and her senses snapped to attention. Now, when the moment she'd been anticipating was at hand, she was a bundle of nerves.

"I'd better go back and let Tramp out," she blurted. "He's been in the camper all evening."

"We'll go in a minute." Taylor was watching her in the dim light. While she inhaled a shaky breath, he lifted his free hand and cradled her chin. His fingertips were warm and rough against her skin. His face was so close she could see the way his pupils had expanded and the slight flare of his nostrils.

"Ashley," he murmured, dipping his bare head.

When she parted her lips to reply, he covered them with his own as gently as a lasso settling over a calf's head. Before she could respond, he pulled back just far enough to look at her. She registered the shock in his eyes and then he kissed her again.

She was barely aware that he had released her chin and wrapped both arms around her. His mouth heated quickly, sliding over hers with a sweet friction that curled her toes inside her boots and made her pulse soar. Her arms circled his neck and tugged him closer as she tangled her fingers in his thick hair. Her knees bumped his. He shifted his legs, sliding a knee between hers. The intimacy melted her control and sent ribbons of desire twisting inside her.

He stroked a hand down her back to her hip. Then he coaxed her mouth open, and she lost track of everything except the way his lips and tongue were making love to hers.

It was only when he finally let her go, stepping back and raking an unsteady hand through his hair, that she noticed he had dropped his black Stetson into the dust at their feet.

Chapter Six

Donovan's buddies dropped him off to rejoin Taylor at a rodeo in Oklahoma. After the usual taunts and back-slapping, Donovan turned to drape a long arm around Ashley.

"I'm glad to see you two didn't kill each other," he drawled. "How did the hazing go?"

"We were unbeatable. He didn't trip over a steer once," she shot back, wishing the handsome blonde had stayed away longer, or that Taylor would decide he couldn't win without her.

Fat chance.

"Thanks for filling in," Taylor told her instead. "We made a good team."

She tried to interpret his expression, but as usual, his face gave away little of what he was feeling. He hadn't kissed her again when he walked her back to her camper after the dance, but she blamed that on Tramp, whose frantic scratching when he heard them outside the door wasn't exactly conducive to romance.

"Does that mean you'll give me a good reference?" she asked lightly.

Instantly, his expression darkened. "Has someone else asked you to ride hazer for them?"

"Not yet," she replied. "But you never know."

They were standing at the arena fence, watching the calf-roping event. The lasso snaked out but fell short when the calf put on an unexpected burst of speed. The rider recoiled his rope and threw it again, but he must have known he hadn't a chance at the prize money. Watching the cowboy flip the calf and hog-tie him, Ashley knew he would soon be loaded up and back on the road, trying to hit at least one more rodeo before the weekend was over.

As the saddle-bronc event started, Taylor touched her shoulder. "Gotta go," he said when she looked up.

Something of her feelings must have showed on her face, because he hesitated. Then he bent his head.

"Kiss for luck," he murmured, surprising her. Briefly, his mouth touched hers as reaction sizzled through her like heat lightning.

"Go for it," she whispered, voice husky.

He straightened and stared into her eyes. "Maybe I'll do that," he muttered enigmatically. Then, before she could recover from his laser-sharp gaze, he was gone.

"Looks like you two have forged a decent working relationship," Donovan observed from behind her.

Blushing, Ashley attempted a casual shrug. "Your brother's not an easy man to know."

Donovan sobered. "He's got his reasons."

She hoped he would say more, but the first saddle bronc burst from the chute, claiming his attention. What was it about the Buchanans that gave them such an air of mystery, anyway?

Later that same evening as she sat in the stands with Bev Heath and Jennifer Mills to watch the rest of the events, Ashley had to swallow a shout of excitement when Taylor's name was announced. She never tired of watching him compete. When his mount burst from the box and ran down the steer, Taylor's predatory grace and sheer masculine power moved her on an elemental level she hadn't been aware of before.

She was already applauding wildly as he lunged for the steer's head and slid from the saddle, kicking out of the stirrups. In that vulnerable second before his heels hit the ground, the steer tossed its head unexpectedly and slipped free of Taylor's hold.

The onlookers leaped to their feet as one long, deadly horn hooked his side, ripping the fabric of his shirt and exposing the vulnerable flesh underneath.

Ashley's heart lurched to her throat, choking off her scream. In the blink of an eye, everything changed. What had been a dance of skill and strength became a deadly threat.

"Oh, no," she moaned, horrified, straining to see. "Oh, God, no."

Donovan reined his horse hard, spinning back toward Taylor. He managed to roll out of harm's way, losing his hat in the process. The steer stumbled to its feet, shaking its head. Donovan rode straight for it, yelling and flapping his arms. After a moment's indecision, the steer bolted for the open gate as Donovan leaped from his horse and ran to his brother.

While Ashley watched, knuckles pressed against her lips to stop their trembling, he helped Taylor to his feet and handed him his Stetson. Taylor waved the dusty hat to show he was okay, and the crowd erupted into applause. Ashley swallowed a sob of relief.

Under his raised arm, the loose edges of his torn shirt flapped open, but he didn't appear to be bleeding or badly hurt. Unable to sit still for another minute, Ashley mumbled a disjointed excuse to her friends and hurried down the steps. She was fighting tears and her legs were shaking with reaction. As strong as her need to see him was her need to get herself back under control. Before she did either, though, she had to prepare for her own event.

She was lucky to finish a poor third, after two women she had already beaten several times this year. As soon as she had taken care of Spinner, she found a seat by herself, high up in the arena where she could brood in peace and private. She spotted Taylor down behind the chutes at the other end, wearing a different shirt and talking to Donovan. She was happy to see that he wasn't limping or favoring his side, but she wasn't ready to face him. Not yet. The stark fear that had overwhelmed her during his ride still hadn't released her from its deadly grip. That and her own mediocre run left her feeling raw and vulnerable.

Taylor was a competitor, just as she was. He faced danger every day that he rode. She had to deal with her sudden fears alone; she couldn't share them with him. Otherwise, one day the idea that she was frightened for him might be just enough distraction to get him killed. She understood that. Dealing with it was something else.

She was in deep trouble. Rodeo was what Taylor did— what he lived and breathed. It was dangerous. People got hurt all the time and she would have said she accepted that. Until today. The thought of *his* being injured, or worse, was too painful to bear.

While Ashley sat alone and pondered this new development, the bullriding finally began in the dirt below. Absently, she watched the first three riders get thrown. Then a boy she hadn't seen before burst out of the chute on a huge black Brahma cross. Two earthshaking leaps and daylight appeared between the bull and the boy's butt. The maddened bull went into a spin and the boy was thrown over his hand, which was firmly stuck in the rigging around the bull's girth. As he kept bucking, the young cowboy's body flopped like a rag doll.

Fearlessly, two clowns moved in to help. One distracted the bull while the other tried without success to free the rider's hand. With a bellow of rage, the bull spun around, catching the clown with the tip of one wicked horn.

Several people screamed as the clown crumbled under the bull's hooves. At the same time, the rigging finally worked loose and the cowboy was freed. He hit the ground and lay still. The remaining bullfighter hesitated, clearly not sure which way to move as the bull swung his head back and forth between the two fallen men.

In seconds, other cowboys had climbed into the arena to help their injured comrades, shouting and waving their hats to distract the furious bull. All of a sudden, Ashley saw Taylor go over the fence and run right at the bull.

"Oh, no, oh, no," she chanted through clenched teeth. This couldn't be happening again. She clutched the edge of her seat, attention riveted to the drama unfolding on the arena floor. Three men were half carrying the fallen clown toward the gate, while two more helped the injured rider who was cradling one arm protectively.

Saliva running from its mouth, the thwarted bull looked first at the open gate and then back at Taylor, who was doing a good job of distracting the animal from his intended victims.

For a moment, it looked as if the bull was going to exit the arena peacefully, but then he swung back around to face Taylor, trapped in the very middle of the big arena.

A roar went up from the crowd below Ashley as the bull lowered his massive head. As soon as Taylor saw that the other men were safe, he wasted no time in sprinting for the nearest fence. The uninjured clown ran back into the arena and tried to get the bull's attention.

Ignoring him, the bull charged after Taylor. Ashley clamped a hand over her mouth, too scared to look away. Taylor was almost to the fence, long legs straining, arms pumping, but the bull was bearing down on him like a runaway freight train.

Hoarse voices shouted encouragement; hands reached down to him from the top of the fence. A white hat tumbled to the dirt, and she recognized Donovan's blond head. Taylor hit the fence midrail. Scrambling for safety, he was yanked up and over as the bull skidded to a stop. A wicked, curving horn missed Taylor by the width of a smile.

His legs were still straddling the top rail when Ashley leaped to her feet, knees knocking, and tore headlong down the grandstand steps. Tears streamed down her face and blurred her vision, but she ignored them.

Chest heaving, Taylor dropped down the other side of the fence to the ground. His legs, quaking like twin aspens, nearly buckled beneath him as he grabbed a fence post for support. Doubling over, he swallowed repeatedly, determined not to disgrace himself by throwing up. Finally, his stomach quit rolling enough for him to straighten cautiously.

Two close calls in one evening were almost more than he could take. His guardian angel, if he still had one, must have been pulling double duty today, he thought distractedly, as a dozen men gathered around and all began shouting at once.

"Are you all right?"

"You're crazy, man!"

"Bravest thing I ever saw."

"Thought you were bull bait for sure."

"God, bro!" Donovan exclaimed, breaking through the crowd to engulf him in a bone-crushing hug. "For a couple of seconds, I thought that bull had you. Are you okay?"

Taylor's laugh came out strained as Donnie released him. "I think so." Now that it was over, reaction was setting in. His teeth chattered so hard that he could barely talk. He had felt the bull's breath, heard his hooves pounding right behind him. Expected to be mowed down before he ever touched the fence.

Part of him still couldn't believe he'd made it to safety.

"Damn, that was close," commented a wizened old judge wearing an admiring expression.

"Too close," agreed another.

All around them, the crowd of spectators was still standing, still applauding and shouting their approval. Before Taylor could ask how badly the other two men were hurt, the second rodeo clown rushed over.

"Thanks, man. I could never have got to them both without you."

"A lot of guys helped," he replied, feeling uncomfortable. "I was too far away to do much."

"Not too far away to distract Hellfire while we got them out," the bullfighter responded. "Facing a bull like that takes real guts. I oughta know," he added, getting a laugh, "since I do it all the time."

Grateful for the release of tension, Taylor chuckled with the others. "How are they doing?" he asked.

"Johnny's got some bruises, but his baggy clothing saved him. That boy has a bunged-up wrist and his side's stove in. They just hauled him off in the aid car." The clown slapped Taylor's back. "Thanks again, man."

Taylor dragged in a deep breath that burned all the way down like campfire smoke. The whole thing had happened so fast that he hadn't thought, just reacted. That didn't make him a hero. He was about to say so when someone barreled into him, almost knocking him down.

"Taylor!" Ashley cried, hugging him hard as his arms automatically closed around her slim body. "Are you okay?" When she tipped back her head to look at him, her eyes were wide with fear, and her freckles stood out like paint spatters on her pale face.

Taylor managed to drag her close. Eyes shut, he inhaled her spicy cinnamon scent and thanked God she was here. When he let her go, his gaze met his brother's over her head.

Donnie's expression was edged with concern.

"Are you all right?" Ashley repeated anxiously. "I've never been so scared in my whole life."

"I'm fine," Taylor rasped. Her admission moved him deeply. He'd been on his own too long, with no one to fuss over him but his brother, and he had no idea how to handle the agitated bundle of soft, sweet womanhood clinging to him as if he really mattered. His gut-level impulse was to carry her away someplace private and reaffirm being alive in the most basic way possible.

While he struggled with his shaky self-control, she laid a hand against his cheek and peered into his face. "Are you really okay?"

He slipped an arm back around her shoulders. "Yeah, I think so. I guess I was lucky."

"Lucky?" she squeaked. "First you almost get gored. And then you get chased by a bull. A half step slower and—" Her lower lip wobbled dangerously, and her dark eyes shimmered with moisture.

For a moment, Taylor thought his own composure would shatter in the face of her distress. "It's all over. Take it easy now." He patted her arm awkwardly.

His clumsy attempts at reassurance must have worked. With a ragged sigh, she blinked away the tears and her lip stopped quivering.

"What happened to the bullfighter and that poor young cowboy?" she asked, voice still shaky.

Donnie moved closer protectively. "They were hurt, but they'll be fine." He herded Taylor and Ashley through the crowd.

"That's good," she said.

"Come on, you need some air," Donnie urged Taylor. "I'll bring Sarge." He grabbed the reins of Taylor's horse and followed them toward the exit.

It was much later when the three of them finally left the bar where everyone who'd heard the story wanted to buy Taylor a drink. Ashley had sat quietly, for the most part, listening to stories of rescues and wrecks in other towns, other times.

It wasn't hard to tell that all the sudden notoriety made Taylor uncomfortable. He had set his Stetson upside down in the middle of the table, suggesting to everyone who offered to buy him a brew that they toss the money into his hat instead, for the two injured men.

"I'll take this to the office in the morning," he said now, still carrying the hat stuffed with money as Ashley preceded him out the door. "The rodeo secretary will know how to get this to Corky and Bobbie Lee."

"I promised Greg Young I'd stop by," Donnie said over his shoulder, walking away. "Catch you later."

Ashley wondered if that were true or if he was only trying to give them a little privacy. Either way, she appreciated the opportunity to be alone with Taylor.

"Why don't you stop by my camper," she invited. "I'll fix some fresh coffee."

"Sounds good." He engulfed her hand in his and led her back to where their rigs were both parked.

When they got to the camper, Ashley opened the door and stepped aside as Tramp leaped out and half-scrambled, half-fell down the steps.

"No, no," she scolded when he jumped up on her legs. He knew better, but he got so lonesome in the camper by himself. During the daytime she often tied him outside, but he seemed to prefer riding in the truck to anything else.

Now he cocked his head and then galloped away to investigate a small tree nearby.

"Tramp's looking fit," Taylor commented as the dog ran in a big circle with his nose to the ground, lifted his leg on a light pole and then came trotting back to them. He was filling out and his coat was clean and brushed. "You'd never know he was the same sorry mutt we rescued only a few weeks ago."

Ashley remembered how Taylor had challenged those boys in order to save Tramp, and the gentle way he had carried the dog to her truck. After witnessing the lengths he would go to just to save a dog, she wasn't surprised that he had risked his own safety today for two injured men he barely knew. The realization that either action could have ended badly made her look at him with a new awareness of his vulnerability, and then her own.

"What is it?" he questioned. "Do I have dirt on my face?"

She shook her head. "Come on in. I'll make that coffee." She called Tramp, who bounded ahead of them into the camper and lay down on a small cotton rug she'd put in the corner for him. Space was at a minimum; when Taylor joined her, it shrank even more.

"You'd better sit down." She turned to find herself a breath away from his big body. Shifting quickly to one side, she scooped a pair of black jeans off the bench seat.

Taylor watched her for a moment, aching to haul her into his arms. Then, realizing they probably both needed a little time to get over the events of that evening, he sat down at the tiny table. Only if he angled his legs was there enough room for them. While she lit the stove and started the coffee, he glanced around at their surroundings.

The camper was crammed full of Ashley's belongings, but she kept it as clean and organized as possible under the circumstances. Next to the table, two doors faced each other across the tiny enclosure, no doubt accessing a closet and a potty. A counter set with stove and sink lined the opposite wall, with a tiny window and cupboards above, more storage and drawers below. Across the front end of the camper was a narrow bunk. Although the table converted to another bed, he could understand why she usually traveled alone. There was barely enough room for one in the cramped enclosure.

The configuration varied only slightly from his own rig, which was bigger and newer but equally as cramped with both him and Donnie inside. A thought sprang into his head unbidden that sharing this camper with Ashley wouldn't seem nearly as crowded.

"That was a brave thing you did today," she said as she busied herself with the coffee and mugs.

"Anyone else would have done the same," he countered gruffly. The whole subject made him uneasy; he didn't deserve laurels for acting purely on instinct. What if that had been Donnie lying in the dirt? If Taylor'd had a thought as he went over the fence into the arena, that might have been it.

"I was afraid for you," she confessed, turning around to face him. Her hands gripped the edge of the counter on either side of her, and he saw that her knuckles were white.

"I'm sorry." He struggled to rise from behind the table. "I never wanted to upset you."

She held out a detaining hand. "No, don't apologize. That's not what I meant." She looked up and he saw that her eyes were once again brimming with tears. The last thing he wanted was to make her cry. How long had it been since anyone had bothered to shed a tear on his behalf? He had no idea.

"Easy, honey," he crooned softly, reaching for her.

She skittered away and Tramp growled softly. Astonished, both she and Taylor swiveled their heads.

"It's okay," she told the dog, whose attention was fixed on Taylor. "Good boy."

Slowly, Tramp rested his head back down on his paws. After a moment, his black eyes closed.

Taylor reached out to touch Ashley's shoulder. "What's the matter?" he asked.

She turned her head aside, but not before he saw the strain on her face. "Nothing."

With a sweet, piercing pain, he realized what the problem was. "Aw, honey, it's okay. Nothing happened to me." He had a desperate urge to comfort her, but he was afraid she'd push him away if he touched her. Then he saw a tear slide down her averted cheek, and something broke loose inside him.

"Don't cry," he groaned, reaching for her. She tried to turn her back, but he wouldn't let her. Wrapping her in his arms, he buried his face in her hair, rubbing his cheek against its softness. "If Tramp sees you crying, he's liable to take a piece out of my ass," he joked lamely.

A tiny hiccup was her only response, but at least she wasn't struggling. Encouraged, he stroked his hands down her back, feeling her tremble under his touch. The idea that she might actually care what happened to him made the hard knot of tension that was always buried inside him begin to relax. He rested his face against her temple, savoring the unfamiliar feelings that radiated through him like tendrils of warmth, slow and easy.

Then, as quick as the fall from a runaway horse, his body responded to the nearness of hers and the tendrils of warmth became coils of heat. He could tell from the way she stiffened in his arms that she felt the change, too. For another moment, he enjoyed the feeling of her body so close to his, her head tucked against his neck with her breath bathing his skin, her soft breasts cushioned against his chest, her hands resting on his upper arms, fingers clinging. Her stomach was pressing against him, too, and she must have felt his response to her nearness, but she didn't pull away.

He dipped his head and nuzzled the side of her throat, breathing in the mingled scents of cinnamon and peaches and the underlying essence that was hers alone. His equilibrium shifted, rocking his control, and his blood turned thick and hot. He was sliding his mouth toward hers when she spoke.

"Promise me you won't take a chance like that again," she murmured. "I couldn't stand to see you hurt."

Surprise jerked through him, and he pulled back as if he'd been slapped.

"Ashley, you know better than to ask that. It's rodeo. The risk is always there. Getting hurt is part of the life. I won't make promises I can't hope to keep." He dragged in a breath and made himself let her go. "I do what I do. The same as you. You're upset now, but don't try to hobble me. I won't stand for it."

He seemed intractable, his voice edged with steel. She hadn't meant to say what she had, but she'd realized somewhere between the walk to the camper and measuring the coffee that she'd lost her objectivity. Without her consent, she'd been plunged into an emotional whirlpool of caring, one that was spinning her out of control. That fast, she was in too deep, heading for a heartache she could not ignore.

"I'm not trying to hobble you," she argued, folding her arms protectively across her chest while the smell of fresh coffee bubbled up around them. "I'm just trying to tell you how I feel."

The muscles along his jaw clamped tight, his whole body rigid with wariness. "And how's that?"

Ashley swallowed, reluctant to set herself up for almost certain rejection. "Well, I'm not exactly sure," she hedged. "I only know that I've never been as scared as I was when I saw you go over that fence." She rested a tentative hand on his chest. "And I never want to be that scared again," she concluded quietly.

He didn't move, didn't blink, but a muscle in his cheek jumped. The tiny chink in his armor gave her hope.

Then he spoke, and dashed it. "I can't make any promises, and I can't give you anything but this right now. If you're looking for anything more complicated than that, you're looking in the wrong place." His voice was as rough as a gravel road, as cold as a blast of wind straight down from Canada. "My only commitment is to rodeo. It's my life and my mistress. That's all there is to it."

Humiliated, she threw up her hands and faced the door. "I wasn't asking for any kind of commitment," she cried, too mixed up to know what she wanted. "Rodeo's my life, too, in case you've forgotten." She whirled, eyes flashing. "I don't want a damn commitment from you or anyone else. I just don't want you breaking your neck when I have to watch, that's all."

His expression thawed slightly. The silence between them grew until she looked away. Then he tucked one finger under her chin. "If I promise not to break my neck when you're around, would you please kiss me?" he asked quietly.

Ashley tried to resist, but the temptation was too strong. Later, there would be time enough to sort through her jumbled feelings.

"Oh, shoot," she grumbled as she stepped into his arms, "who could resist a cowboy who says 'please'?"

The way his eyes flashed, she expected him to sweep her into a hard embrace and a hot, driving kiss that would suck the life right out of her. Instead he cradled her as gently as he might a newborn chick. The touch of his mouth was so soft it made her ache. His lips pressed hers warmly, retreated on a sigh and then returned as if unable to resist. When the tip of his tongue finally teased her into yielding, she was more than ready to deepen the kiss. His arms tightened around her, and his mouth heated on hers as sensations poured through her. Greedily, she pressed against him, seeking more.

His fingertips touched her cheek, smoothing back her hair, and he ambled his way from her chin to her ear. First his breath and then his soft, warm lips explored its curves and hollows. He bit down lightly on the lobe, and a shiver of sensation shot through her like a flaming arrow. Tipping her head back, baring her throat, she silently begged for more.

She leaned into his big body, feeling the press of his buckle and then, as he shifted, the heat of his arousal. An answering need soared within her as she melted against him.

As her hips rocked into the steely strength of his, his breath broke on a ragged hiss of pleasure. Instantly, his gentle, ambling pursuit was kicked aside like an empty beer can. He returned to her mouth unerringly, covering it with his. Caught up in the passion exploding between them, she could only moan helplessly, deep in her throat, and hang on tight as he ravaged her mouth and drove her to the point of madness.

Her entire world had narrowed to him and the tide of emotion rising between them. Then, suddenly, he lifted his head.

"If we're going to stop, it has to be now." His voice was deep, husky with desire, his eyes dark and heavy lidded. His face was stamped with hunger, all harsh planes and jutting cheekbones.

She studied him through half-closed eyes, wanting only to sink back into his heated embrace and put aside all rational thought.

"Ashley." He gave her a shake. "Don't look at me like that or I'll rip the decision right out of your hands."

Decision? she mused. Awareness trickled back slowly as he continued to stare down at her, and she realized he was waiting for her to say something. She'd never been a coward, but she knew with sudden, chilling clarity that this one man had the power to break her as no wreck ever could. Still, she lacked the will to step away.

"I don't want to rush you," he said when she remained silent. "If you aren't ready..."

She looked into his eyes and saw the resignation—the acceptance of the rejection he seemed to expect. She saw past the bleakness to the uncertainty and loneliness beneath. Saw the forlorn little boy step from behind the man and reach out.

Something inside her that she'd forgotten was still there rose to meet him, wanting nothing more than to gather him close to her heart and warm him with her love. At that moment, she knew she was utterly lost.

"I've never wanted anyone the way I want you," she whispered, accepting her fate with a smile as she lifted her arms.

A ragged groan was torn from deep inside him as he squeezed his eyes shut. When he opened them again, there was a flash of aching tenderness in their depths. While Ashley watched, unbearably moved, that tenderness was replaced by an explosion of raw need. Bending to scoop her into his arms, he settled her on the narrow bed.

"Are you sure?" he rasped. He must have seen the answer in her eyes, because he didn't wait for her to speak. Instead, he bent over her, kissing her with such pure need and naked hunger that he set her soul aflame.

Chapter Seven

Taylor's heartbeat thundered in his ears and his fingers trembled as he unfastened Ashley's shirt.

"You're beautiful," he murmured, smoothing it aside and gazing down at the curves covered only by the lace of her bra. Somehow, he had to find the strength to keep from tearing off her clothes and claiming her—like a stud horse on the scent of a ready mare. Even as he tried to clear his head, she sabotaged his efforts, opening his shirt and slipping her hands inside to caress his bare skin.

"You're beautiful, too." The sincerity of her words and the trust in her eyes was almost more than he could bear. Reining in his own stampeding desire, he set out to show her just how precious she was.

Slowly, he finished undressing her, taking the time to explore each new treasure he uncovered. Her unguarded response was more than ample reward for his patience, as she let him know with sighs and wild little sounds in her throat just how much his touch pleased her.

His own breath was strained, his body aflame. Not content to lie back and indulge him, she attacked him with an urgency that threatened to shatter his composure. Her hands stroked and teased, igniting a path of fire. Her lips followed, fueling the inferno.

Trembling, fevered, he clutched at the last fragments of his control and set out to overwhelm hers. He must have succeeded because when he finally allowed himself to slide into her welcome warmth, she raised up to grab his hips and pull him tight against her. It was all he could do to hold back the tide of his passion until he felt her come apart beneath him. Then, as her body arched and she cried out his name, the last thread of his control snapped. He exploded into a climax that stripped him of his life force and left him struggling for breath.

As soon as he was able, he shifted his weight on the narrow bed. There was just enough room for him to lie beside her as long as he stayed very close. His arms were around her and his legs were tangled with hers. Her uneven breathing tickled his chest and her hand was splayed over his heart. He had never been more comfortable.

After several long moments of sheer, total contentment, he found the strength to sit up. Reason came flooding back, and with it, reservations about what they had just shared.

In the soft glow from the light over the stove, Ashley watched his face change and harden. Now that the physical urgency between them had been dealt with, emotional turmoil swept through her. Say something, she begged silently as he leaned down and picked up his jeans from where he had dropped them.

He pulled them on and then he fastened the shirt he hadn't taken the time to remove. Painfully aware of her own total nudity, Ashley scrambled up and slipped past him to grab her robe from the closet and wrap it around herself. When she pushed the door shut, he looked up and his hands stilled.

"That was—" His voice was harsh. He swallowed and tried again. "You were—" He shook his head and reached for her. "Come here."

Ashley barely hesitated before stepping into his embrace. "What was I?" she asked, heart pounding with fear. He hadn't yet met her gaze.

"Incredible," he rasped, resting his chin on the top of her head. When he shifted and kissed her, she returned the slow, thorough caress with renewed hunger.

There were a dozen questions she wanted to ask, a dozen reassurances she needed desperately. Instead, uncurling her fingers from their death grip on his shirt, she forced herself to step back and smile. "You're pretty fantastic, too," she told him.

His hand touched her cheek and he studied her intently, but she had no idea what he was searching for. She wanted to ask him. Instead, she tried to keep everything she was feeling from blazing across her face and scaring the hell out of him. Blushing as she recalled the intimacy of what they had done, she drew the edges of her robe tighter and prayed for control.

Taylor sat back down and pulled on his socks and boots.

"I'd better go." His voice was unusually hesitant. "It's late."

Digging her short nails into her palms, she managed another bright smile. "All tired out?" she teased.

Apparently, it was just the right tone to take with him. His slight frown smoothed out and the firm line of his mouth softened. He curled an arm around her shoulders. "Your fault," he murmured, nuzzling her hair.

Ashley hated the stilted banter between them after what they had just shared. She wanted to ask how it made him feel. She wanted to share the emotions bursting inside her. Sensing that he wasn't ready, she remained silent.

In the corner, Tramp still lay on his rug, but he was watching them both. Funny, she'd forgotten all about him earlier. Now she wondered what he thought about what he must have witnessed.

"Think we embarrassed my dog?" she asked Taylor.

"Naw. He probably had his paws over his eyes the whole time." Taylor raked a hand through his hair, shoving it back from his forehead before he donned his hat.

"The coffee's still on." She wasn't ready to let him go, not yet.

He let his gaze sweep the camper. "I'll take a rain check." The walls were closing in on him. All he wanted was to get away and sort out the confusion swirling inside him. He'd expected to feel differently after he had her and damned if he didn't. Only problem was, he'd thought the edge would be off his hunger, but all he could think about was being with her again. It was the same as it had been after he first kissed her—all he wanted was more.

She had opened up and let him see her vulnerability. Her need made him feel ten feet tall. Bulletproof. Even now, the memory of her passion left him staggered. And somehow, emptier than ever.

Now he had to deal with the consequences of his actions. He'd known getting close to her would only bring him trouble. Hell, he should have hit the ground running out of the box. Instead of listening to his instincts, he'd let his hormones override his self-control and keep him hanging around her like a lovesick bull.

He'd be damned lucky if he got out of this with his hide intact. He wasn't so sure about his heart.

"I'll see you in the morning," he said, feeling painfully inadequate. He knew she needed more from him right now, and he was tempted to tell her he had no more to give—that inside him was just a big empty hole.

Aw, hell, she'd find out quick enough. Sooner or later she would need something from him, something he didn't have and had no idea where to get. Then he would let her down and she'd see what a fraud he really was.

"I'm going home tomorrow, back to Colorado, for Kenny's graduation," she said. "I'll be leaving at first light."

"How long will you be gone?"

Her smile didn't reach her eyes, but he pretended not to notice. "Just a few days. I'll be in Oklahoma by Friday morning."

He thought about asking if he could stay with her tonight, but before he could find his voice, she reached around him to open the door. Suddenly he hated the casualness of leaving her bed to meet up again down the road, but he had no idea how to put his feelings into words.

"See you on Friday," he said instead. Gritting his teeth, he slipped out and shut the door behind him.

Back inside the camper, Ashley poured herself a cup of the coffee she no longer wanted and unrolled her sleeping bag. Tramp got up, stretched and went to the door.

"This is the last time tonight," she said, letting him out. "Make it count." There was no sign of Taylor. She watched the dog while he watered a fence post, then let him back in. As soon as he was settled on his rug, she set her alarm clock and took off her robe. Pulling a night-shirt over her head, she turned out the lamp and crawled inside the sleeping bag.

Tramp sighed and she heard him change position. Outside, all was quiet. Blinking back tears, she wadded up the pillow beneath her head and closed her eyes.

She should have been happy, replete, satiated. Instead, she was as lonely as hell, and she felt as if she had just let something important slip right through her fingers.

Taylor was dismayed by how much he missed Ashley when she went back to Colorado. The days they were apart crawled by like Gila monsters on a warm rock, barely moving at all. Even Donovan commented on his restlessness. Taylor won big in Amarillo, but he was relieved when the show was finally over and he could head out. All he thought about on the road was that every mile he drove brought him closer to Ashley.

When they pulled in to the rodeo grounds, he looked around eagerly, but he didn't see her rig. While Donnie headed for the office to pay their fees, Taylor took their horses to the barn. When he left Sarge's stall, he saw Ashley headed his way with her pinto in tow.

He knew there was a foolish grin on his face as he watched her coming toward him, but he didn't care. Dressed in boots, jeans, a yellow Western shirt and her Stetson, she looked wonderful.

"Hi," she said softly when she reached him. Her cheeks had turned pink. "Did you miss me?" Her expression was such a mixture of hope and wariness that it damn near broke his heart. It was easy to see that his clumsy attempts at keeping his distance were already causing her pain.

"Hell, yes, I missed you!" he exclaimed, pulling her into his embrace. Breathing in her special scent, he dropped a quick kiss on her upturned mouth. Groaning, he kissed her again, long and thoroughly. She felt so good in his arms that it was all he could do to let her go. When he finally did, they were both breathing hard and his body insisted that one taste wasn't nearly enough.

He had to fight the urge to drag her back into the privacy of the stall and prove he had missed her. "How was Kenny's graduation?" he asked to distract them both.

Her dark eyes sparkled in the overhead light. "It was great. He looked so grown-up in his cap and gown. I thought Emma and Joe would burst with pride. Joe even cried, but he tried to hide it."

Ashley had told him the story of how Kenny had become part of their family. Remembering his own checkered childhood, Taylor wondered if the situation had really been all that rosy for the boy. Maybe when it came to foster parents, the Sutters were the exception to the rule. Intellectually, Taylor knew there had to be people who took in foster children because they genuinely wanted to help. In his gut, however, he was still too cynical to buy the idea.

The rancher he and Donnie had stayed with got himself some pretty cheap labor. He'd worked the boys hard. If he cared for them at all, he had managed not to show it.

Taylor glanced back at his horse, who was dozing with his head lowered. "Let me help you with Spinner," he offered. "Then we can grab some lunch at Rowdy's and you can tell me about your visit home."

"Good idea."

He squeezed her hand, wishing he could take her back to his camper instead. A short time later, they left the barn with its familiar sounds and smells behind and walked across the parking lot.

When Ashley slid into a booth at the small café, Taylor surprised her by sitting beside her instead of taking the seat opposite.

"You don't mind, do you?" he asked as he rested his arm across the back of the seat.

"Not a bit." She touched a hand to his cheek. He was so attractive that he took her breath away.

His jaw was freshly shaved. Before she could remove her hand, he rubbed his cheek against her sensitive palm as he watched her through narrowed eyes. Only when the waitress brought menus and Ashley dropped her hand did he avert his gaze.

She gulped in a breath, as if she had just been released from some powerful tractor beam, and tried to make sense of the menu.

After the waitress returned to take their orders, Taylor turned back to her expectantly. "So," he asked, "did you have a good time with your family?"

"It was great." She went on to describe the ranch and to tell him all about the graduation ceremony. "Maybe you could go back with me someday," she suggested shyly. "I'd love to show you Joe's horses."

A gleam of interest lit Taylor's blue eyes, as the waitress brought their lunches. "I'd like that," he said quietly.

She felt as if they had cleared some major hurdle. Greatly encouraged, she took a healthy bite of her club sandwich.

"Donnie wants to head east for a while with Phil and Brian," Taylor told her, toying with a French fry.

Chewing, she remained silent. Would he find a man to be his hazer this time?

When she didn't respond, he curled one hand over hers. "You brought me luck," he said earnestly. "Be my hazer again. Donnie wants to take the truck, so if I could ride with you and share your horse trailer, I'd just find someone else to bunk with. Of course I'll pay my share of the expenses, too."

"I wasn't worried about that." She knew that cowboys on the circuit were used to sharing whatever space was available to grab a few hours' sleep. She had done it herself with other barrel racers, hitching rides, sharing motel space, lending the cramped floor of her camper or the cab of her truck to any woman with a sleeping bag and nowhere else to stay. Someone would take Taylor in.

If he traveled with her and they split the expenses, she could save more money. She wouldn't be on the road alone. It would be difficult, though, to let him walk away when night fell.

Was he serious about sleeping somewhere else or merely trying to give her a choice? She wanted to ask him but couldn't. Instead, she swallowed the bite of sandwich and took a sip of lemonade, knowing he was waiting for some kind of response.

"We can look over the shows coming up and plan our schedule together," he added before she could speak. "Sharing the driving instead of taking two rigs, we can get to more places, and it will be cheaper for both of us."

She leaned back in the booth and studied him, playing for time. Knowing she was going to say yes, but still reluctant to step into a situation that could ultimately prove dangerous to her emotions and destructive to her heart.

"I don't know," she stalled. "Can you cook?"

Clearly, her question caught him off guard. "Cook?" he echoed.

"Yeah. It's cheaper than eating out all the time."

Some of the tension in him relaxed. "I've been on my own for a long time. Do I look like a man who's missed many meals?" He patted his flat stomach.

She eyed his solid physique. "Maybe your brother's the one who does the cooking," she hedged.

Taylor rolled his eyes, falling in with her teasing. "He's younger than I am. He's the cleanup crew."

"Aha!" She leaned forward and waggled a finger under his nose. "You sound like a man who considers KP beneath him. I'm younger. Does that mean I'd have to do the KP?"

"We'll take turns." His face grew serious and his hand tightened on hers. "I'll do whatever I have to," he said quietly. "Now, do we ride together or not?"

She wished she had the will to resist, but of course she didn't. "I was planning on going to Oklahoma next," she told him. "What about you?"

"Oklahoma's fine. I'll call in my entry and we can leave here right after your ride."

For the first week, the partnership went well. Taylor insisted on doing most of the driving. Whenever Ashley wasn't looking, he paid the lion's share of the expenses, as well. He didn't talk much on the road, but she felt at ease with him, radio tuned to the nearest country station and Tramp sitting proudly on the seat between them. A couple of times other cowboys relayed messages from Donnie, who seemed to be winning consistently. If Taylor missed him, he didn't say.

The only flaw in their arrangement was that, so far, Taylor had stuck to his plan to sleep elsewhere. At every opportunity, he kissed Ashley until they were both breathless. It was becoming more and more difficult to let him go when he finally tore himself from her willing arms. She had tried every way she knew to keep him with her, except to come right out and ask him.

That she couldn't do. Not when he appeared willing to go. She thought back over their night together and couldn't come up with a single reason why he continued to leave her alone. Meanwhile, she did his hazing, and he continued to place in the money and to insist she share his purse.

The extra workout seemed only to warm Spinner up for Ashley's event. The barrel racing went well, too. Apparently sexual frustration wasn't a deterrent to winning. If anything, it probably gave her an edge.

They were both in the top fifteen in the standings. If their luck continued to hold, they'd be competing in the national finals in Las Vegas at the end of the year.

That was a long time away, though. The big Fourth of July weekend, nicknamed "Cowboy Christmas" because of the many rodeos to choose from, was coming up next. It was the weekend when everyone would try to hit as many shows as possible to increase their winnings and move up in the standings. Ashley and Taylor were no exception. They spent a lot of time looking at maps and schedules, as well as using the phone to register for their events.

One day in Nebraska, Ashley was sitting at the table in her camper studying the latest *Pro Rodeo Sports News,* when Taylor came in the open door. She glanced up to greet him and then went back to the newspaper.

Shutting the door, he slid in beside her and started massaging her shoulders.

"Mmm." She sighed, leaning against his solid presence. Her neck and shoulders ached from the long trip the night before. She had insisted on taking her turn driving while Taylor caught some sleep on the seat beside her. While he had, she kept sneaking glances at him, admiring his strong profile.

Now the feel of his breath on her neck was enough to send shivers of longing through her like jolts of electricity. He was driving her crazy. She suspected he was doing his best to keep himself under careful control, but she wasn't sure why. Meanwhile, her own feelings only grew stronger.

Now he gentled the touch of his hands on her shoulders and leaned forward to trace a path down her throat with his lips. His breathing sounded ragged. Perhaps his control was getting shaky.

Afraid to turn her head and spook him, Ashley sat quietly. Any hope of making sense of the rodeo listings before her had, however, gone out the window at the first touch of his hands.

"Am I interrupting anything?" he asked.

Her fingers tightened on the edge of the table. "Nothing important," she breathed.

"Where are you in the standings this week?" He caught the lobe of her ear between his teeth and worried the tiny gold hoop with the tip of his tongue.

"S-seven," she hissed as reaction to his nearness poured through her like warm honey.

"And me? How'm I doing?" With his big hands wrapped around her shoulders, he had let go of her ear and was tracing warm, wet circles on the side of her neck.

His ambiguous question brought a bubble of laughter to her throat. "Number f-five, I think." It was getting harder to concentrate.

"What looks good for the fourth?"

"Fourth what?"

His chuckle was deep and rich. "The Fourth of July. What looks good?" Undoing the top snap of her shirt, he slid the fabric aside with his fingers and leaned over to nibble the sensitive skin covering her collarbone.

Ashley gave up all pretense of studying the newspaper. "You look pretty good to me."

He hesitated, and she heard him draw in a quick breath. Daringly, she dropped her hand to his thigh. As she stroked the worn denim of his jeans, his muscles clenched beneath her fingers.

While she waited, afraid to breathe, he turned her gently toward him in the cramped space between the seat and the table. His eyes glittered and his expression was intent. Raising one hand, he brushed his thumb across her lower lip. Slowly, he rubbed it back and forth, watching what he was doing as if he were performing delicate surgery.

Helplessly, gaze locked on his lowered lashes, Ashley parted her lips and caressed his thumb with her tongue. He raised his eyes to stare hotly into hers. Desire sharpened the planes of his face. Then, as she curled her fingers into the front of his shirt, he lowered his head.

With their mouths closer than two heartbeats, he stopped. Perhaps he was still fighting his attraction to her. Perhaps he had second thoughts, although she doubted it. He wanted her—she could tell. Shifting slightly, she joined her mouth to his.

As the kiss exploded between them, a shudder went through him and his hands tightened. Then he angled the alignment of his lips on hers. His tongue delved into her mouth, stroking, savoring. Drowning in reaction, Ashley yielded gladly.

The kiss was wild and hot. She was going up in flames, a conflagration of need and burning desire.

A low growl worked its way up Taylor's throat as his mouth ravaged hers. His hunger was like a lit match, igniting her response. She twisted in his embrace, trying to get closer. In the cramped confines of the tiny seating area, it was impossible.

"This is worse than necking in a car with a floor shift." His voice was deep and husky, yet underscored with reluctant humor.

Ashley dragged open her eyes. His face was flushed. While she continued to watch him, he got to his feet and extended his hand. His gaze was locked on hers, as if he was silently seeking permission.

"I've missed you," he confessed. "It's been hell. Let me stay with you now. Let me do all the things I've lain awake nights thinking about."

Heat flowed through her like a river of lava. She nodded and he squeezed his eyes shut with obvious relief. She put her hand in his and let him pull her gently to her feet. When he started to unfasten the snaps on her shirt, she did the same to his. Sliding the fabric from her shoulders, he bent forward and placed a lingering kiss on the valley between her breasts. When he reached around to unhook her bra, she pushed his shirt off his shoulders. Then she freed the cuffs and it fell to the floor. With frequent interruptions for kissing and stroking, they finished undressing each other.

When Ashley smoothed her hands across Taylor's broad chest, stroking the soft, curly hair, tracing the outline of his muscles with her fingertips, he tipped back his head and closed his eyes as if he were absorbing her touch into his very being. Loving the feel of his warm, satiny skin, she leaned forward and began to kiss a path from his wide chest down to his stomach.

Immediately, his hands closed in her hair and tugged her head gently back so he could kiss her mouth. As he stroked her spine, she moved her hands from his hips to his firm buttocks. While she did so, her breasts pressed against his chest.

Before she knew it, he had her down on the bed and was stretched full length beside her, bracing his head on one hand.

"I need you," he whispered.

Her heartbeat thundered in her ears. For once, everything he was feeling showed on his face, and she wondered if he was aware how much his expression gave away.

"I need you, too." Her throat closed around the words and she wondered if he could hear them. Apparently he did, because his eyes flared and the heat that blazed there sparked an answering heat inside her.

"Taylor," she murmured helplessly, reaching for him. He looked as if he meant to say something, but then he merely leaned forward to kiss her. As he did so, he stroked and caressed her, finding each sensitive spot on her body and setting it on fire with the skill of his hands and his mouth. All she could do was to hang on and ride the sensations building inside her.

Part of Taylor would have liked to slow down and watch her response to his ministrations, but the raw hunger that drove him allowed no time for dalliance. He was a passionate man, but always before there had been one small part of his mind that stood back and observed—never quite relinquishing control until that last throbbing climax that emptied his mind as well as his thrusting body.

Not this time. Not with this woman. She made him feel as if he mattered. Instinctively, he knew she didn't give herself to every cowboy who came along. Her feelings had to be involved. Selfishly, he was glad. Perhaps later it would only make things more complicated, but for now the idea of being with someone who saw value in him, someone who cared, was the headiest aphrodisiac of all.

His control was about to snap, like a rubber band stretched too thin. Before that happened, he wanted to give her every bit of pleasure that he could. Hanging on to even a shred of sanity was almost more than he could manage.

With new urgency, he stroked the insides of her thighs down to her knees and back again. When her legs parted slightly, he leaned over her, taking her mouth as his questing fingers found their target.

She arched against him, clutching his shoulders. Conscious thought began seeping out of him like water from a leaky bucket. Groaning, he covered her body with his and knelt between her legs.

Ashley was lost in a swirling sea of sensation. More, she thought dazedly, she wanted more. He slid his hands beneath her hips. Just when she thought she would fly apart if he didn't claim her, he thrust into her. As soon as he was sure she had adjusted to his invasion, he began to move—long, powerful strokes that set her on fire.

There was no way she could withstand the mastery of his possession. Helplessly, she gave herself up to him. Even as she soared, she felt him drive into her one last time. He went rigid and then, with a hoarse cry, he gave himself up to the firestorm they had created together.

She had hoped that making love again would be the beginning of a new closeness between them. That maybe now Taylor would be willing to tell her about himself, to share his thoughts and feelings so she could get to know him on more than just one level. She was wrong.

Physically, he couldn't resist her. All pretense of his staying elsewhere while they traveled together had been abandoned. In public, he was far less reserved than she might have expected, sometimes taking her hand or slinging an arm around her shoulders when they were at the arena or the barn. He hugged her when they won the steer wrestling. He kissed her when she ran the barrels successfully. At the rodeo dances, he hardly let her out of his arms.

Obviously, he wasn't ashamed of their relationship. He just had no desire to deepen it past a certain level of physical intimacy.

The realization almost broke her heart.

He loved watching her ride, her body crouched low over Spinner's neck, her loose hair streaming from under her Stetson like a fiery flag. Arms pumping, heels drumming against her mount's heaving sides as they raced across the arena like one entity.

Boot braced on the bottom fence rail, Taylor tracked her progress around the first barrel as Spinner slammed on the brakes and made the tight turn. Ashley clung like a burr. In a blink, they were headed toward the next barrel. Hearing her whoop of elation, Taylor smiled.

Damn, she was good. He was thinking about the finals when he saw her horse go down as if he'd been shot, taking Ashley with him. It happened so fast that for a moment Taylor couldn't believe what he saw.

The breath whooshed out of him as if he'd been suckerpunched. She and the horse were still down. In a heartbeat, he cleared the fence and ran toward her. As he slid to his knees at her side, he saw that her eyes were shut. At least she wasn't pinned beneath the pinto.

"Ashley, honey, are you okay?" His heart was in his throat, its beat thundering so hard in his ears that he couldn't make out what the attendant who had rushed up behind him was trying to say.

"Ashley!" Taylor cried again, fear like a knife in his gut as he reached for her hand. He was vaguely aware of Spinner thrashing his head and screaming with pain. Then Ashley opened her eyes. Her hand squeezed his and relief threatened to swamp him.

"Taylor? What happened?"

"Spinner fell."

"Excuse me," said another paramedic, urging Taylor aside. "Let us look at her."

Still shaking, Taylor forced his fingers to release her hand and stepped back while the two men began checking her over. Her horse hadn't yet got to his feet, but someone was at his head, soothing him, and the vet was checking him over.

Taylor stayed close while they asked Ashley several questions. Then they put a splint on one of her legs and brought out a stretcher.

"Oh, God, my knee," she groaned, trying to sit up.

"Lie back," instructed one of the uniformed attendants. "Try not to move." They lifted her carefully onto the stretcher and carried her toward the gate, while Taylor followed. His gaze was riveted to her face. It was pale, her features drawn with pain. When she saw him looking down at her, she tried to smile. Tears seeped from the corners of her eyes.

"You'll be okay," he found himself telling her. Injuries were common in rodeo. They happened all the time. He had seen plenty of men hurt. Women, too. "Everything is going to be all right."

The words had barely left his mouth when one of the attendants stumbled, jostling her and she cried out in pain. Seeing her in such agony was almost more than Taylor could bear. He had never felt more helpless in his life.

Desperately, he wanted to help her. All he could do was to grip her hand tight and mouth a silent prayer while he tried not to let his own fear show.

Chapter Eight

"I need to see about my horse," Ashley insisted as the paramedics loaded her stretcher into the waiting ambulance. She tried to sit up, but the pain in her leg streaked through her body, making her grit her teeth to keep from crying out. Wildly, she twisted her head around. Taylor was standing behind the ambulance, his face lined with concern.

"Where's Spinner?" she cried. "He went down. Do you know if he's hurt?" Tears of pain and worry spilled from her eyes. When she tried to dash them away, the movement sent fresh agony shooting through her.

"You need to go to the hospital," one of the attendants told her. "That leg has to be examined."

"I can't go until I find out if my horse is hurt. He needs me." She bit her lip, struggling for control over her mounting frustration. She didn't dare even think about her own injured leg.

"Taylor, would you see about Spinner for me? I need to know how he is."

"I want to go with you," he replied. "I'm sure Spinner's fine. You're more important to me than any horse."

While she appreciated Taylor's sentiment, she had to be sure her pinto was being looked after. She couldn't stand thinking about him, possibly injured, left alone in his stall and wondering why she wasn't there to take care of him.

"We have to go," the attendant told her, one hand on the door.

"No, wait," she pleaded. "Taylor, would you check on him for me? Please?" The pain in her knee was agonizing when she tried to lift her head, worse than anything she had ever felt, but at least *she* was able to understand what was happening. Spinner could be frantic with fear. She couldn't bear to think of him, terrified, so panicked that he might do himself a further injury.

Taylor reached up to touch the ankle of her good leg. "If that's what you want me to do, I'll go see about him right now."

"You can catch up with us after you do that," offered one of the attendants waiting by the back door. "The hospital isn't far from here."

Taylor nodded, clearly torn. He must have seen Ashley's concern and known it would only be worse if she had to worry about her horse, too.

"Okay," he said reluctantly. Only then did he release his hold on her hand. "I'll take care of Spinner and check on Tramp, and then I'll be at the hospital as soon as I can."

Ashley thanked him tearfully. "I'll be waiting for you."

It seemed like hours later that Taylor finally showed up at the emergency room, but she knew she had lost all track of time. One look at his face and Ashley knew the news wasn't good. Fresh tears filled her eyes and she did her best to blink them away as she tried to brace herself for whatever he had to tell her.

It had happened so fast. One moment, everything had been fine; the next, she'd been facedown in the dirt.

"Tell me," she demanded when Taylor stopped at her bedside and gently brushed the hair back from her forehead.

His eyes avoided hers and a muscle worked in his cheek. He dragged a chair over to the side of the bed and sat down heavily. Then he took her hand and laced his fingers through hers. "I'm sorry. The bone was shattered. There was nothing anyone could do."

"Oh, God," she whispered. "No, no, no." She loved that horse. Ever since Joe had given him to her, the two of them had been a team. Spinner had offered her everything he had and then, when she asked for more, he had always reached down and found it for her.

Taylor gripped her hand in both of his. He was watching her anxiously. "Have you found out anything yet?"

She shook her head, unable to think of anything but her horse as she struggled for control. "Where is he now? Have they given him something for the pain? Is anyone with him?" Surely Taylor wouldn't have left unless there was someone else to watch over him. She couldn't bear to think of him hurting, confused, wondering where she was. "I have to—" She lifted the thin blanket.

Taylor jumped to his feet and wrapped an arm around her, staying her. His eyes were bleak, his stare unflinching. "Honey, there's nothing you can do. It's too late," he said in a rock-solid voice. "He was in so much pain that the vet went ahead and put him down."

"No, that's not possible. He's young, he has years ahead of him. When he's too old to rodeo, I'm taking him back to Joe's, where he can enjoy his retirement. He's not gone!" Her voice rose to a wail at the end.

Slowly, eyes moist, Taylor shook his head. "I'm sorry, honey. He's gone. It had to be done."

The flood of fresh tears threatened to choke her as she finally accepted the news. Part of her had known it was serious. Spinner wouldn't have fallen otherwise.

She bit her lip to stop its trembling. Damn, but she should have been there to hold his head, to say goodbye. Barely aware of what she was doing, she pressed her face into Taylor's hard chest and sobbed.

Murmuring disjointed words of comfort, he rocked her slowly, giving her time to absorb the dreadful news. Some part of her was grateful for his ministrations, even as she mourned Spinner's loss.

Finally, when the storm of tears began to abate, Taylor levered her gently away and lowered her back down on the cot. He handed her a box of tissues. "Have you seen a doctor yet? Have they given you medication for the pain?"

She almost choked on the lump of sadness wedged in her throat. "They haven't given me anything. They took X rays of my leg, but it's my knee that hurts the worst."

He sat back in the chair, hand still holding hers tightly. "Everything will be okay," he said. "I'm here for you. When we find out something specific, I'll call your family, if you want me to. Evie's looking after Tramp. She'll keep him with her as long as need be."

With those simple words, he soothed away for the moment all the underlying worries that were beginning to gather like storm clouds. She was used to taking care of herself, and she hated to ask for help of any kind. Although she had to remember that Taylor might not always be here for her, having him with her now was enough. Exhausted, she lay back down against the pillows. "Thank you."

His smile was crooked. "You're welcome. Why don't you try to rest while we wait for the X rays?"

She didn't think she could, but the doctor had to wake her when he came back. When he was through discussing the extent of her knee injury, she knew she had no choice but to go to Joe's ranch to recover for at least a couple of weeks.

The doctor wasn't sure whether she would need surgery or how soon she could get back in the saddle. Not that she had a horse to ride anyway, she thought sadly. The fresh reminder of poor Spinner brought on another flood of tears.

Looking helpless, the doctor muttered something about finishing his paperwork and then he fled.

"I'll have to call Joe and see if he can come for me," she said when he left. Rubbing her swollen eyes with her fists, she tried to figure out what to do first.

"You don't have to ask Joe. I'll take you home." Taylor's deep voice startled her.

"I can't ask you to do that. You're going—"

"I'm taking you back to Colorado as soon as you're released from here. You didn't ask—I offered." He looked as if he wouldn't let her argue with him. "Now, do you want to call your family and tell them what happened, or shall I?"

"You should be in a wheelchair," Joe scolded, turning to speak to Ashley. He and Taylor had been standing at the corral fence, watching a pure white mare show off her matching colt.

Taylor turned, too, and then he hurried to Ashley's side. She was using aluminum crutches, and her leg was in a well-padded brace. Tramp was with her.

"I couldn't have gotten out here in a wheelchair," she argued as Taylor hovered, not sure just what to do to help her. "The path isn't paved."

Tramp and Paddy, Joe's Irish setter, sniffed each other as Joe made an exasperated sound in his throat. "Don't come running to me when they put you in traction," he told Ashley.

Taylor gave him a startled glance, only to see his weathered face break into a grin. Earlier, he had admitted how worried he was about her knee, but now he hid his concern.

"You sound just like Mom!" Ashley exclaimed. "She used to say that when I climbed the tree in the front yard."

Joe's grin widened. "I know. She said the same thing to me, when she wasn't threatening to wring my neck if I hurt myself." His attention shifted to Taylor, who wasn't sure what to make of the exchange. "She never appreciated it when I tried to point out the irrationality of that threat."

"She got angry when you were hurt?" Taylor asked cautiously. His own father had often gotten angry at him and Donnie.

Joe shook his head. "No, she got angry at the *idea* of us getting hurt. When we really were hurt, she was great. Cried and everything."

While Joe had been talking, Ashley stumped over to a bench and plopped herself down with a grateful sigh. Tramp ran back to check on her, and then he and Paddy sprawled out in the sun. She put her crutches aside and peered up at Taylor. Her eyes were still shadowed with sadness and worry and the edges of her mouth quivered, but she was doing her best to put on a brave face. "Joe's turning into our mother." Her tone was light. "He tells his kids the same things she used to tell us. Things we swore we'd never get caught repeating."

"No, I don't," Joe began to argue hotly. "I never lecture them about green vegetables or remind them to do their homework or ask if they've washed behind their ears." He paused for effect. "Emma's the one who says those things."

As Ashley chuckled along with him, Taylor figured Joe was doing his best to distract her. Both men knew how much she mourned the loss of her horse. Before she came out, Joe had been discussing with Taylor the animal's possible replacement. The horses they looked at were impressive, beautiful creatures with outstanding bloodlines and flashy colors: pintos, albinos and a couple of sassy buckskins with black stockings and stripes down their backs. Not a plain chestnut or a bay in the bunch.

Although Joe maintained a huge herd of beef cattle, he'd been quick to admit that when it came to the animals, the horses were his first love. The horses and Paddy, the Irish setter that had followed them around all morning.

Both dogs rose and went back over to Ashley. Crooning to them, she scratched behind their ears as they competed for her attention.

While she was fussing over them, Taylor spoke to Joe in an undertone.

"How's she look to you?"

Joe studied her thoughtfully for a moment. "Tired," he muttered back. "It's going to be damn hard to keep her from overdoing it, though. As you may have noticed, she doesn't much like sitting still."

"I suspected that," Taylor drawled.

"What are you two whispering about?" she demanded as the dogs wandered back into the sun. "I bet you're talking about me."

"You aren't the center of the universe," Joe replied.

"We have more interesting things than you to talk about," Taylor said at the same time.

They must have looked as guilty as hell. She stared at them through narrowed eyes. "I'll just bet."

As both men shuffled and stared at their feet, Ashley felt her determined good mood begin to crumble. On top of everything else, it had been two days since Taylor brought her back to the ranch, and she had no idea how much longer he could afford to stay. Every day he lingered cost him prize money and, more important, the points that kept him at the top of the standings. If she had been less selfish, she would have insisted that he leave.

Instead, she couldn't bear the thought of his going without her. Having him around distracted her from dwelling on the loss of her horse and from worrying too much about her own future. Not that Joe and the rest of the family didn't do their best—they just didn't have the edge that Taylor did.

That same edge seemed to have stolen her heart when she wasn't looking.

She grabbed her crutches, intending to struggle to her feet. Both men rushed over to her before she could rise.

"Where do you want to go?" Taylor asked.

"You're going to wear yourself out," Joe accused.

"Let me take you back to the house," Taylor suggested.

"I'm sick of being in the house," she cried. Sick of being fussed over, sick of the discomfort and the inconvenience and, most of all, not knowing what was going to happen to her.

The doctor in Denver where she'd gone yesterday had been noncommittal about her chances for a full recovery. They would know more when the swelling went down and they could assess the damage to tendons and cartilage.

"Let's wait and see" was all he'd said.

She'd wanted to slug him.

Now Taylor glanced helplessly at Joe.

"Why don't we all go look at the rest of the horses?" her brother suggested in a soothing voice that made her want to slug *him*, too. "We can take the Jeep. If we go slow, it shouldn't bother her knee."

"Why don't I take her to see the horses," Taylor countered. "If you'll trust me with the Jeep. I'm sure you have chores you should be doing." His smile bared his teeth.

Sudden comprehension filled Joe's face. "Oh, yeah." He was clearly nonplussed. "Sure." He looked as if he would have liked to grill Taylor about his intentions.

Swiftly, Ashley intervened. The idea of spending some time alone with Taylor brightened her mood as little else could.

"That's a great idea," she said, as she grabbed her crutches and lurched to her feet, nearly overbalancing. "I'll just walk back to where I saw the Jeep parked."

Her attempt at distracting Joe worked beautifully. He dived at her. Before he could touch her, though, Taylor swept her into his arms. The look he sent her brother was openly territorial.

"I'll take her."

"I'll take her."

Ashley ducked her head, smothering a satisfied grin.

"I hate like hell to go and leave you here, but I have to meet Donnie in Dallas the day after tomorrow," Taylor told her as they sat in the Jeep and watched the mares and their offspring showing off in the near pasture. It was a beautiful day, the sky overhead as blue as his eyes, the land stretched out before them like an old-fashioned green-and-gold shag carpet, dotted with red and black cattle in the distance. In the immediate foreground, the mares grazed contentedly while their babies played and chased one another.

"You can take my camper, if you'd like," Ashley offered, refusing to let her disappointment show. "I won't be needing it for a while." She shifted her leg to a more comfortable position, glad that Taylor was tall enough to drive with the seat shoved all the way back.

He was watching her, narrow eyed, no doubt attempting to gauge her reaction to his news. "Thanks for the offer, but Kenny's going to take me to the airport in Denver. I'll fly to Dallas from there and Donnie can pick me up."

Kenny and his friend David had gone hiking, but they were due back the next day.

"I see," she murmured, unsure what else to say except to thank Taylor for all his help. When she did so, a look of frustration crossed his face.

"Damnation, but I wish you were going back with me," he ground out, pulling her close. "I'm going to miss you more than I can say."

"I'll miss you, too." His warm breath bathed her cheek as desire, pure and strong, rose within her. They'd had little privacy in the two days they'd been at the ranch. Both Emma and Ashley's mother had hovered around her like well-meaning nursemaids, helping tremendously but leaving little opportunity for more than a couple of hurried embraces with Taylor.

Yesterday Emma had walked in on them kissing in the kitchen. Even though she'd excused herself and beat a hasty retreat, the mood was shattered. After settling Ashley in the living room with a book, Taylor left to seek out Joe. The two of them had spent more time exploring the ranch together than Taylor had with her, except when the family gathered in the evening to visit and watch movies on television.

For once, there wasn't a passel of foster children over-running the place. Joe had confided in Ashley shortly after her arrival that since Kenny was graduating, he and Emma had decided to take the summer off and spend more time with each other. Obviously, he hadn't figured on the arrival of his half sister to complicate things.

Grumpily, Ashley hoped the two of them were better able to find privacy than she and Taylor had been so far.

"I can't wait to get back on the road," she told him now as they sat with their arms around each other. Taylor was sifting his fingers through her hair, examining it in the sunlight as if it were spun from gold. "I've always loved the ranch," she continued, ignoring the little shivers of desire his touch stirred so effortlessly, "but it's so... so settled here. So tame and predictable. Hardly anything ever changes but the seasons."

Taylor was watching her profile. "You love rodeo, don't you?"

Startled by his question, she turned to stare at his profile. "Of course. Don't you?"

He was frowning, but his brow cleared instantly. "Yeah, it's all I ever wanted to do."

"Did you learn to rodeo on the ranch in Idaho?" she asked cautiously. For a long moment, she thought he wasn't going to answer.

Then he shifted on the seat, taking his arm from around her shoulder and grasping the steering wheel instead, as if he had to brace himself in order to talk about his past.

"The ranch I told you about was a foster home where Donnie and I stayed," he said quietly. "But it wasn't anything like this. I guess Old Man Tulley just figured he was getting two cheap ranch hands and a monthly check besides."

Ashley gasped at the resignation behind Taylor's statement. "But you must have been just boys," she said indignantly. "How long were you there?"

"I was twelve when he took us in, and Donnie was ten. As soon as he'd graduated high school, we hit the road. The old man was a stickler about school, I'll give him that. He made sure we went, and that we got decent grades."

"You were so young," she said. "It must have been very difficult to support yourselves on the road, at least at first. Couldn't you have stayed at the ranch and rodeoed locally?"

Taylor must have been remembering how it was, because a shadow crossed his face. "The old man died," he said. "When it came to family, Tulley had some pretty traditional ideas. He left the ranch to a nephew. There was no place for us then, so we cleared out."

"You were never adopted?" she asked, sad for the boy he had been. No wonder he didn't like to talk about it.

He ran one hand around the steering wheel, tracing its shape. "He wasn't mean to us or anything like that; he'd just never been married or spent much time around kids.

If he cared about us at all, he didn't know how to let it show."

Ashley's heart ached for him and for Donovan, too. It was easy to see why Taylor kept his feelings to himself, but even more amazing was his brother's outgoing nature. How odd that the two men were so different, at least superficially.

"Do you remember your parents at all?"

He looked surprised. "Sure I do."

"What were they like?" She waited for him to retreat behind his usual wall.

Instead, he ran his hand around the back of his neck, rubbing it absently. "Our dad wasn't abusive, not by today's standards, but he didn't tolerate much mischief. Mom was always sticking up for us when we got in trouble. Looking back, I think that two little boys just put more strain on his temper than he could handle. Instead of blowing up, he'd pull back inside himself."

Taylor's expression had a bitter edge. "He could freeze you with a stare, make you spill your guts and confess things you'd only thought about doing. Knowing he was displeased with me—and the wall of silence that went along with it—was worse than any beating he could have given me. I always felt like I let him down. He'd tell me how much I'd disappointed him and I'd wonder if he hated me."

"Oh, Taylor," Ashley murmured, stroking his hand as it lay on the seat between them. "How awful."

He glanced at her and shrugged, clearly uncomfortable. "Maybe it was to offset that, but Mom was always telling us how much she loved us and how terrific we were. Even when we got in trouble or broke something of hers. I know that she gave me whatever security I felt back then."

"She sounds wonderful," Ashley told him. "What about your sister? What was she like?"

A shadow passed over his face. "Kirby was the love of Daddy's life. He called her his little princess."

In the pasture before them, a coal black filly squealed as a full-grown pinto kicked at her. In the blink of an eye, the filly's mother was between her and the other horse, teeth bared. Then all three fell to grazing as if nothing had happened.

"It must have been hard for you to watch your father favor Kirby so much," Ashley ventured. "Were you jealous of her?"

"Oh, no. She was the baby of the family, eight years younger than me. I was nuts about her. Plus Donnie and I figured if we treated her good, our daddy would notice and be pleased."

The picture he painted was a painfully familiar one. At least her father's favoritism of Joe had been unintentional. She knew he had cared about her, even if she always felt as if he would have loved her more if she had been prettier, smarter, or just a son. She tightened her grip on Taylor's hand.

He glanced down and cleared his throat. "I didn't mean to go on so."

"You didn't. How did the two of you end up in a foster home? Did something happen to your folks?"

Immediately, his face closed up like a slamming door and he withdrew his hand. "I don't talk about that," he said, the warmth that had been in his voice only moments before completely gone now.

While Ashley tried to deal with her disappointment at his sudden withdrawal, he shifted in the seat and looked down at her with obvious regret. "First time I get you alone in way too long and all I do is talk."

As farfetched as it seemed, perhaps he just couldn't believe she was really interested. She hoped there would be time together to convince him otherwise. Meanwhile, his innate sensuality was a powerful lure.

Encouraged by his wry comment, she leaned forward and batted her eyelashes provocatively. "Got any other ideas, cowboy?"

Groaning deep in his throat, he pulled her closer. "Oh, honey, do I ever." Despite the awkwardness of her knee brace, it was all the talking either of them did for quite a while.

Taylor hated to think about leaving Ashley behind when he left for Dallas. That night in his upstairs room in Joe's house, he tossed and turned on the narrow bed. Out of deference to her injured leg, Ashley was settled in the only bedroom on the main floor. As far as Taylor was concerned, she might as well have been in a castle surrounded by a moat full of alligators.

Getting up to stand naked at the tall, open window, its lacy curtains pushed aside, he toyed with the idea of braving the moat and the alligators, sneaking barefoot down the upstairs hallway past the master suite and Ashley's mother's room. Was that why Joe had put him at the far end, away from the staircase?

Taylor was well aware of Joe's protective streak when it came to his baby sister. He hadn't actually warned Taylor off, but he'd come damn close, pumping him subtly about their relationship and his intentions when she wasn't around to overhear.

Taylor had avoided telling him anything, because there really wasn't anything to tell. He cared about Ashley, but he had no idea what the future held, and he refused to spend time worrying about it. Not that he didn't understand the other man's attitude, because he did.

Taylor would have done the same damn thing with Kirby, if he'd only been given the chance. Not for the first time, he wondered where she was, if she was happy, in good health, married. Did Taylor have nieces and nephews growing up somewhere—family he'd never even met?

The worry that she might be in desperate need of his help and he would never even know twisted the familiar knot of anxiety in his gut that never completely dissolved. A debilitating sense of helplessness curled his fingers into the sheer fabric of the lace curtains until it threatened to rip. Realizing what he was doing, he released his death grip carefully. Turning, he stared at the door to his room, picturing Ashley sleeping below.

He listened to the silence of the old house. Was that his own heart he heard thudding in his ears, or the hot blood pounding in his veins, draining from his head to settle much lower in his painfully aroused body? Dammit, she was so close and yet so inaccessible.

He had to be crazy to even consider going to her. Even as he acknowledged that, he grabbed his jeans off the chair where he'd tossed them and pulled them on. He told himself she wouldn't appreciate his sneaking into her room in her brother's house, but it didn't keep him from crossing the floor and easing open the door to the silent hallway.

With a little luck, he'd be in bed with her before she had her eyes open. Fresh desire surged through him as he remembered how responsive she was. When he kissed her, she melted against him like hot wax. Once he got his hands on her, she'd forget all about scolding him for seducing her beneath her brother's nose.

The only flaw in his plan was that when he got downstairs and opened her door, her bedroom was empty.

Ashley lay on the chaise longue on the big back porch and contemplated the stars twinkling overhead like delicate Christmas lights. She had been too restless to sleep, despite the pain pill she had taken before bed. It dulled the ache in her knee but was no help against the one in her heart.

She missed Spinner with a sharp ache that hadn't yet begun to dull. Her knee, still as sore as a bad tooth, worried her. What if it didn't heal completely? Sighing, she searched the heavens for answers she knew weren't there.

Selfishly, she wished that Taylor could stay at the ranch with her until her leg was strong enough for her to start training another mount. She hoped to buy a barrel racer so the training time would be minimal. At least working with a new horse would help to keep her mind off Taylor, but she couldn't even ride without the doctor's okay. Even if she had been foolish enough to try it, Joe wouldn't let her.

More than the excitement and the people and the adrenaline rush of competition, more than the aching satisfaction of doing something well or the brief, intense glory of winning, she was going to miss Taylor. His touch, his kiss, his presence beside her on the road, the sound of his voice, even his scent, soap and sweat and leather, were firmly implanted into her brain. And her heart.

Fresh tears gathered behind her eyes and threatened to spill over. Annoyed with her own weepy weakness, she was about go back inside when the screen door creaked quietly open.

Glancing up, she saw the familiar outline of Taylor's big body in the gloom. His powerful chest was bare and his jeans rode sinfully low on his narrow hips.

The sight of him made her forget all about her problems. "What are you doing up?" she asked softly.

His crack of laughter was like a gunshot in the silence of the night. "It's your fault that I'm up, as you so delicately put it," he drawled. There was a dangerous edge to his voice, like the purr of a big cat that could turn predator in the blink of an eye.

As Ashley struggled to read his mood and his deliberate misunderstanding of her question, he leaned over the chaise where she was lying.

"I figured since you caused the problem," he said in a low, rough voice, "that you'd want to have a hand, so to speak, in the solution."

As she tipped back her head, trying to make out his expression in the darkness, he captured her shoulders. The heat of his palms soaked into her skin like sunshine, and her lips parted on an involuntary gasp of delight. His desire for her was almost palpable.

"What the hell have you done to me?" he demanded, and then his lips covered hers in a scorching kiss.

Chapter Nine

Their renewed closeness made leaving Ashley behind in Colorado a hundred times more difficult for Taylor. Never before had it been a problem to clear from his mind, once he was back in the arena, everything but the steer and the coming few seconds. No one but Ashley had ever been able to intrude on his thoughts when he was about to compete.

"Hey, bro?" Donovan called as they waited tensely for the steer to enter the chute. "Are you okay?"

Furious with himself, Taylor gave his brother a sharp nod and focused on the steer. It broke from the chute and he felt his horse gather itself beneath him. Taylor managed to maintain his concentration until the timer dropped his flag, but his time wasn't quite good enough to finish in the money. Had it been because the steer was a little too quick, or because he had hesitated that extra fraction of a second before dropping down off Sarge's back? Not knowing was enough to clench the muscles along his jaw and tighten his chest until he felt something inside him would surely snap from the strain. He raised his head to search for Ashley, and then he remembered she wasn't here.

"Tough break," Donovan said as he dismounted behind the chutes and clapped Taylor on the back. "You'll do better next time."

Without looking up, Taylor grumbled some halfhearted response and began leading his horse back to the barn.

"What do you hear from Ashley?" The question had him swinging around, hands knotted into fists as he dropped Sarge's reins.

"I haven't checked in with her today," he snarled. "Why don't you call her yourself if you want a goddamn update?"

To his credit, Donnie didn't punch him, which was what his uncalled-for outburst probably deserved. Instead, his brother gave Taylor a searching glance.

"Maybe I'll do just that," he drawled, frowning. "Do you want me to give her a message for you?"

With a muttered curse, Taylor spun away and tugged on Sarge's reins. Then he thought about what she must be going through, stuck at the ranch, when all she undoubtedly wanted was to be here, with the noise and the dust and the excitement that had wormed its way into her blood, just as it had his.

He relented, aching like a bear with a bad tooth. "Yeah, tell her I miss her."

Donnie's frown faded. "Will do." He smoothed down his mustache with his thumb. "She'll be back before you know it," he offered, and then he led his showy palomino away without giving Taylor time to respond.

Sure, he consoled himself as he led his own horse out, nodding to a couple of other riders without speaking, she was too stubborn to let this setback keep her down for long. She'd be back with bells on as soon as she could bend her knee enough to sit a horse.

"It's orthoscopic surgery—no big deal. I've got a line on a horse, too, a barrel racer from Montana. If everything works out, I could be back in a couple of weeks." Ashley shifted the receiver to her other ear, guiltily wishing it were Taylor on the phone instead of his brother.

She knew two weeks was pushing it, but she missed Taylor so much. Ignoring the knot in her stomach and the tears of self-pity that swam behind her eyes, she listened to Donovan's reassurances.

"That's right," she agreed. "They don't expect to find anything but a little flap of cartilage that needs to be trimmed off—just like a hangnail. I won't even be staying at the hospital. It's an outpatient procedure." She told him when the surgery was scheduled, the next morning in Denver, and thanked him for the yellow roses he had sent.

Donovan wished her luck and passed on Taylor's message.

"Tell him to take care of himself," she responded, longing rising in her throat and threatening to choke her. "You too." She knew Donovan probably had things to do, but she was reluctant to sever the connection. His voice was a link to the life she loved as well as the man who had captured her heart. Finally, there was nothing left to say. She thanked Donovan again for calling and forced herself to let him go.

Taylor called frequently, but he always sounded hurried and distracted. She would have liked to ask him if he missed her—she needed to hear it from him directly—but it was an impossible question to voice over the phone.

Dammit, but she wanted to see him. She needed the comfort and strength of his embrace, the reassurance of his hard body tight against her. If he had been anywhere within a couple of hundred miles, she would have gone to him, but he was in Texas. Besides, she wasn't sure he wanted her there. Her own insecurity was more of a tether than her injured knee.

Taylor wanted to be there when she had the surgery, but she was adamant that he not leave the circuit.

"You've already missed too much time on account of me."

"Are you sure?" he demanded, studying the schedule in his hand. "I could fly in first thing. I'd only have to miss—"

"No," she interrupted before he could finish. "I'll be in and out in less time than it would take you to get here. I'll be fine."

He knew she was exaggerating, but he let it pass. Hell, maybe she didn't want him there. Perhaps she had enough to deal with, getting back in shape and figuring out what to do about a replacement for Spinner. Unlike steer wrestlers and calf ropers, barrel racers didn't share their mounts. The bond between horse and rider was too strong, too interdependent. If the quarter horse from Montana panned out, it would still take time to forge another winning team. No matter how fast her knee healed or how quickly she came back, she might not really be competitive for months.

Meanwhile, it was obvious to Taylor that she didn't want him hanging around the hospital.

"All right," he agreed reluctantly. "I'll call you tomorrow night and see how it went, okay?"

As soon as she agreed, he wished her luck and broke the connection, feeling shut out and frustrated. He wanted to lend her his support and assure himself that she was really okay. Hell, he wanted to wave a magic wand and undo her wreck. He *wanted* her back in his arms and his bed.

Her self-sufficient tone when she told him she didn't need him around did little to placate him.

"I'm so sorry, honey." Her mother's wrinkled cheeks were streaked with tears, her voice full of a parent's special heartache for a child in pain.

The lines in Marian Gray's face had deepened at the doctor's news, but she had been widowed twice and was used to looking for the bright side of adversity. Now as she sat by Ashley's bed, she sighed and patted her daughter's hand. "There must be something else, something better, waiting for you down the road, my darling."

The familiar rodeo term for moving on brought new tears of despair to Ashley's burning eyes. "I suppose you're right," she whispered, trying to give comfort, even though she couldn't take comfort herself. From somewhere deep inside herself, she dragged up a brittle smile for her mother's sake. There was a cold lump in her stomach that wouldn't dissolve, but she put off thinking about the future.

What future? Since the doctor had come in to discuss the results of her knee surgery, she'd had trouble assimilating the news. She'd been given one talent and now it was gone. Snatched away with a ruined knee. How did she begin to live with that?

As she did her best to put on a brave face, a fresh thought stopped her cold. How was she going to tell Taylor that her life in rodeo was over?

He wanted to slam his fist into the wall beside him in sheer frustration. Lately, his schedule had been a killer, as many as three shows a week in three different towns as he fought to stay at the top of the standings. For him, Colorado might as well have been the moon.

Through the receiver in his ear, Ashley chattered on, telling how well physical therapy was going. It was only when he asked how soon she was going to be back on the road that she became evasive. Despite her cheerful tone, a premonition shivered down Taylor's spine.

Something wasn't right, and it went beyond mere loneliness. He gripped the receiver tighter and broke into her stream of questions about mutual acquaintances.

"Sweetheart, what aren't you telling me?"

At the other end of the wire, there was a pregnant silence. The breath he heard her take was shaky, but her voice, when she finally spoke, was pure, undiluted sensuality.

"Maybe I forgot to tell you how much I miss you," she purred, raising his temperature and sending flaming arrows of need straight to his groin.

Curling the receiver into the hollow between his neck and shoulder, he turned his back to the room and closed his eyes. "Why don't you tell me now," he rasped.

Her chuckle slid over his nerve endings like the teasing scrape of her fingernails. Damn, but he missed her. If he could have gone through the phone wires to get to her, he would have done it in a heartbeat.

"You tell me first," she whispered.

Lowering his voice, he did just that, pouring out his hunger and loneliness. It was only after they had both hung up and he'd walked away from the pay phone, wishing he could hold his hat in front of his body as a shield, that he realized she had once again evaded his questions.

At the other end of the line, Ashley replaced the receiver with a hand that trembled. Her diversionary tactics had backfired—big time. She hadn't expected him to be so candid about missing her, but his deep voice had swept away her doubts on a tidal wave of longing. Ultimately, his admission only made the news she had yet to tell him that much more difficult.

"Thanks for driving me to town, Mike." As they approached Joe's house, Ashley noticed an unfamiliar pickup parked in the driveway, but she didn't think much about it. Neighbors came by all the time. Most of them drove trucks. Even a few friends from high school had come to visit after word of her injury got around, although no one she could think of drove a new red three-quarter ton with fancy wheels and a pair of spurs dangling from the rearview mirror.

"Ask me anytime," Mike replied. "Driving you around sure beats chasing cows and eating dust." The young ranch hand had taken her into Caulder Springs to leave Tramp at the vet's for minor surgery. As far as Ashley was concerned, neutering was the only responsible option for a mixed-breed pet, and she'd been meaning to have it done as soon as he was totally recovered from his other injuries.

Since all the vehicles at the Blue Moon had manual shifts, including her own, Joe had asked Mike to drive her whenever she needed him. From the interest in his hazel eyes and his rapid-fire questions about life on the road, it was clear he was impressed by her background in rodeo.

Now he hurried around to her side of the truck to help her out of the high cab. When she thanked him again, his cheeks flushed a dusky red.

"I was wondering if you'd like to see a movie in town this weekend," he asked.

Ashley was about to gently turn him down when she looked up to see Taylor striding across the lawn toward them. Beneath his Stetson, his glittering eyes were riveted on her and his jaw was set. In one hand, he wielded a bunch of flowers wrapped in green paper.

With a guilty start she pulled away from Mike, who was still holding her elbow. A flush stained her cheeks as she searched Taylor's unsmiling face.

"When did you get here?" she asked, barely aware that Mike was still waiting for an answer.

Taylor stopped in front of her and gave the young cowhand a look that would have sent a lesser man scrambling for cover.

"Just in the nick of time, I'd say," he replied. "Son, don't you have somewhere you ought to be right about now?"

His superior tone filled her with a mixture of annoyance and pleasure. She was about to introduce Mike when Taylor grabbed her free arm. "I'll take it from here." Gimlet-eyed, he stared Mike down.

"Ashley?" The boy's voice had risen slightly, but he wasn't retreating. Considering that Taylor was a half head taller and probably fifty pounds heavier, she had to give Mike points for tenacity.

"It's okay," she told him, biting back a grin at his obvious relief. "Taylor's a friend of mine. Thanks again for the ride to town."

"Sure," he said, swallowing so his Adam's apple bobbed. "About this weekend—"

She felt Taylor stiffen beside her. No point in pushing him too far. "I'll get back to you later," she told Mike quickly.

He glanced down at Taylor's possessive grip and the half-forgotten bouquet. Understanding dawned. His flush deepened. "Okay, sure." He wasted no time in circling the pickup and climbing behind the wheel to drive away.

"Who was that?" Taylor asked, shoving the flowers into her arms. His expression had closed up, revealing nothing of what he might be thinking. Despite his forbidding demeanor and his caveman attitude, Ashley was so happy to see him that she barely glanced at the riot of colorful blooms.

"He's my driver," she said. "I can't manage a stick shift yet and I had to take Tramp to the vet."

Taylor frowned. "What's wrong with the dog?"

"Nothing. I'm having him neutered."

The expression of empathy all men seemed to get at the mention of messing with another male's reproductive parts flickered across Taylor's face. "I guess I acted like a possessive jerk," he muttered finally.

Ashley moved closer to slide her hands possessively around his waist. She was happier than she had been in weeks. Still holding the flowers, she tilted her head back to look him full in the face. "Thank you for these. You can act as possessive as you want. Just quit apologizing and give me a proper greeting."

When he complied, raising his head again after a kiss that left her breathless, he scraped the knuckles of one hand down her cheek. His eyes were shadowed.

"What's wrong?" she asked. Maybe, despite the floral offering and the warmth of his kiss, he had come to give her bad news, to tell her in person that he was tired of waiting for her and had decided to break things off between them.

Ashley did her best to brace herself for whatever he might say.

"I came because I've been worried about you," he surprised her by replying. "I suspect you haven't been entirely straight with me, and I'm here to find out what's really going on."

His perceptiveness shocked her. "Going on?" she echoed with a squeak in her voice. "What do you mean?"

They had been walking toward the house arm in arm, but now he turned to face her. Glancing down, he said, "I want the truth. I know you've been hiding something, and I need to know what."

Blinking back the sudden flood of tears, Ashley dug her short fingernails into the palms of her hands and admitted what she had been struggling so unsuccessfully to accept herself.

"I'll be able to ride again, but I can't compete," she said in a husky voice. Oh, God. Saying it out loud made it impossible to ignore. "The damage to my knee is too severe."

With no recollection of how he'd gotten there, Taylor found himself leaning against the side of the pickup he'd just bought in Texas. Ashley's news had caught him totally off guard. He didn't know what he had expected—

maybe that she'd hooked up with an old boyfriend or had fallen for her surgeon—but not this.

"The doctor could be wrong," he said, voice grating as he tried to absorb the shock. "Have you gotten a second opinion?"

She nodded, staring down at her hands. Her face was turned away from him, but he saw a tear splash against her knuckles. It felt as if someone had just poured acid on his heart.

"My doctor consulted two other specialists." Her voice quavered. "They agree that competing would put too much strain on what's left of my knee. If I were to damage it further, I'd lose the ability to bend it at all."

The words lay between them as cold and final as an obituary notice. Taylor didn't know what to say. "Good God," he finally burst out. "People in rodeo get injured all the time. Half the cowboys at any given show are wearing braces or casts, but their careers aren't over. Not for a damn knee injury."

His eyes blurred and he blinked several times. Chafing at his feeling of utter helplessness, he brought both fists down hard on the top of his truck. "I can't believe this."

"I'm sorry," Ashley gulped.

At the sound of her apology, remorse sliced through him like a knife. "Oh, honey, no. *I'm* sorry. This is about you, not me. I'm the one who should be apologizing for being such a selfish bastard." He pulled her trembling body against his, wrapping his arms around her as if he could still shield her from the hurt she must have been feeling.

As if *he* could do anything to help her. He didn't even know how to give comfort. "Why didn't you call?" he demanded desperately, hoping she wouldn't notice the lack in him that had kept him away when she needed him most. "I should have come sooner."

She raised her head to look at him, eyes like drowned pennies. "Don't say that," she whispered. "I needed some time to absorb all this, but I'm so glad you're here now."

She rested her head against his chest and a tiny sigh escaped her. "So glad," she repeated in a sad little voice that had none of her usual vitality.

If he was any kind of a real man, he would have been here for her surgery, instead of putting his own agenda first. How could he have been so selfish, unwilling to give up a chance to increase his winnings?

The bitter taste of his own shortcomings filled him. She had needed him and he'd been out chasing rainbows. Rainbows she would never chase again.

God, it was more than he could deal with. He shook his head and swore bitterly, then he tightened his arm around her and kissed her hair. He ached to tell her that it didn't matter, that things would work out fine, but he couldn't. He had no idea what would happen now that she couldn't compete.

He wasn't quitting—he had decided long ago that nothing and no one was worth quitting rodeo.

Gently, he rocked her, wishing there was some reassurance he could make without mouthing promises he couldn't hope to keep, but there was none.

The two of them had gone to dinner in town, but the evening was less than successful. Although Ashley tried to put on a happy face and make conversation, her thoughts kept returning to the inescapable truth that her rodeo days were over. She wanted to ask what that meant to their relationship, but each time she'd nerved herself to do so, her courage failed her.

It was obvious he was trying hard to distract her, but his own preoccupation was plain to see in the tense lines and evasiveness that stamped his features. The idea that he was trying to think of a tactful way to escape hurt so much that she could hardly get through the meal without breaking down and begging him not to leave her at all.

"So," she said finally, ending the silence between them that had begun when they left the little Italian restaurant. "When do you have to go?"

Joe had already invited Taylor to stay at the house as long as his schedule permitted. As soon as she had the chance, she'd thank her half brother for his understanding. She knew he hadn't made up his mind about Taylor and didn't want to see her hurt any more than she already had been, but still he'd put his own reservations aside and done what he could to help.

Now Taylor glanced at her briefly in the growing darkness. "I have a few days," he replied. "Let's not think about it tonight, okay?"

As if she could *stop* thinking about it. For all she knew, this would be the last time they were together. The only thing she could possibly do without flying into a million tiny pieces was to savor every precious moment until he walked out of her life.

Plastering a smile on her face, she lifted her hand to his hard cheek.

"Fine with me," she murmured, tracing the line of his jaw.

He slowed to turn onto the road to the ranch, and then he grasped her hand and brought it to his lips. The openmouthed kiss he placed on her palm sent tingles all the way up her arm like tiny shock waves. His warm breath and the touch of his tongue against her sensitive skin made her shiver with longing.

He stopped at a narrow dirt road.

"Where does this go?"

"Down by the creek," she replied.

He turned onto the track and drove slowly, braking by a stand of cottonwoods.

"Just what I was looking for," he said, looking around. "It's a pretty night and I want to be alone with you."

At his glance, her heart rate doubled. It was dark out now, but the moon had risen. At night this spot was completely private.

Taylor set his hat on the dashboard. He released his seat belt and then reached over to free hers. "I need you," he whispered, taking her into his arms. "I can't get enough of you."

With a soft cry, Ashley went into the haven of his embrace. The kiss they shared was both tender and passionate. As always, his touch burned through her, heating her blood and caressing her nerve endings. Needing more, she opened her mouth beneath his and tightened her fingers in his hair. She heard his breath catch, and then he hauled her closer, careful not to bump her knee, and changed the angle of the kiss.

His mouth heated, hardened, his tongue claiming hers. She twisted to get closer, moaning in frustration when she couldn't. After a few moments of futile maneuvering, he lifted his mouth and a ragged groan tore through him.

"I brought a blanket." His voice was rough with hunger.

Ashley's blood surged. She was on fire for him. Leaning forward, she let her lips drift across his cheek to his ear. When she made a whispered suggestion about the blanket, his fingers bit sharply into her shoulders. Then he pulled away, eyes glittering darkly.

"Honey, you've got yourself a deal," he drawled. "Stay put while I spread out our magic carpet. I'll be right back for you."

Moments later, he helped her through the long grass to a flat spot at the base of a tree. Overhead, the full moon provided enough pale light for her to see the desire burned into his face. She shivered when he widened his stance and pulled her close. His obvious need threatened her already shaky control.

"You can't know how much I've missed you," he whispered after he kissed her again. "Here, let me help you." He gripped her hand and lowered her to the blanket.

Leaning back on her hands, she tipped up her head and watched him. "Show me how much."

"Oh, babe, I intend to." Gaze locked with hers, he stood over her like a conquering hero straight out of the Old West. Slowly, he began unfastening his shirt.

As she watched, he bared his chest to the moonlight, the patch of silken hair a seductive shadow. He freed the tails of his shirt and stripped it off, the powerful muscles of his shoulders and arms bunching as he moved. Tossing the garment aside, he knelt down beside her.

Ashley was wearing a peasant blouse that bared her shoulders and a full skirt that spread out around her on the blanket, covering the light brace on her knee. Taylor curled his warm hands around her upper arms, slipping his fingers beneath the hems of the short, puffed sleeves. The innocent caress was surprisingly erotic.

She settled her palms against his chest, losing herself in exploration. When her fingers brushed his nipples, he tugged down the wide neckline of her blouse and peeled away her bra. For a moment, he simply sat and looked at her, until she shifted and tried to cover herself.

Gently, he lowered her hands. "You're beautiful," he whispered. "I'd almost be content to sit and look at you for the rest of the night." His chuckle was wry. "Notice I said 'almost.'"

When Taylor bent his head, the perfume of her skin threatened to snap his control like a twig. He wanted to take it slowly, watchful of her injured knee, but the scent and feel of her quickly swamped his noble intentions. Shifting, he laid her carefully down on the blanket and leaned over her to skim one hand up her thigh, bare beneath her skirt.

"How's your leg?" he asked, suddenly remembering her injury.

Her chuckle was husky. "What leg?"

His fingers brushed the edge of her panties and slipped underneath the soft lace, seeking out her moist heat. Gasping, she shifted restlessly and the nails of her hand pressed into his back. He wondered absently if he could get his jeans off without removing his hand.

When it proved to be impossible, he released her and tackled his pants and boots. When he came back down on the blanket, she was sitting up, divesting herself of her blouse and bra. Making a sound of pleasure, she reached out to run her hand over his stomach.

He froze. His muscles quivered as she kept going, slipping beneath the waistband of his shorts. When she boldly stroked his throbbing flesh, he had her on her back so fast she let out a squeak of surprise.

"Did I hurt you?" he demanded.

"No." Her reply was a breath of sound in the night. "I'm just...empty."

Her words inflamed him. With fingers that shook, he reached up under her skirt to strip away her panties. Kicking aside his shorts, he pushed her skirt up around her waist and touched her intimately.

"No," she moaned, reaching for his hand. "I want you. Now."

Her words shattered what little control he had left. Trying desperately not to hurt her, he made a place for himself between her legs and buried himself inside her as she sobbed out his name. As soon as he felt her convulse around him, he exploded. His body surged as he emptied himself into her welcoming heat.

When he was able to move again, he shifted so they were facing each other. "I hope I didn't hurt you," he muttered, aware of her brace rubbing against his bare leg. He'd been inconsiderate to take her on the ground in her condition. Even a bed would have been uncomfortable for her; instead he'd all but thrown her to the grass and ravaged her.

"The only way you could have hurt me was to drive straight back to the house," she replied, reaching up to stroke his cheek.

He caught her hand and kissed the knuckles. What did this woman see in him that she could make him feel so treasured? Obviously, she didn't see him clearly, or she would have known better. The thought sent a shiver through him.

Then he realized how selfish he was being, thinking about himself again, when it was Ashley whose whole life had been turned upside down.

"How you doing?" he whispered. "Are you cold?"

She shook her head. "I'm fine." Her voice sounded small.

"What is it?" Maybe his rough handling had hurt her knee after all and she just didn't want to admit it.

"Thank you," she said quietly, shocking him.

He reared back and peered into her averted face. "For what?"

"For making me forget everything for a little while."

Her voice was like a knife stabbing him. He gathered her close, doing his best to ignore his body's urgent response to her nearness. Hoping she wouldn't notice his fresh arousal. Instead, she smoothed one hand over his hip and circled him with her fingers.

"Ah, honey—" he began, intending to warn her that she was playing with fire. Knowing she might be too uncomfortable to deal with his renewed passion.

She reached up and kissed his lips, shocking him when she slipped her tongue into his mouth even as her fingers caressed his length.

His breath exploded in a long hiss. Without letting him go, she studied his face. "Now," she mused in a throaty voice, "I know there are more ways we can accommodate my knee, and I'm not letting you go until we've explored them all."

Heart bursting with emotion, Taylor did the only thing he could. He gathered her close and helped her to explore.

Chapter Ten

Later that same night Taylor slipped down to Ashley's bedroom and made slow, delicious love to her. Without uttering a word, he explored her body from the roots of her hair to the tips of her toes as thoroughly as if he were charting a gold mine without a lantern. When she was certain she could exist not one moment longer without him buried inside her, his control finally broke and he slid into her pulsating heat. Finally he left her limp and boneless, too satiated to move, as he shifted his big body and collapsed beside her. An electric fan on top of the dresser played over their damp, heated skin while Taylor dozed, his leg thrown over hers and one big hand still fastened around her wrist like an ID bracelet.

Exhausted, Ashley stared into the darkness and listened to the quiet hum of the fan. When she had first returned to the old house, the silence kept her awake. Now, despite herself, she was adjusting to the mind-numbing routine and the utter predictability of life on the ranch. She would rather get used to waking up beside Taylor in a new town each morning, she thought rebelliously. That was a routine that would never get boring.

"Are you still awake?" His voice was gravelly in the darkness. His warm breath danced over her skin, replacing lethargy with longing.

"Mmm-hmm." Since she had told him about her knee, he hadn't said a word about the future. She was dying to know how he felt and what he foresaw happening between them now that her life had altered so drastically. Wanted to ask how he could make love to her so completely, stripping away her sense of self and merging with her so completely, yet still managing to withhold a part of him from her. She wanted—no, needed—to know if his heart was involved as was her own.

Stroking the patch of silky hair on his wide chest, she swallowed all the questions she lacked the courage to ask. Swallowed, too, the declaration of love she wanted so desperately to give and to hear in return.

Beside her, Taylor propped himself up on one elbow and leaned over to brush her mouth with his. Her breath caught as he lingered, teasing the corners of her mouth with his tongue. Then he pulled away as she sighed, disappointed.

"I have to go before Joe wakes up," he said. "I don't think he'd care to run into me sneaking out of your room." Turning back the covers, he swung his legs off the bed and began groping for his jeans. They were the only thing he'd been wearing when he'd opened her door earlier.

"I'm a big girl," Ashley protested in a whisper as he pulled on his jeans. "Joe can't very well ground me."

"Grown-up or not, you're still his baby sister. And I guess you've already been grounded." Taylor's tone was impossible to read.

She was sitting up in bed, staring at him in the moonlight from the window, but his face was in shadow. Was that how he saw her? As someone who'd been grounded and was to be left behind? Did a long-distance romance between them have any chance of survival? Did he even want it to?

He circled the bed and sat down beside her, cradling her face in his hands. His fingers were rough and callused against her tender skin, a working man's hands—strong but with an infinite capacity for tenderness. She could only hope his heart was the same.

"I can't stay," he murmured.

Again, she wondered if he meant he couldn't stay in her bedroom or in her life. Again, she swallowed the words.

"I know." She chose to assume he was referring to tonight.

"I'm riding out with Joe in the morning while you're at physical therapy, but I'll see you when you get back." Kissing her again, he rose and padded to the door. He opened it quietly and listened for sounds from upstairs. Apparently satisfied, he slipped from the room without looking back.

It was crazy to feel a chill. The night was warm. Sitting up in her bed, Ashley stared into the darkness and wondered what she was going to do when he left her for good.

"This is Taylor. He'll be helping us out this morning." Joe introduced him to the foreman, Pete French, and the other men seated at the long bunkhouse table.

Taylor bade them hello. He recognized Mike as the young man with Ashley the day before. He returned Taylor's greeting with no visible curiosity and then returned his attention to his breakfast. The cook brought out heaping plates of hotcakes and bacon for Joe and Taylor, and an older hand with a grizzled beard slid his chair over to make room.

"Taylor's a steer wrestler," Joe said, handing him the coffeepot. "I've seen him in action and he's pretty damn good." His relaxed grin deepened the lines on his weather-worn face.

Acknowledging the compliment, Taylor poured syrup on his hotcakes and took a healthy bite. He knew no one would question him. Cowboys were used to working side by side without ever knowing each other's last name or where they were from. They would accept what he chose to tell them and judge him only on how he sat a horse and did his work. With a pinch of nostalgia, he remembered the men on the ranch in Idaho and the way they had looked after him and his brother. None of them cared that the boys weren't family.

Taylor sipped the strong, hot coffee while Joe and his foreman discussed the days' chores and who was needed where. Ashley's physical therapy appointment would keep her busy until noon. He had offered to drive her, but Emma had errands in town, too. Ashley seemed relieved when Joe suggested Taylor spend the morning in the saddle instead. It was good to be back on a ranch, doing honest work with animals dependent on him for their welfare. He enjoyed brushing elbows with cowboys who led a simple life governed by the seasons, the welfare of the herd and their own traditions.

With a sigh of near contentment and a surreptitious glance around the rustic room, Taylor dug in to the rest of his food.

A couple of hours later, narrowing his eyes against the brilliant sunshine, he urged his rangy gray gelding into a trot. They rode with Pete across an endless pasture toward a scattered band of cattle that needed to be rounded up and moved.

Taylor was glad for the work. Staying busy kept him from brooding.

The creak of saddle leather beneath him, the smells and sounds of the herd, even the slight ache in the small of his back reminded him of the days back on John Tulley's spread. Over the years Taylor had forgotten how much he enjoyed the outdoors, the animals and the companionship of other men with similar ideas of what was really important.

One of the hands had lent him a bandanna when they rode out; another offered him work gloves. Once Pete determined that Taylor really could ride without spooking the cattle, he gave him a few simple orders and left him to carry them out.

The night before, after he had crept back to his own room before getting up to leave with Joe, Taylor dreamed about Ashley's accident. In his dream, they were in an outdoor arena. The grandstands were deserted and the only sound was the howl of the wind. It kicked up the dust around his feet as he stood alone in the arena.

Ashley raced in, heading for the first barrel. A tumbleweed blew across Spinner's path and he shied, sending Ashley somersaulting over his head as Taylor tried to get to her and failed. She landed at his feet in a crumpled heap and lay still, her eyes wide and staring.

In a cold sweat, he awoke to the sound of the shower running next door. The nightmare had brought back vivid images of the accident and his fear when he saw her go down with her mount. Pure terror had sucked the breath from his lungs. Now he barely managed to bite back a hoarse cry.

How did you stand by and watch helplessly when someone you cared about did something dangerous?

He remembered Ashley's fear when he'd gone after that bull and almost been trampled. Funny, he hadn't thought about that after she'd been hurt. Now he recalled how she'd begged him to promise he'd be careful and his own impatient response.

How had she kept herself from slapping him for his insensitivity? Had he ever bothered to tell her he understood now just how she felt?

If she had been physically able to return, could he have found the courage and understanding to watch her compete again or would he, too, have asked for promises that were impossible to give? Thanks to a cruel twist of fate, it was a decision he might never have to face.

A cow bolted from the group he was herding. Taylor kicked his heels into the gray's sides and cut the animal off.

He liked working with cattle, always had. Someday he would probably settle down to ranching full-time, if he ever got rodeo out of his blood.

When he won against tough opponents or finished high in the national standings, he couldn't imagine that day ever coming. At other times the day was easier to visualize—when he misjudged a steer and ate dirt, or when the next show was three hundred miles away and all he wanted was to grab some shut-eye. He also thought of the day when he drew a spooked steer and didn't place, or his body chose to remind him he was no longer twenty-two. Maybe fate would step in as it had for Ashley, and decide the time for him.

Hell, he had a big enough stake put by for a piece of land and a small herd. What more did he need? He had championship buckles and mended bones and stories to last him a lifetime. Once he'd thought he would keep on truckin' until he either won a world championship buckle or was too old and brittle to take down a running steer. Now he wasn't so sure.

Maybe he was just scared that if he ever stopped in one place long enough, the emptiness in his life would have time to catch up with him.

Taylor followed the last of the herd through the gate and shut it carefully behind him. He thought about leaving the ranch the next day, leaving Ashley. For only the second time that he could remember, he didn't *want* to go back on the road. The first time had been when he'd first brought her home after her wreck.

As the sun climbed higher, he rolled back his sleeves, mopped his neck with the borrowed bandanna and remembered similar mornings in Idaho. Thinking about that reminded him of Kirby, his baby sister. When he and Donnie had gone to Tulley's ranch, another couple had taken Kirby, who was almost four at the time. Taylor had tried to keep in touch, but phone calls from the ranch were long distance and he had no money to pay for them. The years went by. Eventually, Kirby had been adopted and moved even farther away.

When Taylor was old enough to look for her, he discovered there had been a fire and her records were lost. Every path he and Donnie took ended in frustration, but they hadn't given up. Someday, somehow, they would find her again.

Now Taylor rubbed one gloved hand across his eyes and pushed the memories aside. As soon as the cattle were settled, he was going back to the house to clean up before Ashley got home from town.

"You want to go on the road with me?" Taylor asked, breaking into Ashley's thoughts. The family was seated around the dinner table, and she had been reviewing in her mind the exercises the physical therapist had given her that morning.

Unable to believe her ears, she lifted her gaze from the fried chicken and potatoes she had been pushing around her plate. He wanted her to go with him!

"If you'd do the cooking, my brother and I would pay whatever you asked." Taylor was talking to her mother with a roguish twinkle in his eye. Her cheeks were pink with embarrassment and pleasure.

"You'd better watch yourself," Marian replied with a delighted smile. "I just might say yes."

Snagging another corn muffin from the serving plate, Taylor leaned toward her. "I'd be the best-fed bulldogger on the road."

"And the heaviest," Joe interjected.

"We'd escort you to the dances, too," Taylor added. "My brother is real good-looking. Just ask Ashley."

When he looked at her, she took a sip of her milk, congratulating herself for holding her hand steady. For a moment, she had thought he was asking *her* to go with him. Her insides were still trembling, too.

"That's right," she managed in a teasing voice. "Donovan's the handsome brother."

"Aw, gee," Taylor grumbled, wincing at the put-down.

Kenny whooped, Joe slapped his knee and even Marian admonished her for the remark. Only Emma's expression was thoughtful.

The other two women turned down Ashley's offer to help with the cleanup, chasing her out of the kitchen instead. She went up to Joe's office, where he was doing the ranch books on the computer.

"Come on in," he invited when she poked her head around the open doorway. "Emma set this system up for me years ago, and I can't tell you how many hours it's saved."

She mumbled an appropriate response and took the empty chair. A bowl of small candies sat on the desk at his elbow. She scooped up a few and ate them absently.

"How's it going?" Joe asked when he got to a stopping place. "Have you had a chance to make any plans?"

"Plans?" she echoed, deliberately obtuse. She had no idea why she'd sought Joe out when Taylor was right downstairs. She had years to spend with her brother.

Now he swiveled his chair around and caught her hand in his. "Honey, you know you have a home here for as long as you want. This ranch is as much yours as it is mine. You can help Emma, work with the horses, get a job in town or watch the daily soaps, if that's what you want," he said earnestly. "Anything you decide is fine with me."

She started to thank him, but he held up a detaining hand. "I just want you to know," he continued with a determined gleam in his silver eyes, "that if you decide to do something else, get a place of your own, whatever, I want to help. I can afford it and you have it coming, you know."

Technically, the ranch was part hers, although Joe had been the one to live here and run things since her father died.

"I have money put away," she protested.

"I figured that," he said. "And I know you're still getting used to the idea of not going back on the road." His frown was sympathetic.

Ashley swallowed the sudden lump in her throat. She knew if he said anything more, she'd end up in tears. "I appreciate the offer," she told him, getting to her feet. "I have no idea yet what I might do."

He rose, too, and eyed her with brotherly concern. "I didn't mean to rush you."

She shook her head. "I know that." Despite her best efforts, tears filled her eyes and she blinked them hastily away. With a wobbly smile, she gave Joe a hug and he wrapped her in a comforting embrace.

"I love you, honey," he whispered. "You've had a rotten break, but you're a strong woman. You'll come out of this okay."

She wanted to tell him how much his reassurance meant to her, but all she could manage was a shaky thank-you. Ducking her head, she slipped out of his arms and dashed from the room.

After she had gone into the bathroom to dab cold water on her red eyes and blow her nose, she took the time to put on fresh lip gloss and a spritz of cologne before going back downstairs to find Taylor.

"Is your knee strong enough for a walk down to the stable and back?" he asked. "After that meal your mother put on, I could use a little exercise."

Not to mention a little privacy, she thought as Kenny burst into the living room where they were standing close together.

"I'm looking for my car keys," he said.

"Sorry, I haven't used them," she replied.

Kenny looked puzzled. Then he grinned. "I'll find them."

Ashley turned her attention back to Taylor. "I'd like to go for a walk," she told him. "My therapist wants me to start bending my knee more. Walking is good for it, as long as I take my time."

"We've got all the time in the world," Taylor replied.

Leading the way outside, Ashley didn't bother to respond, but both of them knew that was anything but true.

When they got to the stable with Paddy, the Irish setter, trotting behind them, they wandered down the wide aisle. Many of the stalls were empty. At this time of year most of the horses stayed outside.

"It will be nice to pick Tramp up tomorrow," Ashley said, patting an old pony whose head was hanging over his stall door. "I can only imagine what the poor dog is thinking, cooped up at the vet's for so long. He probably has himself convinced he's been abandoned again, only in fancier surroundings this time."

"Think how glad he'll be to see you when you do show up," Taylor told her as they walked out the other end of the stable. Stopping by an empty corral, he rested his arms on the top railing. "You'll be his hero for rescuing him."

"Yeah, there is that." Standing beside him, she looked at the faint outline of the mountains in the distance and wondered how she could get Taylor to talk about his own feelings instead of the dog's.

What she wanted to hear was how he felt about her. Did he love her even a little? Was he going to try to come back and see her? Above all, how much longer was he going to stay?

Together, they gazed out past the empty corral where the sky was starting to change color. Except for the occasional sound from one of the horses or the faint lowing of the cattle, it was so peaceful she could have screamed. God, but she wanted to go back to what she loved.

And to whom she loved. She looked at Taylor, standing there ready to catch her if she stumbled. Her heart ached. *Love me,* she cried silently as he returned her stare with a puzzled one of his own.

"Knee getting tired?"

She shook her head, disappointed that he hadn't somehow understood her silent plea. Instead, he took one of her hands in his. For a moment her heart soared. Was he finally going to put his feelings for her into words?

Instead, he cleared his throat and looked away, frowning. His hand tightened on hers.

Oh Lordy, he was going to break it off. Her lower lip wobbled and she bit into it ruthlessly. She refused to cry in front of him. Not now. If all she had left was her pride, she would hang on to it with both hands.

By the time he shuffled his feet and brought his attention back to her face, she had herself firmly in hand. Then he shattered her composure with one question.

"Sweetheart, how would you feel about coming with me on the road?"

Her mouth fell open in shock.

"No, wait," he continued hastily, "don't answer right away. I know it wouldn't be easy for you, not being able to compete, watching the others doing what you're dying to do, too." He was talking faster, the words tripping over each other. His expression was etched with tension and his eyes seemed dark and unreadable. "It would be tough, I know, getting in and out of the camper, riding for hours in the cab." He took a breath and searched her face. "But we could be together, that way. It would be fun, too. Seeing old friends, checking out new places." He took off his hat and raked a hand through his hair, leaving it sticking up in spots. "Surely there are a few towns out there where you've never been."

She could scarcely believe what she was hearing. "You want me to go with you? To travel with you?" She had scarcely heard anything he said after *"we could be together."*

He nodded emphatically. "That's right. That truck I bought can haul a decent-sized camper. I saw one back in Texas that I liked. Course it would be cramped, but I think we could manage."

His smile was crooked, his hand squeezing hers just short of pain. "It's a cabover with a big bed." She must have looked confused. "The camper," he said, charming her utterly when his cheeks turned dusky pink. "I could help you climb in and out of the bed until it was easier for you, but your knee's getting more flexible."

He wanted her with him. He didn't plan to leave her behind because she was no longer a part of rodeo. He wanted to make a place for her in his life. He cared.

Tears welled up in her eyes. She was about to throw her arms around his neck when she realized he had said nothing about how he felt, or how long he wanted her with him. Doubts rose, crowding aside the first real happiness she had felt in weeks. There was so much else to consider. She would be dependent on him financially; at least she wouldn't be earning money. The more time she spent with him, the more she would love him. And wasn't she just postponing the inevitable? Sooner or later, she had to make a new life for herself.

"Honey, what do you think?" he coaxed when she didn't respond.

Swallowing nervously, she looked into his unreadable eyes and gave him the only answer that made any sense.

Chapter Eleven

"If this is Thursday, it must be Oklahoma, right?" Ashley muttered to herself as she stood in the middle of the new camper Taylor had bought two weeks before. Right now, he was working his horse in the outdoor arena, and she was making herself useful wiping off the counter that didn't need wiping and straightening up the compact living space that was already neat as a pin.

The side windows of the camper were open to catch any breeze that might drift through the area. From outside, Ashley could hear women's voices and an occasional burst of laughter. If she had wanted, she could have joined the knot of wives and girlfriends who traveled with their men. They were friendly enough, and had been quick to include her in their ever-shifting circle.

Ashley's hand stilled on the counter. The group of women who *accompanied* contestants wasn't where she wanted to be. On the back of a barrel-racing quarter horse was where she belonged, she thought fiercely. Then she shifted, tripping over a tennis shoe she had left on the floor, and pain speared her knee, reminding her why she was here with a dishcloth in her hand instead of back in the arena wielding a riding crop.

Her knee was better than it had been. She could bend it without pain, and she had climbed on a horse the other day, while Taylor hovered like a mother hen. Donovan had offered her the use of his palomino, since he traveled with other bullriders now and did no hazing. She thought his offer had been an extremely generous one, considering that she was the main reason he and Taylor no longer traveled together.

Both men insisted it was because Donovan wanted to concentrate on the bullriders-only competitions, but she had her suspicions. Rinsing out the kitchen rag, she hung it over the faucet to dry. In this heat, that should take about fifteen minutes.

She glanced at her watch and pushed her hair off her forehead, wishing she hadn't left Tramp back at the ranch. She could use the company. Maybe she'd take a quick shower before Taylor got back. The fancy new camper had an oversized water tank and a tiny bathroom, complete with a hand-held shower attachment, as well as the huge bed Taylor had mentioned before. There was a microwave, an elaborate sound system and an intercom that connected with the cab of the truck, along with the usual compact kitchen and roomy seating area. The wood was oak and the cabinet doors were inset with stained-glass panels.

Life on the road had never been like this before. Of course, she had never traveled with a man before and she'd always been a participant, not a combination cook, one-person cheering section and lover.

With a restless groan, she opted for the shower. Dinner was already waiting in the tiny propane refrigerator. After they ate, there was the evening show and Taylor's ride to watch and then a night in his arms before they pulled up stakes again.

In the tiny bathroom, she heard the sound of Taylor's hello over the splash of running water. She shut it off and was wrapping a towel around herself when the bathroom door opened.

Ashley took one look at the expression on Taylor's rugged face and her question about his workout died on her tongue. Even though they had spent most of the night before wrapped in each other's arms, his eyes glittered with raw hunger as his gaze raked down her body. Pushing the door open wider, she let the towel fall and stepped into his embrace.

"I'm all dirty," he protested, even as he leaned down to gather her close and bury his face, streaked with dust and sweat, into her shoulder.

She turned her head and kissed his hard cheekbone. "I don't care."

Sudden tension tightened his arms around her. She could feel his warm breath feathering across her bare skin. Like a cat, she arched against him. The denim of his jeans abraded the inside of her thigh as she raised one leg and rubbed it along the length of his.

His hand trembled as it trailed down her naked back. Then he let her go and her heart plunged.

Shooting her a look of raw longing, he locked the camper door. Relief poured through her, followed by shivers of arousal as he turned back to her and dropped to his knees. Grasping her hips in his big, rough hands, he strung sizzling open-mouthed kisses across her stomach. When his head moved lower, her knees threatened to buckle. Swaying, she gripped his shoulders.

"Let me," he murmured, fingers tightening.

Unable to deny him anything, she yielded.

Later, Ashley cleaned up from their meal of pasta salad and sliced ham while Taylor showered, shaved and put on the clothes he would wear in the arena that evening. He kept darting looks in her direction, remembering her generosity earlier. The depth and honesty of her response never ceased to amaze him. Despite his own reticence, she held nothing back.

He must have reeked of sweat and horse, but she hadn't cared. Now he was tempted to ask her if she was happy with him. She seemed to be, but sometimes he caught her watching the same people she used to compete against, and he wasn't so sure.

What if being here with him wasn't enough? What if *he* wasn't enough? Sooner or later, she would realize how lacking in substance he was and how little he had to give her. Then she would leave him, the same way everyone he knew eventually left him, because he didn't have whatever it took to hold those he cared about. First his parents had gone, then his ex-wife had turned to others for whatever she needed—and someday when he least expected it, Ashley would go, too.

When she had dressed after their lovemaking, she'd put on a soft green Western shirt with tight black jeans. Her red-gold hair was caught into a ponytail at the base of her neck, the ends curling softly. Remembering how she had looked earlier when he had lain with her on the thick carpet, her eyes dark and soft, her lips swollen from their kisses, sent a reaction sizzling through his body and made his jeans uncomfortably tight at the inseam.

Would he ever get enough of her?

"I like the color of that shirt on you," he told her when he realized the silence had stretched between them for too long. "Is it new?"

When she turned from putting away their freshly washed supper dishes, she was smiling. Obviously, his comment pleased her. He would have to remember to compliment her more often. "I'm glad you like it. Emma gave it to me when I was home. She knew I needed cheering up."

Fresh guilt hit him for leaving her in Colorado to face her fate without him. He hung his head. Not suspecting the seriousness of her injury was no excuse. She had needed him and he was gone. "I wish I could have—"

Quickly, she pressed her fingers to his lips, stopping the flow of words. "You came back for me," she told him softly. "That's all I ever wanted."

"And are you where you want to be now?" he demanded, fearing her answer.

A shadow appeared in her eyes, disappearing when she blinked. "Of course I am. I love being with you."

He sighed, knowing there was more she wasn't telling him. "There's no one else for me, either," he said fervently, clasping her around the waist and drawing her between his thighs. "No one." It was the closest he dared come to admitting his feelings.

Ashley hugged his declaration to her later that evening when they walked back through the tunnel from the arena. As he led Sergeant Pepper, lathered and head hanging, Taylor's expression was remote. The event hadn't gone well. First his Appy had refused to settle into the box. Then one of those flukes occurred, when the steer refused to take a clean fall no matter how strong the bulldogger, how flawless his technique. Seconds had ticked away on the clock until Taylor finally managed to power him over.

Since Taylor had spent so much time in Colorado with Ashley, she knew that every win from now on was crucial. There was nothing she could say to comfort him, so she remained silent.

A stunning blonde in a red satin shirt and dark jeans was walking toward them, hips swaying seductively. Her long hair was full and curly. More than one cowboy turned and stared as she sauntered past.

When the woman spotted Taylor, a smile curved her red lips and she came to a stop in the aisle, propping one hand on her hip.

"Well, hello," she purred up at him, batting long, thick lashes that framed china blue eyes. "Taylor Buchanan, long time, no see."

Ashley sensed his immediate tension. It wasn't uncommon to run into women who knew who he was, but someone had showed Ashley a newspaper photo of this one.

Lorrie Ann, his ex-wife.

"Hello, Lorrie." His voice was remote, revealing nothing.

Lorrie glanced at Ashley and then dismissed her. Taylor's former wife was a tall woman. Her skin and makeup were flawless, the scent she wore seductive. It made Ashley want to sneeze. Next to the other woman, she was reduced to the tomboy she had always been, plain and awkward. She wished she'd bothered with more than a swipe of lip gloss before they had left the camper.

"Too bad about what happened out there." Lorrie nodded in the direction of the arena. "You always did have the worst luck." Her voice was husky. "How have you been?"

Ashley glanced at Taylor, whose jaw had hardened. "We've been fine," he replied firmly.

Lorrie's eyes narrowed as she shifted her attention, looking Ashley up and down. Ashley returned her stare with a level one of her own, even though she was quaking inside. Taylor had loved this woman enough to marry her. How could Ashley hope to compare favorably with someone so gorgeous, so totally feminine?

"Aren't you going to introduce us?" the other woman coaxed, a smile playing on her red mouth.

He performed the introductions perfunctorily. "We have to get going," he added after Ashley murmured something polite and blatantly insincere.

"Ah, yes," the blonde commented, tossing back her golden hair. "How well I remember the hectic schedule." Her gaze touched on Ashley again. "The cramped camper, the long drives from one show to the next." She flicked her gaze back at Taylor. "The nights," she murmured.

"What are you doing here?" he demanded. "I heard you were living in Dallas."

Ashley wondered if he had made an effort to keep track of her. Despite what he had told Ashley, did he miss her?

Lorrie Ann made a dismissive gesture with a red-tipped, ringless hand. "That didn't work out. I'm singing again and some prominent people are interested in me."

"Good luck with it." He tugged on his horse's reins and grabbed Ashley's elbow with his free hand. "Come on," he said in a clipped voice. "I need to take care of Sarge."

"Nice seeing you again." Lorrie Ann's laughter floated after them as he hustled Ashley away.

"I'm sorry about that," he said under his breath. "She always was a witch."

Then why did you marry her? Ashley wanted to ask. Instead, she said, "Don't worry about it." What she really needed from him was reassurance.

What she got instead was brooding silence. Even when his Appaloosa had been taken care of and they got back to the camper, he was quiet. Then, when he hauled her against him and kissed her passionately, desperately, his eyes squeezed shut so his dark lashes fanned his cheeks, she couldn't help but wonder who, in his mind, he was holding, her or his lovely ex-wife.

"Do you miss her?" As soon as he released Ashley's mouth, the question popped out without her consent.

"Miss who?"

She glanced down at her hands, clasped tightly to keep them from trembling. "Lorrie Ann."

To her astonishment, he uttered a sizzling curse. "You don't know what you're talking about."

"She's beautiful. You must have loved her a lot." Since she'd already jumped in with both feet, she blurted, "Do you still love her?"

Taylor swore again. "How can you ask me that? It's you I'm with, not her."

"But I don't know how you feel," she cried, frustrated.

"This is ridiculous." With a last disgusted look, he grabbed his hat and pushed past her. The door slammed behind him, shaking the camper with its force.

Oh, damn. She'd spoiled everything. Now he was angry with her and she still didn't know which woman he had really been kissing when he held her.

* * *

"Hey, bro, what brings you out tonight?" Donnie asked over the music and noise as Taylor claimed the bar stool next to him. "I thought you'd be home snuggling with your lady love."

Taylor shot him a look meant to shut him up, and then he took a long drink of the beer the waitress set before him. "You thought wrong."

He could feel Donnie's eyes boring into him. Hunching his shoulders, Taylor glared down at his schooner. It had been a mistake to come here; the last thing he felt like discussing was Ashley.

Donnie clasped his shoulder and leaned closer. "Let's get a table," he said quietly.

Annoyed, Taylor shrugged off his brother's hand, then regretted the action immediately. Donnie was only trying to help. "Yeah, okay," he relented, grabbing his beer and sliding from the bar stool. "Come on."

"What's wrong?" Donovan asked as soon as they were seated at a small table in the corner. "You look like you could bite through horseshoe nails."

A reluctant grin tugged at Taylor's mouth. "I probably could. First I got a steer whose knees wouldn't bend," he confessed ruefully.

"Yeah, I saw. I don't think that particular steer had knees, but it happens." Donnie's tone was philosophical. "You didn't let that make trouble between you and Ashley, did you?"

Taylor lifted a brow. "Why do you ask?"

Donnie blew out a breath. "Personal experience, I guess. We only hurt the ones we love."

The edge to his voice prodded Taylor's curiosity. Women flocked around Donnie like flies on horse apples, but he never seemed to pay much attention. It was something Taylor meant to ask him about one of these days, but now sure as heck wasn't the time.

"We ran into Lorrie Ann after my run," he said instead, voice flat. Damn the woman. His feelings toward her had died a quick death when he caught her in bed with Hank Hall, but he figured meeting her had upset Ashley—although why it should he had no clue. Compared with Ashley's natural loveliness, the woman looked like a tarted-up Barbie doll.

"What happened?" Donovan asked.

Taylor shrugged, avoiding his brother's eyes. "Not much. Lorrie Ann did her usual number, assuming I'd be interested in hearing all about her resurging career." He snorted with disbelief. "She wasn't exactly rude to Ashley, but she never did get along with other women that well. She always claimed they were jealous of her." He snorted again.

Donovan set down his beer mug, stroked his mustache idly for a moment and then leaned closer. "Some people might think your ex is still a beauty."

Taylor shrugged. "If you like the type." There had been a time her perfectly made up face, potent perfume and bleached hair had appealed to him, but not anymore. Especially not since he'd been exposed to the natural attractions of freckles, laugh lines and peach shampoo.

"She drips self-assurance," his brother continued impatiently. "You loved her enough once to marry her. That could be intimidating to a woman who's not sure where she stands."

Taylor stared, perplexed.

"I take it you haven't told Ashley how you feel," Donnie said.

"What are you saying? Ashley's the woman I'm with now, and she's a lot prettier than Lorrie Ann in her war paint." Ashley didn't need the attention-getting props his ex used, thank God.

Donnie's voice was dry. "Have you bothered to tell Ashley any of this?"

Taylor took a long swig of his beer. "Why should I? She knows how I feel about her."

Donnie raised his eyebrow. "Does she?"

"Hell, yes. Besides, I'm not after Lorrie Ann." He shuddered at the thought.

"Are you after Ashley?"

The question made Taylor set down his glass and sit back in his chair as he mulled it over. "I guess I am." Putting the declaration of intent into words made him nervous. What had happened to all that self-protective common sense he'd been so proud of? No doubt he had lost it right after the first time he took her to bed—he just hadn't been willing to admit it before.

Draining his glass, he shoved back his chair and got to his feet. "Hell, I guess I'd better find Ashley and tell her..." He fumbled to a stop as panic surged through him. "Tell her not to rush out and buy any bright red nail polish," he amended.

Donnie rose, too, and clapped him on the shoulder. "I guess that'll do for a start."

All the way back to the camper, Taylor worried about what he had meant by that last remark.

Ashley was surprised to hear the camper door open this early. After the way Taylor left, she figured he would be gone a lot longer. Had even thought he might be out searching for Lorrie Ann. Maybe he just hadn't been able to find her.

Embarrassed to be caught crying, Ashley sat up in the darkness and scrubbed at her cheeks with her sleeve.

For a moment, Taylor was silhouetted in the doorway, the outline of his broad shoulders and cowboy hat stealing her breath. Oh Lord, but she loved this enigmatic loner.

"Hey, babe, I'm back." He shut the door behind him. She hadn't bothered with the lights, but the moon shone faintly through the curtains. Moving forward slowly, he stubbed his boot on the table leg and swore colorfully.

"Why are you sitting here in the dark?" Before she could protest, he switched on the battery light over the table. Then he saw her and froze.

She must have looked even worse than she thought.

"What's wrong?" he demanded, coming closer and squatting down to peer at her face as she ducked her head. "Has something happened? Is your knee bothering you?"

She turned her face away from his intense scrutiny and shut her eyes. "Nothing happened." Oh, great. She sounded as pathetic as she probably looked.

She heard his intake of breath. "You've been crying."

Tempted to deny it, she simply didn't reply. Ashamed, she said instead, "I was just listening to the radio." It played softly. "You startled me, that's all, and I'm a little sleepy, I guess." Hating herself for being such a coward, she got to her feet, careful not to touch him. When she inched her way past him, he turned to watch her. In the lantern light, deep lines etched his face and his eyes were narrowed.

She busied herself getting a small bottle of juice from the fridge.

"I'm sorry," he rasped, surprising her.

"What for?" Without looking at him, she tried to untwist the cap on the bottle. It refused to budge. He reached for it, but she yanked it aside. She rapped it once, sharply, on the counter and succeeded in getting it open.

Carelessly, Taylor flung his hat on the bed. He braced his hands on the edge of the counter on either side of her, effectively penning her in front of him. Ignoring him, she turned her head aside and took a drink of the juice. While the silence grew, she set the bottle on the counter and stared pointedly at his hand.

"Excuse me."

He didn't budge. "I'm sorry we ran into Lorrie Ann," he continued. "It must have been unpleasant for you."

Ashley let herself look up, searching for any tell-tale signs of longing in his expression. "Do you miss her?"

He gave a sharp crack of laughter. "Hell, no."

"Are you sure?"

"You know why we split up. She was cheating on me." His voice had taken on an edge, what she thought of privately as his no-trespassing tone.

"Maybe you changed your mind afterward," she suggested. "Maybe you wanted her back, but it was too late." She held her breath, waiting for him to deny it.

Instead, he moved his hands, settling them at her waist. "Maybe your imagination is working overtime," he countered. "The only woman I want is right here in front of me."

Relief made her sag against him. His hands burrowed beneath her T-shirt, seeking bare skin. When he found it, he stroked up her rib cage, pausing at the edge of her bra. Awareness made her shiver and her nipples harden, wanting his touch.

When he bent to kiss her, she dodged him. There were too many questions still churning up dust in her brain like a herd of restless cattle.

"So you don't have any feelings for her?" she asked.

He stiffened and she knew she had displeased him with her prying. He snaked his hands out from under her shirt and backed away to prop one shoulder against the closet door. Folding his arms across his wide chest, he said, "Yeah, contempt. Anything else I felt died when I found her screwing someone else in my bed." His mouth had flattened into a grim line, but a muscle danced in his cheek.

Ashley reached out to him with some vague idea of offering comfort, but he shifted away. "If you're looking for some corny declaration of love from me, forget it," he growled. His eyes were as cold as ice. "Heaven knows I want you, but that's as far as it goes. I'm done with anything more complicated than that. I won't go through it again."

She blinked back tears. Oh, she understood, all right. She had wanted to know how he felt, and now she did. To protect his own heart, he would willingly sacrifice hers.

Before she could reply, he added softly, "I'm sorry if the truth hurts, but I can't promise you more than there is inside me to give. I don't want to lose you, so I hope it's enough."

Pride might have forced her to walk out right then if she hadn't believed there was anything more behind his stony facade. She would be taking a terrible risk if she stayed and was wrong about him, but she wasn't ready to give up. Not yet.

She studied his set face, and then she realized he was braced for her rejection. A tiny flame of hope flickered inside her. As long as he cared whether she stayed or

went, she couldn't give up. There had to be a way to un-
lock the feelings she was certain still existed deep within
him. All she had to do was to find it.

All she needed was a sign, some small indication that
he was able to trust her on some level. Then she would be
able to believe that the rest would eventually come.

Slipping by him, she took her juice and sat down at the
small table. "Let's talk about something else," she suggested. "You never told me how you and Donovan ended
up on that ranch in Idaho. Why don't you grab a beer
from the fridge and tell me about it now?"

She held her breath, praying he would find the willingness to open up to her about his past. The idea might
be farfetched, but surely it would be a start.

He stood in the glow of the battery light and stared
down at her, obviously perplexed at her abrupt shift in
topics. Then, while she held her breath, he glanced at the
fridge and then back at her. Finally, he shook his head
and she felt her heart begin to crack apart.

"I don't understand why you want to talk about that
now," he said as she struggled with the pain spreading all
through her. "That's just something I don't discuss. Not
with anyone."

"I see," she managed to reply through lips that felt
stiff. "Well, it was just a thought."

"Come on, it's getting late. Let's go to bed."

She stared, wondering whether he truly couldn't feel
the undercurrents between them, or if they just didn't
matter to him.

Taylor watched her anxiously, willing her to agree with
his suggestion. If he could just hang on to her a little
while longer, she would eventually come to see that what
they had was enough, without searching for something
more that just didn't exist. She had to.

"Okay." Her voice was subdued, but he had no doubt that he could make everything all right again, once he had her back in his embrace where she belonged.

Relieved that she agreed, he quickly shucked his clothes and climbed into the big bed. Then he saw what she was doing, and his heart iced over.

Ashley had repositioned the table and was making up the other bed.

He lay awake for hours, staring into the darkness and wondering what she was thinking. He was dying to ask, but every time he opened his mouth, courage failed him. Finally, the pale light of morning filtered through the window shades and he decided to get up.

When he leaned over Ashley, she was either asleep or pretending to be. He could see faint shadows below her closed eyes. She needed the rest. If she was sleeping, he hated to disturb her.

When he got back from the rodeo office, she had coffee made and the camper packed up for travel. It was only when she turned and handed him a steaming mug that he noticed her duffel bag on the seat. From its bulging shape, he knew it was full. Automatically, he took the coffee she handed him and sipped it, burning his lip.

"I've made a decision," she said in a voice that sent ice sliding down his spine.

"What is it?" he growled, braced for the worst.

"There's no place for me in rodeo, and there's no place for me with you."

"That's not true," he protested as dread clawed at him like a living thing. He'd known what he offered wouldn't be enough, but it was all he dared to give.

She shook her head. "My mind's made up. Your life is here on the road. Mine isn't, not anymore."

"There's more to it than that," he guessed. "There has to be."

Her chin rose a notch. "That's right, there is more. I love you."

At her startling announcement, he reached for her, but she backed away.

"Don't worry, I'll get over it," she added coolly. "Without trust and sharing between us, the love I feel will die. But don't expect me to stick around here while it does."

"Is this about my not wanting to talk about my childhood?" he demanded disbelievingly. "Is that the problem?"

"Oh, Taylor," she sighed, "it's about so much more than that. If you can't understand, there's just no way I can explain it."

He had no idea what she was getting at. She loved him. Why wasn't that enough? Frustrated, he gripped the coffee mug so tightly that all feeling left his fingers, just as the feeling drained from his heart.

"What are you going to do?" he asked.

Her faint smile was so sad it almost broke him. "I'm going to do the only thing that makes any sense to me now," she said, tears glistening in her big brown eyes. "I'm going home."

Chapter Twelve

Ashley hadn't realized until she actually spoke the words that she had already subconsciously made the decision to return to Colorado. Watching the barrel-racing competition the day before had been like fertilizer to the growing seeds of discontent inside her. She still mourned the loss of her horse. She missed the excitement of competition and the satisfaction that being damn good at something she loved had given her.

Now it was time to find something else she could love—something else she could be good at and in which she could submerge herself while she tried to mend her broken heart.

She loved Taylor. Deep inside she knew she could be very good at that, if only he let her close enough to try. With a lump in her throat, she waited for his reaction to her announcement. One word of love from him and she'd stay. She knew that. All she needed was some sign that she mattered enough for him to lower that protective wall and let her in.

Holding her breath, she watched him. For a moment, hope soared inside her as his face paled and longing darkened the blue of his eyes. His lips parted. Fiercely, she willed him to say something, anything, that would convince her he thought what they had was worth fighting for.

"How soon are you leaving?" In a blink, his expression had been wiped clean of feeling, the clarity of his eyes clouded and unreadable.

The fragile flame of hope inside her winked out. Later she knew there would be pain, but for now she was grateful for the numbness that gripped her.

"This morning," she said, turning away. "No point in putting it off. I'll catch the bus to Denver and someone from the ranch can meet me there."

"Maybe I could drive you—" he began.

"No!" Immediately, she softened her strident tone. "You can't afford the time. Let's just keep it simple, make a clean break." It was her heart that was breaking, but even now she had the feeling that she was doing the right thing.

He released a gusty sigh. "All right, if that's the way you want it." Just that easily, he let her go.

She wanted to scream that it was the last thing she wanted. She *wanted* him to fight for her. She had gambled on his wanting her enough to fight, and she had lost.

Staring at her back, Taylor struggled to find some sense in the feelings rioting through him. Her announcement had caught him by surprise. He had really thought she cared—enough at least to hang around for the rest of the season before she cut out on him. His mouth took on a bitter twist. It only went to show how little he knew about her.

Why had he thought she was different? By the time she turned back around, he was stone-faced and outwardly composed. By sheer grit he managed to stay that way until she was ready to climb onto the bus that would take her from him for good.

For a moment before she boarded he thought she might relent. Her eyes filled with tears and her lower lip trembled. He had to blink a couple of times himself, control wavering dangerously, and he damn near bit the end of his tongue off to keep from begging her to change her mind.

One thing he couldn't stop himself from doing, though, was kissing her one last time. He took her mouth fiercely, pouring the feelings he didn't dare express into this last echo of the intimacy they had shared. Then he released her and turned away, but not before he noticed that she had gone pale, her eyes huge and dark. He would have sworn she whispered his name, but he knew it was only his own imagination playing tricks on him—telling him what he so badly wanted to hear.

Resolutely, vision blurred, he set one foot in front of the other, and with a force of will he hadn't known he possessed, he kept moving until he was standing back at his pickup.

Without sticking around to see her bus pull out, he got in and drove away, back to the fairgrounds. Then he went out to win his next event.

"Why don't you call her?" Donnie asked, the familiar question stirring Taylor's temper. His brother had been asking the same thing for weeks now, and Taylor was getting damn sick of hearing it.

"If you don't have anything better to talk about, find yourself a different table." His tongue stumbled thickly, so he gave up on talking and took another drink instead. It didn't matter. The saloon was well within walking distance of his camper and his sense of direction was still intact.

"I hate seeing you so unhappy." Donnie looked as worried as an old mother hen.

With an effort, Taylor raised his head and blinked his brother's image into focus. "Unhappy?" he echoed. "Dammit, man, I can't lose. I'm number three in the standings. Why the hell should I be unhappy?" His belligerent tone dared Donovan to answer.

"You're lucky you haven't killed yourself," he said quietly. "You're careless, you take god-awful chances. You're winning because no one competing against you is willing to risk breaking his neck."

Taylor slapped his hand on the table, deeply offended. "Well, thanks a hell of a lot," he sneered. "It figures that you don't think I'm winning because I'm the best, just the craziest."

"I know you're the best. I also think you've stopped caring—about anything. That might give you a hell of an edge in the arena, but it scares the bejesus out of me when I watch you ride."

Angrily, Taylor drained his glass and shoved back his chair. Rising, he almost lost his balance, but then he caught himself and managed to straighten up. "What would you know?" he demanded bitterly, for once beyond caring what he revealed about himself or what anyone thought. "You aren't hollow inside. You don't have to worry that people will see into you and realize there's nothing there. Everyone likes you. Women fall all over you, and you barely notice. When you open your mouth, everyone wants to hear what you have to say. People connect with you, they care about you. No one looks into you and sees how empty you are, down deep where it counts." He stumbled to a stop, noticing for the first time that several people were turning to stare.

Before he could escape, Donovan grabbed his arm. "They left me, too," he said quietly.

His words made Taylor freeze in place. "What?"

"Our parents," Donnie said. "You weren't the only one they went away and left. They left me and they left Kirby, too."

A blast of old anger and hurt surged through Taylor, dispelling some of the haze the liquor had woven around him. He hung his head, struggling to regain his control.

"Come on." Still holding on to his arm, Donovan urged him toward the door. "We need to talk."

"No we don't," Taylor protested, his head beginning to throb. He wondered if it was possible to suffer the bends from sobering up too fast, like a diver surfacing too quickly. His head felt as if it were full of bubbles, painful ones. When they walked outside, the fresh air hit him like a wave. He shook his head to clear it and nearly fell down.

"Whoa, there." His brother's grip tightened. "Don't collapse on me. You're too damn heavy for me to carry by myself."

Taylor was barely aware that they stepped off the porch of the old-fashioned saloon. As soon as they reached the parking lot, he swung around.

"I'm fine," he said. "Don't need your help." He swatted away Donnie's hand on his arm. "I just need some sleep."

Donovan hesitated. "You're wrong, you know. About being empty inside." His gaze sharpened and Taylor felt as if he were being probed with a laser. "You couldn't love her if you were empty, and you do, don't you? You love her and it hurts like hell."

Taylor was about to deny it, but then his shoulders sagged. What did it matter? "It's not enough," he mumbled, staring at nothing. "There wasn't enough of me to give her and she left me."

"Go after her."

Pain was replacing the lovely numbness he'd worked so hard to develop. "I can't."

For a long moment, Donovan just looked at him. Then he released a sigh of frustration. "Come on," he said. "I'll walk you back to your camper."

Taylor waved his arm. "It's right over there. You can see it from here. Stand here and watch, if it makes you feel any better."

Donovan must have decided that any more talk tonight was pointless, because he agreed with the suggestion. Folding his arms across his chest, he waited while Taylor made his way home, trying not to stumble in the near darkness beyond the lights from the saloon.

The last thing Taylor wanted was for his baby brother to swoop down on him again, babbling about their parents' disappearance not being his fault. Or making him admit out loud the feelings for Ashley he didn't want to acknowledge even to himself.

He had accepted that their parents had to be dead by now. Knew that, even if they had abandoned the two brothers, they would never have voluntarily left their little princess behind. They had planned to come back. After all these years, it was cold comfort, but it was all he had.

It beat hell out of thinking about Ashley. When he reached his camper, he glanced back at the saloon. He could see Donovan's familiar figure standing right where Taylor had left him. He raised his hand and Taylor returned the salute before he went inside to the silence and the loneliness, shutting the door behind him.

It was late morning when Ashley came out of her room. She was still in her robe, hair uncombed and face unwashed. Although she had been in bed for hours, she was still tired. Someone had come and gotten Tramp, who slept in her room, and let him outside. He was probably playing with Paddy, Kenny's Irish setter.

Everyone else had eaten and left hours earlier, but there was hot coffee on the stove and a plate of Emma's blueberry muffins on the counter. A copy of *Pro Rodeo Sports News* lay on the table where Ashley was sure to see it, open to the page that listed the season's standings in each event.

She ignored the newspaper until she sat down with her coffee and a muffin. Then curiosity got the best of her, and she read the list of top fifteen steer wrestlers.

Taylor's name was number three.

With mixed feelings, she raised her mug and sipped her coffee. She wanted him to do well, didn't she? It wasn't in her to wish him bad luck, and she was glad he hadn't been injured. So why did a selfish little part of her twist into a hard knot of disappointment when she was confronted with his success?

The answer was easy. She wanted some clue that he was as miserable as she—that he missed her and wasn't doing well without her.

Hellfire, he was doing great. She was the one who needed to take her life off hold and get on with it, just as she had told him she was going to do, right before he'd let her walk out of his.

She knew that Joe and their mother were concerned for her. She saw the worry in Emma's eyes whenever Ashley turned down an invitation to go shopping or to visit friends.

She glanced down at herself. It was almost noon and she wasn't even dressed. She hadn't showered and her hair needed a trim. Joe had suggested last week that the two of them talk to a real estate agent about finding some property closer to Denver where she could begin training barrel racers, teach riding and give clinics in competing. He'd even offered to start her out with some horses handpicked from his own herd. That and a few ads in rodeo publications should bring enough business to get her started. She had money saved. If she was careful until she built up her clientele, she'd manage.

The only thing she had really been doing for herself since she came back to the Blue Moon was the exercise regimen to strengthen her knee. Just the other day, the doctor had told her it was probably as good as it was going to get. She could walk and run, and she could even ride as long as she didn't compete.

Now she stared down at her coffee. Taylor wasn't coming after her, and she was fast running out of excuses to wait for him. It was high time she stopped.

She was helping her mother with lunch when she heard Joe and Emma walk in the back door.

"Hello, Ashley" was all he said, but the look he gave her across the neatly set table was filled with gentle encouragement and approval. It shamed her that she had worried him so. Was it her imagination, or were there more gray hairs in his sideburns?

"Would you have time to go with me to talk to that real estate agent one day this week?" she asked him as they all sat down to eat. Only Kenny was missing; he had been working for a neighboring rancher, earning money for college in the fall.

"I'd be happy to." He passed her the bowl of green salad they were having with chili and biscuits, and there were smile lines creased into his weathered cheeks. "Have you thought about what kind of place you want to look for?"

She sprinkled grated cheese on her chili before she answered. "Actually, I was hoping you'd have some ideas."

It was obvious that her answer pleased him. They spent the rest of the meal discussing what she had to have, what she might hope for and what she could reasonably do without.

It wasn't until lunch was over and Ashley helped Emma clean up and stow dishes in the dishwasher that she realized she hadn't thought about Taylor for over an hour. It might take time, but she knew now that she could overcome this and move on if she tried hard enough.

In the general noise of the arena, the group of men was quiet when Taylor walked up, leading his Appaloosa by the reins. Several heads were bowed, and other faces etched with shock.

"What is it?" he asked Ernie Boyd, who was standing the closest to him. "What's happened?"

Ernie raised his head and a chill went down Taylor's back. The younger man's eyes were red and there were tear tracks in the dust on his face.

"It's Jerry Shields," he said hoarsely. "We just heard."

Taylor's heart squeezed painfully in his chest. Bad news was a part of the life. "Heard what?" He hated asking.

Ernie's mouth trembled and he turned away, shaking his head. Taylor looked around the ragged circle of silent men. They all looked grim and he knew the worst. His hand tightened on Sergeant Pepper's reins and he swallowed a lump of dread.

Before he could repeat the question, a timer named Judd cleared his throat. "He got gored down in Beaumont. Bled to death. The funeral's day after tomorrow in Dallas."

Despite Taylor's premonition, shock and regret swept through him at the words. Jerry had been one of the new breed of competitors, trained athletes rather than working cowboys. He had guts and talent and what cowboys call try. He'd been good, too. Damn good.

Now it was over for Jerry. With the unexpected twist of a steer's head and perhaps an unguarded moment on his part, life for him was done, poured into the dirt of some arena like so much spilled coffee.

No matter how often he heard it, Taylor never got over the finality. He clapped Judd on the shoulder and glanced around the circle of drawn faces. "I'm sorry. Anyone needs a ride to the funeral, let me know."

Ashley forced excitement into her voice, knowing that Joe was watching her closely. "It's perfect!" she exclaimed as the agent took them back to his car after they had toured the outbuildings.

"You can keep your own horses in the one stable and boarders in the other," Joe volunteered. "There are plenty of stalls in each."

"The arena will be perfect for lessons," she added, mentally reviewing what she had just seen. "The corrals are all well fenced, and there's enough parking for cars and horse trailers, good water. We're close enough to

Denver to attract business from there. Even the house is just right for me.''

The property wasn't large, less than ten acres altogether, but it was big enough for her immediate needs. The house was small and far from new, but it was nicely maintained and the kitchen and bathroom had been remodeled only three years before. Best of all, the owner was willing to lease the property with an option to buy. If Ashley found that it wasn't what she wanted after all, she wouldn't have the trouble of reselling it.

"Shall we go back to the office and draw up some papers?" Bill Newton, the agent, suggested.

It was hot in the sun. Ashley was wearing a cotton blouse, and Joe had on a T-shirt with his ever-present Stetson, but Bill was bareheaded, dressed in a long-sleeved dress shirt and dark slacks with his Western boots. He had to be uncomfortable.

"Do you want to think about it?" Joe asked her.

She shook her head. They had been looking for two weeks without luck and this property had just come on the market. If she dawdled, she might lose it.

"No," she said, smiling at Bill. "Let's go back to that air-conditioned office of yours and tend to business."

He had taken out a bandanna-print handkerchief. Now he mopped his beaded brow and grinned. "Fine with me."

Taylor stood in the blazing sun, eyes downcast, as the minister's voice droned over the flower-draped casket. The little churchyard was packed with Jerry's friends. His widow, ghostly pale in a black dress that was too big for her, looked slightly dazed by the service. Two little boys in white shirts and blue jeans clung to each of her hands and two older couples Taylor assumed must be her par-

ents and in-laws stood on either side, as if to protect her
and her children from the ceremony going on around
them.

The minister stopped talking and Taylor glanced up.
As the voices of the men around him joined in reciting
"The Cowboy's Prayer," he studied their faces. Young,
old, weathered or smooth, they all had the same mix of
sorrow, pride and strength, the same determination to
win and the same love of the life he had thought was all
he would ever need for a measure of contentment.

Now he wasn't so sure. Even later, when he had paid
his respects to Jerry's family and rounded up the two
cowboys who had ridden to Dallas with him, his mind
wasn't on the scene he had just witnessed. It had already
moved on to the contemplation of his own future.

During the long ride back to Mesquite, the other two
bulldoggers alternated between talking and sleeping. After a couple of tentative attempts at including Taylor in
their conversation, they gave up good-naturedly, willing
enough to leave him to his own thoughts.

In general, rodeo people were a tolerant bunch. These
two were no different from most. That their conversation contained as much joking and humor as sad tales
was no surprise to Taylor. They had paid their respects to
Jerry and would mourn his passing in their own way, but
life went on and the road ahead was long and winding.
Humor and camaraderie were only two of the weapons
cowboys used to keep away the fear and the doubts about
their own mortality.

Taylor, on the other hand, was totally focused on his
mortality. Ever since he first heard the news about Jerry's death, he had been keenly aware of how short and
unpredictable life could be. And how lonely, especially if

a man was afraid to go after whatever happiness wandered his way.

For years now, Taylor had thought happiness lay in the only life he had ever wanted—in capturing a National Finals Rodeo championship buckle and in knowing he was the very best at what he did. The pursuit of that dream had helped allay the disappointment he felt in not being able to locate his sister, as well as the numbing, hollow, ever-present ache of not knowing what had happened to their parents more than twenty years before.

Now he couldn't help wondering if rodeo had just been a place to hide and an excuse to keep from taking real chances. Not the ones he took every time he leaped from horseback onto a racing steer, but the real threats in which a man's heart could be ripped out and trampled. The kind of threat that had kept him from trying to stop Ashley when she announced she was going home, and the kind of dry-mouthed fear that could freeze a man in his tracks and keep him from ever succeeding at what really mattered.

Even now, thinking about the alternatives was scary enough to make Taylor long for a cigarette, although he had kicked the habit years ago. Beside him in the cab, one of the other men shifted in his sleep, leaning slightly against Taylor, and began to snore. As he drove steadily down the road, Taylor wondered if his passenger's dreams were peaceful or full of fears like Taylor's own.

Exhausted, face streaked with perspiration and dust, knee throbbing with weariness, Ashley sat on the back porch of her new house and gazed into the darkness. From one of the stables a horse whinnied and kicked the wall of his stall. Beside her on the porch, Tramp raised his head. After he had sniffed the air for a moment, he settled back down with his muzzle resting on his paws.

"What do you think of our place?" Ashley asked idly.

His ears pricked up, but he didn't move his head. No doubt he, too, was exhausted from the events of the past week. There had been papers to sign, furniture and equipment to buy and move, deliveries of hay and feed to arrange, advertising to order, insurance to set up and unpacking to do. She'd moved in two days before and her family and old friends from Caulder Springs had properly warmed the place with a party just last night. Her refrigerator was still full of leftover salads, cake and other goodies.

Today, Joe had delivered the four horses she had already started training to barrel race back at the Blue Moon, and a stock contractor had brought four more she intended to use for basic riding classes. Her ad had appeared in the local newspaper for the first time this morning, and already there were several queries on her answering machine. In time, she would schedule barrel-racing clinics, as well.

Now that everyone was gone and the chores were done, she found herself struggling against the surge of loneliness that threatened to swamp her. Thank God for Tramp's company. As soon as she had time, she intended to pick out a couple of cats at the local shelter. Tramp hadn't bothered the barn cats at Joe's, and she assumed he would treat the ones she brought home with equal disdain.

She tipped back her head and looked up at the stars, silently reminding herself just how lucky she was to have come out of rodeo with her body nearly intact and enough money to set up a future.

She was well aware how many performers less fortunate than herself lost everything in their pursuit of the elusive dream of success. Marriages failed, children were neglected, huge debts were incurred and lives were lost. Yes, she was lucky to have escaped with nothing more than a damaged knee and a shattered heart.

Despite her feeling of satisfaction over her new endeavors, she would give it all up in a wink if Taylor loved her. Since he didn't, she'd best remember to count her blessings. Even though she had faced adversity and hardship in the past and come out on top, getting over Taylor was sure to be the most difficult challenge she'd ever faced.

Blinking back tears, she promised herself it was one battle she had every intention of winning.

Chapter Thirteen

Ashley was standing in the middle of her outdoor arena teaching a riding class of beginners when the phone inside the barn door rang, startling her. "Keep going around," she instructed them as she slipped through the fence.

Donovan was one of the last people she expected to call her here. As soon as she heard his voice, her stomach dropped to her toes.

"Is Taylor all right?" she asked, voice shaky.

"He's not hurt," Donovan replied quickly. "Not yet, anyway."

She pressed the phone more tightly to her ear, watching her students through the open doorway without really seeing them. "What do you mean, not yet?"

"I'm worried about him." Donovan's voice sounded grim. "Ever since you left, he's been taking terrible chances." He sighed. "Hell, I'm a bullrider and he frightens me."

"He's been doing well," she replied, then bit her lip. She hadn't meant to admit she'd been following the standings.

"Sure, he has. He doesn't care what happens to him. No one without a death wish can hope to beat that kind of recklessness."

Ashley's fingers tightened on the phone as she watched her students again. They were all doing fine, walking their horses in a slow circle around the corral. "What do you expect me to do?" she asked. "I'd offer to talk to him, but I don't think he'd listen."

"I want you to come to Denver next weekend and tell him how you feel. He'd listen to that."

Her blood turned cold at his words. How did Donovan know how she felt? Had Taylor told him about her declaration of love? How humiliating.

"What do you mean, how I feel?" she bluffed.

"You care about him, don't you? Do you want to see him hurt, or worse?"

"Of course not, but Taylor doesn't care how I feel," she argued. "Besides, I have a business to run. I can't just leave when I feel like it."

"If you don't show up in Denver, I'll bring him to you," Donovan threatened.

"He wouldn't come."

"I'll figure out a way if I have to hog-tie and mount him on the hood of my truck like a trophy deer." The frustration in Donovan's voice had her convinced he was dead serious.

Her shoulders sagged and she turned away from her students so she could compose herself. "I'll try to come," she said. "But I can't promise anything. Tell me exactly when you'll be there."

She listened closely while Donovan gave her the information, and then she noticed that one of the children in the arena had let her horse move too close to the one in front of it. Even though she had deliberately chosen placid mounts for these classes, there was always a danger of kicking.

"I have to go," she told Donovan. "Don't you dare bring him here."

"That's entirely up to you," he replied with steel in his voice. What had happened to the easygoing brother?

Without bothering to answer, she broke the connection.

"Tracy," she called, "pull up on the reins a little and make some more room between Dusty and Megan's horse, okay?"

If she had thought for a minute that talking to Taylor would change anything, she would have gone in a heartbeat. She had told him she loved him. As far as she was concerned, there was nothing left to say. If she thought for a minute he would let Donovan drag him out here, she'd hire a security guard to stand at her front gate, but she knew that wasn't going to happen. She had told Taylor she loved him and he had let her go. He wasn't about to follow her now.

"Just come with me and see her!" Donovan was so frustrated that he was yelling. Good thing he and Taylor had the barn adjacent to the rodeo arena to themselves. "We can be on our way again in ten minutes."

Taylor had been edgy all weekend, worried that Ashley would be at the rodeo and he would run into her. He had a crick in his neck from looking over his shoulder, and his eyes were bloodshot from searching the stands for a glimpse of her. His concentration was shot, and his temper was in shreds. Donnie's harebrained suggestion that they pay her a visit gave Taylor a good idea why his brother had been so jittery.

"Did you talk to her about this?" Taylor demanded. "Have you been scheming behind my back?"

Suddenly, Donovan was too busy messing with his saddle to meet Taylor's accusing gaze. "What makes you think I'd do anything like that?"

Thoroughly annoyed, Taylor uttered a curse that jerked Donnie's head around. "I ought to beat the tar out of you," he added for good measure.

Donnie straightened and his voice got quiet. "Go ahead, if you think it will help."

Bunching his hands into fists, Taylor spun away and hit the wall hard enough to make Sarge scramble to the other side of the stall, eyes rolling.

"Easy, buddy," Taylor crooned, feeling contrite. None of this was the Appaloosa's fault, nor was it Donovan's. Deep down, Taylor knew that.

Stepping into the aisle to face his brother, he parked his hands on his hips and hung his head. "Sorry, man," he muttered.

"Does that mean you'll go with me?"

Taylor's head snapped up. "Hell, no. And if you don't drop the subject, I just might reconsider whipping your sorry butt." His voice held a warning, but the anger that had threatened his control moments before had dissipated. As misguided as Donnie was, he'd only been trying to look out for Taylor's welfare. "A man's got his pride, okay? I'll be fine," he added, "so mind your own business." His tone was still friendly, but it was underlined with determination.

Donovan rubbed his jaw while he studied Taylor. "Is your pride more important than your heart?" he asked finally.

"My heart's just fine, so drop it before I have to get ugly."

Instead of taking advantage of the golden opportunity for razzing him that Taylor presented, Donovan searched his face for a moment, and then he shrugged. "I'll mind my own business if you'll promise to quit trying to kill yourself in the arena."

Taylor didn't need his brother to tell him he had been pushing his luck. The anger and pain that had spurred him so hard for the first few weeks after Ashley left was pretty much burned out of him, anyway, replaced by a lump of ice that sat in his gut and chilled him no matter how hard he tried to thaw it out. Nevertheless, he knew he couldn't continue without inviting serious injury to either himself or his horse.

"I'll be more careful," he promised in a low voice. Then he pointed an accusing finger. "But you have to quit interfering or all bets are off."

Taylor extended his hand. Once they had shaken on a deal, neither could welsh. It had been an unbreakable rule between them since they were boys.

As Donovan hesitated, obviously frustrated, his stare clashed with Taylor's. Finally Donnie swore, low and bitterly, and then he clasped Taylor's outstretched hand. "Deal."

Taylor sighed with relief. Deep inside, he wasn't all that sure he could have withstood seeing Ashley again without falling on his knees and begging for a second chance—one he knew he didn't deserve.

* * *

Ironically, it was right after Taylor had promised to be more careful that he narrowly escaped serious injury.

He was in the arena, leaning from his horse to grab the steer's horn, when the unpredictable happened. The steer missed a step, the cinch Taylor had carefully checked before his run broke, the saddle shifted beneath him and he ended up somersaulting in the dirt. How he managed to miss being skewered or trampled, Taylor had no idea.

More shaken than he cared to admit, he retrieved his hat and walked from the arena on trembling legs while the stands erupted into a burst of applause. It wasn't the worst wreck he had endured by any means, but somehow as he had tumbled out of control, it was the most frightening.

Even later, when he saw the accident in slow motion on videotape, he could only conclude that either an alert guardian angel or random luck had been all that stood between him and disaster. Maybe someone besides his brother thought his miserable hide was worth saving, after all.

"I'm proud of what you've done with this place," Joe said. He had stopped by on his way home from Denver and watched Ashley conduct another session of her beginning riding class for children. She had five students now, and was leasing an old Arabian mare from a neighbor to round out her own string.

When the class was over and she had released her students to their parents, she took Joe on a quick tour of the stables and the other outbuildings before they went into the house for tall glasses of iced tea. Furniture in the little rambler was still sparse and most of the walls were bare, but she was in no hurry to fill the place up with meaningless possessions. During the years she had been on the road after giving up her apartment in Amarillo, she'd learned to travel light. Right now, tack and feed for the animals were more important than lamps, pictures and end tables.

"It's taking shape," she agreed, glancing around the kitchen where they sat at a small round table with matching chairs that Kenny had repainted a soft blue. "I'm starting to get inquiries about my first barrel-bending clinic, too."

Joe took a long swallow of iced tea. "Is your knee ready for that kind of stress?"

She didn't let his brotherly protectiveness annoy her. "Yep. Doc Lee said it would be fine as long as I don't let a horse fall on me." For a moment, she thought of Spinner and how much she missed him. Then she lifted her chin.

Joe was watching her through narrowed eyes. "You're stronger than I suspected," he said quietly. "It took a lot of courage to begin again after your last wreck. I know how much rodeo meant to you." He glanced down at his glass and traced a long drip in the condensation with one finger. "I'm sure that walking away from Taylor Buchanan wasn't easy, either."

"No, it wasn't." She hadn't told Joe why she'd left Taylor. Although her brother's words warmed her heart, she shifted uncomfortably in her chair. The last thing she wanted to talk about was the man she was trying so hard to forget.

"I'm here if you need me," Joe said. "Sometimes talking helps."

"I know." She hesitated. "Part of it was rodeo," she began slowly. "It's his life. He made that very clear, right from the start. Before I got hurt, it wasn't a problem. But when I went back with him, I didn't seem to fit in anymore.''

"I can understand that. Didn't he?"

Ashley realized she hadn't really tried to explain her feelings to Taylor. She'd thought he'd shut her out, but now she wondered if she hadn't been guilty of just the same thing. "That wasn't all of it," she told Joe. "I wanted more of an emotional commitment than he was willing to give."

"You loved him," Joe said flatly. "And he didn't return your feelings."

She shrugged. "I guess not. He let me go."

Joe shook his head and she saw a wry grin curve his mouth. "What is it?" she demanded. "Why are you smiling?"

His eyes took on a faraway expression. "I was just remembering something. Love doesn't always mean not letting go."

"What do you mean?" she asked.

He took another swallow of his iced tea. "Emma threatened to leave me, too, and I was going to let her."

"Why?" she asked. Joe loved Emma. The idea that he might have let her go despite his feelings puzzled her.

Joe sat back in his chair and studied Ashley for a long moment. "You know that Emma was married before?"

Ashley nodded. Emma had been getting over a painful divorce when their mother had invited her to visit the ranch. "You were married before, too."

"That's right. Do you know why my first wife left me?"

Ashley frowned. She'd assumed Joe and Stephanie had merely grown apart. "I guess not."

"Did you know that Emma lost a baby during her first marriage?"

Ashley's eyebrows rose. She hadn't known that, either.

"Emma had a baby girl who was stillborn," Joe continued.

"Is that why you haven't had any children of your own?" Ashley asked. "Because she couldn't?"

He shook his head and leaned his forearms on the table. "Emma's not the one who can't have children. I am."

Ashley stared. She had never suspected. "Is that why you almost let Emma go?"

"That's right. Because I was convinced she deserved more babies, to replace the one she lost. She tried to tell me it didn't matter, but I wouldn't listen. Because I refused to believe I could make her happy, I almost lost her and ruined both our lives."

"I'm sorry."

"It's okay. I didn't tell you this so you'd feel sorry for me. Believe me, there's no need for that."

It was all Ashley could do to assimilate what he had told her. He had always been such a powerful, perfect figure to her. It was a shock to realize he had flaws, if one could call his sterility a flaw.

She stared down at her hands for a moment, wondering why Joe had chosen now to tell her all this. When she looked up, he was watching her closely. "Is there a message here?" she asked lightly, knowing the last thing he wanted was her pity. Knowing, too, that neither he nor Emma needed it. What they had built together was solid and strong. Their love for each other was easy to see.

Joe's grin was crooked, but it held no regret. "There could be," he told her. "Taylor strikes me as a man who would cut out his heart before he would ever hurt someone he cared for. When he stayed at the ranch, I got the distinct impression that he cared about you."

She flushed at Joe's raised eyebrows. Was he referring to Taylor's nocturnal visits to her room? It wasn't something she could ask him. Instead, she frowned. "Letting me go hurt me," she insisted.

"Maybe he doesn't see it that way. Anyway, I'd bet it hurt him, too, and I can't help but wonder why he did." Joe glanced at the clock on the stove and slid back his chair. "Well, I've got to get home. Mom says to tell you to come by for dinner anytime and Emma sends her love."

Ashley rose and he circled the table to envelop her in a brotherly hug. "You need anything at all, you just ask," he said gruffly.

"Thank you." She knew he understood that she was really thanking him for a lot more than his last offer. With the generosity that was so typical of him, he had shared something she suspected few people knew about. Silently, she vowed not to let his act of kindness go to waste.

The afternoon was hot, and for once, Ashley would be glad when the last class of the day was over. The rodeo had come and gone from Denver and she presumed the Buchanan brothers had, too. Two weeks had passed since Joe's visit. She still didn't know what to think about his suggestion that Taylor had let her go for some twisted reason of his own. Besides, she had no idea where Taylor was, only that he was at a show somewhere, risking his hide in the race toward the finals.

As she glanced at her watch, Tony, the teenager she had hired to work part-time appeared in the doorway of the smaller stable. "I'm done in here," he called.

"That's great." She shaded her eyes with her hand. He was a tall, gangly boy, all elbows and knees, but he was a hard worker and he seemed to have an affinity for animals. "Take a break until class is over," she told him. "Then you can help put up the horses."

He nodded and turned away. She was about to tell her students to trot when she noticed a truck coming down the driveway in a cloud of dust. It was early for any of the parents to arrive, and she didn't recognize the truck.

Beside her, Tramp began to bark excitedly. She glanced down at him. "Hush, boy. You'll spook the horses."

It was an idle threat. Very little would bother the placid mounts she had chosen for the beginner class. Still, Tramp didn't usually raise such a fuss. From the corner of her eye, she noticed that Tony had reappeared in the stable doorway. No doubt he was curious, too.

Ashley was about to scold the dog again when she got a better look at the driver of the truck. Speechless with shock, she watched while Taylor parked the rig and got out. Immediately, Tramp ran over to him, tail wagging, while Ashley stood rooted to the spot, staring.

"Want me to finish the class?" Tony asked, making her jump. He probably assumed Taylor was here to talk to her about business.

"Sure, thanks," she said absentmindedly. Why *was* Taylor here? Could Joe have been right? Immediately, she dismissed the idea.

"Hi." Taylor walked over and stopped in front of her, removing his hat and raking a hand through his hair. She noticed that his face looked thinner and there were new, deeper lines cut into his tanned skin.

"Hi." She had no idea what else to say. Her throat had gone so dry that her tongue was sticking to the roof of her mouth.

Taylor looked around curiously, and she wondered what he thought of her little operation. Before she could dredge up the will to speak, he brought his attention back to her.

"This is quite a place. You must have worked hard to get so much done so quickly."

"I've had a lot of time on my hands," she said. "And a lot of help from my family and friends."

Dull color spread across his cheekbones. "I suppose you have." For a moment, he studied the band of his hat, turning it around in his hands as if he were searching for possible flaws. Then he raised his head. Something in his eyes reached down into her chest and gave her heart a painful twist. It began to thump in double time.

"Why are you here?" she asked.

"Uh, could we talk?" His expression revealed nothing, but a muscle jumped in his cheek.

"I guess so," she replied slowly. "Let's get out of the sun." She led him to the tiny office she had set up in the near stable. She was painfully aware of him, and she wondered why he had come to torment her.

As soon as they were inside the little office and she had shut the door, she searched his face expectantly. Damn, but he was as attractive as ever. It was almost physically painful to be this close and not be able to touch him.

"All right," she said. "What did you want to talk about?"

He set his hat down on the scarred desk, upside down so the brim wouldn't break. "I've decided to retire."

If he had told her he decided to switch to barrel racing or goat tying, she couldn't have been more stunned. "Retire?" she echoed. "From rodeo?"

"That's right."

"But why?" she demanded. Rodeo was his life.

He shrugged. "Why not?"

"Because it's what you do," she sputtered. "You love it, and you're good at it. You have years left before you'd even have to think about quitting." The idea of his voluntarily giving up what she would have done almost anything to hang on to infuriated her. "Why would you do such a fool thing?" she shouted. Then an awful suspicion came to her. "You didn't get hurt, did you?"

He shook his head.

"Are you sick? Do you have some incurable disease?" Oh, God, don't let anything be wrong with him. Even though he didn't love her, she would never wish him bad luck.

He actually grinned as he shook his head. "No, I'm not sick."

"Then why?"

"Because I've come to realize it's time," he said quietly, his gaze never leaving hers. For a moment, he looked as if he might say more, but then he just glanced around the tiny room.

"You've put your mark on this place," he said. "You're making a home here."

She wondered how he could say that when he hadn't even been in her tiny house. Then she understood that he was talking about more than that. He was talking about putting down roots.

"I'm trying." Somewhere along the way, she had lost the need to win just to prove her worth. It had been Taylor who brought the excitement to those last weeks she was able to compete. Perhaps if she had stuck it out longer when she'd gone back with him, she would have found that excitement again.

Now it was too late. Now, when she realized that she wasn't getting over him—she loved him more than ever.

She almost groaned aloud, casting about instead for some way to get him out of here before she humiliated herself with tears.

"Was that your last class?" he asked, gesturing to the outdoor arena.

Puzzled, she admitted that it was. He'd better not ask her to dinner or anything dumb like that, for old time's sake. She'd never get through it in one piece. Even now, she didn't understand why he had bothered to come all this way just to tell her he was retiring.

"Well," she said briskly, "I wish you luck in whatever you decide to do next." She didn't ask him about his plans; she didn't want to know. All she wanted was for him to leave.

"Do you know the Kettering place out by your brother's?" he asked.

Warily, she nodded. "Yes, it's a beautiful spread." Then she remembered that Joe had said something about it being for sale. Panic shot through her like the blast of a gun. Oh, no, Taylor couldn't be thinking of buying it. She'd never have any peace if there was a chance she might run into him in Caulder Springs. She wouldn't be able to visit her family or friends without thinking about his living a few miles away.

"It's probably overpriced," she babbled. "Vern Kettering always did put too much value on everything he owned. And I hear he's let the buildings run down." She cast about for more reasons to discourage him, but couldn't think of any.

"It didn't look too run-down to me."

"You've already looked at it?" she asked.

"Yep. I was wondering if you would go over there with me and tell me what you think."

She was instantly suspicious. "Why me?"

Nonchalantly, he shifted his weight, cocking his hip and relaxing his knee. The movement drew her attention to the body she had held and touched so intimately. Fresh pain welled up inside her.

"You're a native," he said. "You might be able to spot things I can't and I'd appreciate your opinion."

She couldn't argue with his reasoning. Call her a fool, but neither could she turn down the chance to spend a little more time with him, despite her frayed self-control.

"Okay," she agreed reluctantly, silently calling herself ten kinds of a fool. "Let me tell Tony." She felt a little guilty leaving the boy to take care of the horses from the riding class all by himself, but she would make it up to him some other time.

When she came back with two cans of soda from the cooler, Taylor was leaning against the unfamiliar truck. "New pickup?" she asked, handing him a soda.

"Mine's in the shop. I borrowed this one." Thanking her, he popped the top on his can and took a long swallow while she watched, fascinated despite her best intentions.

"Ready to go?" he asked.

She nodded, pushing aside her doubts about the wisdom of going as he opened the passenger door. When she scrambled into the cab without assistance, he asked how her knee was doing.

"It's fine," she said shortly.

Taylor circled the truck and climbed in beside her, turned the key in the ignition and tuned the radio to a local country station. All the way to the Kettering ranch, as they made awkward small talk, Ashley regretted her decision to come with him.

When they finally got to the ranch and turned down the long driveway, Taylor glanced at her across the width of the seat. "The Ketterings aren't here, but they left me a key to the house."

Ashley's eyebrows rose. He must be a serious prospect for them to do that. Her hopes that he would change his mind about moving so close to her family plummeted. Her spirits sank even lower when he stopped the truck behind the house and she looked around. The rambler itself was old but wore a fresh coat of white paint. Surrounding it were neatly tended flower beds and several shade trees. Farther down the driveway were the outbuildings, including a solid-looking barn, all painted matching white.

After they got out, Taylor pointed to a bare area near the barn. "I thought that would be a good spot for a stable."

"Are you thinking of raising horses?" she asked, curious despite herself.

He shrugged. "I might do like your brother, raise cattle to pay the bills and horses to satisfy my soul."

She couldn't help smiling at his description. "You figured Joe out." Then she realized Taylor wouldn't live on a ranch like this alone for very long. One day soon he would get married and start a family. The thought of his living here with somebody else was almost enough to buckle her knees.

"What's wrong?" he asked, watching her.

"Nothing. What did you want me to look at first?"

They started with the house. It needed some remodeling, but he didn't seem concerned. With every room they saw, Ashley struggled against the unwanted images of the two of them living there together, raising children as well as livestock.

"Well?" he asked, breaking into her thoughts. "What do you think?"

"It's nice." She was relieved to hear how steady her voice was, despite her inner turmoil. How much longer could she maintain her composure? Glancing at her watch, she faked surprise. "Oh, my. The drive here took more time than I thought. I should be heading back pretty soon. Do you mind?" By sheer determination, she kept her expression one of polite interest and mild concern.

He frowned and glanced at the open door. "There's one more thing I want to show you," he said. "Then we'll go. Okay?"

Reluctantly, she agreed. When they were back in the pickup, he turned onto a side road that was little more than two faint wheel tracks in the grass.

"Where are we going?" she asked, glancing back at the barn.

"You'll see."

In a few moments, he pulled up beside a gentle swell of land. Shutting off the engine, he took a deep breath. When he turned to her, she thought she saw tension in his eyes. "Come on," he said, voice husky. "It's over here."

Curious, she got out of the truck and looked around. The area was quiet and peaceful without being too far away from the other buildings.

Taylor startled her by taking her hand and giving it a gentle tug. "I want to show you the prettiest spot on the whole place."

She followed him silently up the rise, part of her wishing he'd release her hand and the rest absorbing the warmth of his skin and the firmness of his touch with nearly obsessive intensity. The idea that this might be the last time he touched her filled her with sadness and made her stumble.

Immediately, he stopped and reached out to steady her with his free hand. When she automatically shied away, his mouth twisted bitterly and he let her go. "We're almost there."

The top of the rise was flat and spacious. Far in the distance, Ashley could just make out the shadow of the Rocky Mountains. In the other direction, the land rolled away like a flat golden carpet, dotted with cattle. She had barely begun to absorb the beauty of the sight when Taylor spoke.

"Let's sit down for a minute."

Her defenses were crumbling. She had to get away. "I'm sorry," she began. "I have to—"

"Ashley, if you ever loved me at all, please sit down."

His words stopped her in her tracks. Biting her lip, she sat in the grass and crossed her legs.

With a sigh, he came down beside her, wrapping his arms around his bent knees and staring at the creek that meandered through the nearest pasture. Then he started to talk and she went still, almost forgetting to breathe.

"When I was twelve and Donnie was ten, my folks left us to watch our baby sister while they went out for the evening. They never came back."

He turned to look into Ashley's eyes. In his, she could see all the pain he'd been hiding away. "No trace of them was ever found. That old rancher took in Donnie and me, and Kirby went to a young couple with no children of their own." His face was set in harsh lines as he pulled up a blade of grass and began separating it into long strips.

"You don't have to tell me this," Ashley said. Her heart was breaking for his pain, but she didn't know how to help him.

"Yes I do." Absently, he pulled up more grass and let it sift through his fingers. "Eventually, Kirby was adopted and we lost track of her. We've searched, but we haven't been able to find any trace of her. Nor have we ever heard what happened to our parents." He bowed his head. "It's been twenty years. I think they must be dead."

"I'm so sorry," Ashley whispered, wanting desperately to comfort him.

When Taylor turned to look at her, the hurt was still in his eyes, but something else blazed there, as well. "You were right," he said after a moment. "I'm glad I told you. It helps to get it out."

She was still too moved by what he had shared with her to reply. While she was searching for something to say, he got to his feet and extended a hand to her. When she took it, he pulled her up beside him.

"Why did you decide to tell me this?" she asked as a breeze teased the hairs that had worked their way loose from her braid. She was painfully aware that he was still holding her hand.

Instead of answering her question directly, he turned in a slow circle. "I'm thinking of building a house right here," he said. "What do you think?"

Confused by his sudden change of subject, she could only nod. "That sounds nice."

Tugging her along with him, he began walking this way and that, describing the layout of the house he envisioned. At first, still puzzled, she was barely able to concentrate. Then as she fought for control of her emotions, a phrase broke through. She listened, wide-eyed, as he mentioned several more details they had discussed late one night as they drove down a long, dark road to the next town. They had planned an imaginary dream house, filled with everything they both wanted. A big deck with a hot tub—

"I'd want the deck here, where we could watch the sunsets from the hot tub," he said, pointing.

Had he really said "we"? Did he have someone else in mind already? The crack in her heart widened. Then she recalled some of the other things they had listed. A big office with two desks facing each other—

"There'd be plenty of room off the kitchen for a good-sized office," he continued. "Of course the kitchen would have an island and one of those appliance barns on the counter, and a built-in grill."

A tiny ember of hope began to glow deep in Ashley's heart. Taylor wasn't a cruel man. He wouldn't bring her here to describe their dream house if he meant to share it with another woman. Terrified that she was assuming too much, she searched his face for some clue to his intentions.

Whatever he read in her eyes must have pleased him, because his harsh expression softened just a little. "For a long time, I was afraid to let anyone see what was inside me," he said. "Then you came along, poking and prying into things I'd gotten used to keeping hidden away. It scared the hell out of me."

Sudden tears filled Ashley's eyes, blurring her vision. She wanted to speak, but he pressed a finger gently to her lips.

"No, honey," he said. "Let me finish."

While she waited anxiously, heart thundering with hope and love, he dragged in a deep breath. As he stepped closer and captured her hands, his blue eyes blazed with all the feelings he'd kept hidden. Despite the warmth of the day, his palms were damp, his fingers clammy.

"Hell," he said softly, "I knew five minutes after we met that you were special. Now you hold my heart and all my dreams in these two hands.'' He bent his head and kissed her palms. ''I'm sorry that I hurt you before. Please, please let me show you that I can change and be the man you need.''

Now she understood why he had told her about his parents. ''You've already changed,'' she replied, the terrible tension around her heart starting to ease up a little. ''And I love you even more than before.''

''I love you, too.'' His voice had thickened. ''Will you marry me?''

His unexpected question filled Ashley with pure joy. She could hardly speak. Laughing and crying at the same time, she threw her arms around his neck.

''Is that a yes?'' he muttered against her hair, holding her close.

''Cowboy, you bet your boots that's a yes!'' she exclaimed, and tipped back her head for his kiss.

Epilogue

"I now pronounce you husband and wife." The minister's expression was properly solemn as he drew the traditional ceremony to a close.

Standing on the same grassy rise where he had proposed just a month ago, Taylor gazed at his brand-new wife. In the bright Colorado sunlight, her long red-gold hair glowed like a river of fire, and the full skirt of her white dress swirled around her in the breeze. The garland of old-fashioned daisies and green leaves she wore in her hair matched those in her bouquet.

Tears trembled on her dark lashes, but he knew from her smile that they were tears of joy. For a moment, his own eyes burned as his love for her nearly overwhelmed him.

"Cowboy, you can kiss your bride now, if you've a mind to," the minister suggested, drawing a chuckle from the family and friends surrounding them in a ragged half circle.

Heart thundering with happiness, Taylor cradled her face tenderly between his hands.

"I love you, Mrs. Buchanan," he murmured, and then he bent his head. Her lips were warm and welcoming.

Since their engagement four long weeks before, Taylor had been a reluctant guest at the Blue Moon Ranch under her brother's watchful eye while Ashley slept alone at the property she was leasing. As soon as the reception was over, he looked forward to showing her exactly how much he had missed her.

"I love you, too," Ashley told him, heart overflowing, as soon as he broke the kiss. In new jeans and a Western-cut jacket that hugged his wide shoulders, he stole her breath.

"I give you Mr. and Mrs. Taylor Buchanan," the minister announced.

Possessively, Taylor tucked Ashley's hand through his arm as they turned to face their guests. "Now that I've got you, I'm never letting you go," he murmured into her ear.

Before she could answer, Emma handed back her bouquet. "Be happy," she said softly.

As the circle of family and friends closed around them, Donovan stepped forward to pump Taylor's free hand. "I'm proud of you, bro. You didn't even faint."

Taylor's grin was brimming with humor. "Your time will come, little brother."

"That'll be the day," Donovan retorted. "No offense to you, darlin', but I don't plan on gettin' lassoed and hog-tied any time soon."

"Trust me," Taylor told him, but he was looking right at Ashley. "When you find the right woman, you'll stick your head in the noose yourself."

When Ashley saw the warmth in her husband's eyes, she could no more take offense at his words than she could cry over the career she had lost when she'd injured her knee. Taylor's love was a hundred times more precious to her than all the championship buckles on the PRCA circuit.

"The sooner we get this reception started," he told her, "the sooner it'll be over and everyone else will head on home." He glanced around them and lowered his voice. "Then I can show you that even an old retired rodeo bum can find the strength to wrestle a heifer when he needs it."

"Just remember, cowboy," she murmured, tracing the groove in his cheek with her finger, "I've got a few moves of my own." Chuckling at the sudden gleam of interest in his eyes, she tugged on his hand. "Come on, darlin', let's get this show on the road."

* * * * *

COMING NEXT MONTH

#1015 SISTERS—Penny Richards
That Special Woman!

Cash Benedict's return meant seeing the woman he'd always wanted but felt he had no right to love. Skye Herder had never forgotten Cash, and now he was about to find out that Skye wasn't the only person he left behind all those years ago....

#1016 THE RANCHER AND HIS UNEXPECTED DAUGHTER— Sherryl Woods
And Baby Makes Three

Harlan Adams was used to getting his way, but feisty Janet Runningbear and her equally spunky daughter weren't making it easy for him. Janet sent Harlan's heart into a tailspin, until he was sure of only one thing— he wanted her as his wife!

#1017 BUCHANAN'S BABY—Pamela Toth
Buckles & Broncos

Not only had Donovan Buchanan been reunited with Bobbie McBride after five years, but he'd just discovered he was the father of her four-year-old daughter! Now that he'd found her, the handsome cowboy was determined to be the best father he could be—as well as future husband to his lost love.

#1018 FOR LOVE OF HER CHILD—Tracy Sinclair

Erica Barclay always put the needs of her son first. But when she fell for Michael Smith, she was torn between passion and her child. Could she still protect her son and listen to the needs of her own heart?

#1019 THE REFORMER—Diana Whitney
The Blackthorn Brotherhood

Strong, loving Letitia Cervantes was just the kind of woman Larkin McKay had been waiting for all his life. And when her son's rebellious spirit called out to the father in him, he wanted to bring them together into a ready-made family.

#1020 PLAYING DADDY—Lorraine Carroll

Cable McRay wasn't interested in taking on fatherhood and marriage. But Sara Nelson made those thoughts near impossible, and her son was proving irresistible—and Cable was soon playing daddy....

Take 4 bestselling love stories FREE

Plus get a FREE surprise gift!

Special Limited-time Offer

Mail to Silhouette Reader Service™

3010 Walden Avenue
P.O. Box 1867
Buffalo, N.Y. 14269-1867

YES! Please send me 4 free Silhouette Special Edition® novels and my free surprise gift. Then send me 6 brand-new novels every month, which I will receive months before they appear in bookstores. Bill me at the low price of $3.12 each plus 25¢ delivery and applicable sales tax, if any.* That's the complete price and a savings of over 10% off the cover prices—quite a bargain! I understand that accepting the books and gift places me under no obligation ever to buy any books. I can always return a shipment and cancel at any time. Even if I never buy another book from Silhouette, the 4 free books and the surprise gift are mine to keep forever.

235 BPA AW6Y

Name	(PLEASE PRINT)
Address	Apt. No.
City	State Zip

This offer is limited to one order per household and not valid to present Silhouette Special Edition® subscribers. *Terms and prices are subject to change without notice. Sales tax applicable in N.Y.

USPED-695   ©1990 Harlequin Enterprises Limited

INTRODUCING…

A collection of award-winning books by award-winning authors! From Harlequin and Silhouette.

Heaven In Texas
by Curtiss Ann Matlock

National Reader's Choice Award Winner— Long Contemporary Romance

Let Curtiss Ann Matlock take you to a place called *Heaven In Texas,* where sexy cowboys in well-worn jeans are the answer to every woman's prayer!

"Curtiss Ann Matlock blends reality with romance to perfection!"
—*Romantic Times*

Available this March wherever Silhouette books are sold.

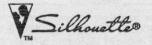

As seen on TV!
Free Gift Offer

With a Free Gift proof-of-purchase from any Silhouette® book,
you can receive a beautiful cubic zirconia pendant.

This gorgeous marquise-shaped stone is a genuine cubic
zirconia—accented by an 18" gold tone necklace.

(Approximate retail value $19.95)

Send for yours today...
compliments of ▼ *Silhouette*®
TM

To receive your free gift, a cubic zirconia pendant, send us one original proof-of-
purchase, photocopies not accepted, from the back of any Silhouette Romance™,
Silhouette Desire®, Silhouette Special Edition®, Silhouette Intimate Moments®
or Silhouette Shadows™ title available in February, March or April at your favorite
retail outlet, together with the Free Gift Certificate, plus a check or money order for
$1.75 U.S./$2.25 CAN. (do not send cash) to cover postage and handling, payable
to Silhouette Free Gift Offer. We will send you the specified gift. Allow 6 to 8 weeks for
delivery. Offer good until April 30, 1996 or while quantities last. Offer valid in the U.S. and
Canada only.

Free Gift Certificate

Name: _____

Address: _____

City: _____ State/Province: _____ Zip/Postal Code: _____

Mail this certificate, one proof-of-purchase and a check or money order for postage
and handling to: SILHOUETTE FREE GIFT OFFER 1996. In the U.S.: 3010 Walden
Avenue, P.O. Box 9057, Buffalo NY 14269-9057. In Canada: P.O. Box 622, Fort Erie,

---

FREE GIFT OFFER
ONE PROOF-OF-PURCHASE

079-KBZ-R

To collect your fabulous FREE GIFT, a cubic zirconia pendant, you must include this
original proof-of-purchase for each gift with the properly completed Free Gift Certificate.

079-KBZ-R

Silhouette

SPECIAL EDITION®

TM

THE MACKADE BROTHERS

the exciting series by

NEW YORK TIMES BESTSELLING AUTHOR

Nora Roberts

The MacKade Brothers are back—looking for trouble,
and always finding it. Coming this March,
Silhouette Intimate Moments presents

THE HEART OF DEVIN MACKADE

(Intimate Moments #697)

If you liked THE RETURN OF RAFE MACKADE (Silhouette
Intimate Moments #631) and THE PRIDE OF JARED MACK-
ADE (Silhouette Special Edition #1000), you'll love Devin's
story! Then be on the lookout for the final book in the series,
THE FALL OF SHANE MACKADE (Silhouette Special Edition
#1022), coming in April from Silhouette Special Edition.

These sexy, trouble-loving
men heading out to you in
alternating books from
Silhouette Intimate Moments and
Silhouette Special Edition. Watch out for them!

NR-MACK3

You're About to Become a

Privileged Woman

Reap the rewards of fabulous free gifts and
benefits with proofs-of-purchase from
Silhouette and Harlequin books

Pages & Privileges™

It's our way of thanking you for
buying our books at your
favorite retail stores.

**PROOF OF
PURCHASE**
Offer expires October 31, 1996

SSE-PP100

Harlequin and Silhouette—
the most privileged readers in the world!

For more information about Harlequin and
Silhouette's PAGES & PRIVILEGES program call the
Pages & Privileges Benefits Desk: 1-503-794-2499

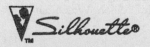

SSE-PP100